THE FIRST MOUNTAIN MAN
PREACHER'S KILL

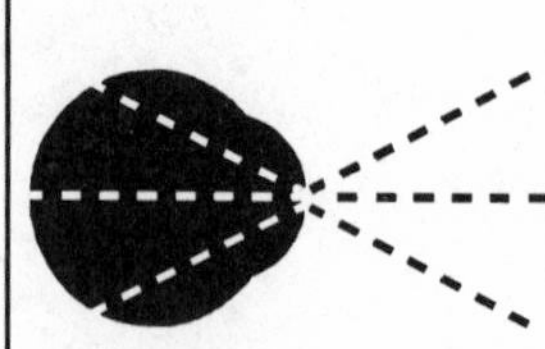

This Large Print Book carries the Seal of Approval of N.A.V.H.

The First Mountain Man
Preacher's Kill

William W. Johnstone
with J. A. Johnstone

THORNDIKE PRESS
A part of Gale, a Cengage Company

Farmington Hills, Mich • San Francisco • New York • Waterville, Maine
Meriden, Conn • Mason, Ohio • Chicago

Thorndike Press, a part of Gale, a Cengage Company.

Following the death of William W. Johnstone, the Johnstone family is working with a carefully selected writer to organize and complete Mr. Johnstone's outlines and many unfinished manuscripts to create additional novels in all of his series like The Last Gunfighter, Mountain Man, and Eagles, among others. This novel was inspired by Mr. Johnstone's superb storytelling.

Thorndike Press® Large Print Western.
The text of this Large Print edition is unabridged.
Other aspects of the book may vary from the original edition.
Set in 16 pt. Plantin.

**LIBRARY OF CONGRESS CIP DATA ON FILE.
CATALOGUING IN PUBLICATION FOR THIS BOOK
IS AVAILABLE FROM THE LIBRARY OF CONGRESS**

ISBN-13: 978-1-4328-5166-8 (hardcover)

Published in 2018 by arrangement with Pinnacle Books, an imprint of Kensington Publishing Corp.

Printed in the United States of America
1 2 3 4 5 6 7 22 21 20 19 18

THE JENSEN FAMILY FIRST FAMILY OF THE AMERICAN FRONTIER

Smoke Jensen — *The Mountain Man*

The youngest of three children and orphaned as a young boy, Smoke Jensen is considered one of the fastest draws in the West. His quest to tame the lawless West has become the stuff of legend. Smoke owns the Sugarloaf Ranch in Colorado. Married to Sally Jensen, father to Denise ("Denny") and Louis.

Preacher — *The First Mountain Man*

Though not a blood relative, grizzled frontiersman Preacher became a father figure to the young Smoke Jensen, teaching him how to survive in the brutal, often deadly Rocky Mountains. Fought the battles that forged his destiny. Armed with a long gun, Preacher is as fierce as the land itself.

Matt Jensen — *The Last Mountain Man*

Orphaned but taken in by Smoke Jensen, Matt Jensen has become like a younger brother to Smoke and even took the Jensen name. And like Smoke, Matt has carved out his destiny on the American frontier. He lives by the gun and surrenders to no man.

Luke Jensen — *Bounty Hunter*

Mountain Man Smoke Jensen's long-lost brother Luke Jensen is scarred by war and a dead shot — the right qualities to be a bounty hunter. And he's cunning, and fierce enough, to bring down the deadliest outlaws of his day.

Ace Jensen and Chance Jensen — *Those Jensen Boys!*

Smoke Jensen's long-lost nephews, Ace and Chance, are a pair of young-gun twins as reckless and wild as the frontier itself . . . Their father is Luke Jensen, thought killed in the Civil War. Their uncle Smoke Jensen is one of the fiercest gunfighters the West has ever known. It's no surprise that the inseparable Ace and Chance Jensen have a knack for taking risks — even if they have to blast their way out of them.

CHAPTER 1

A rifle ball hummed past Preacher's head, missing him by a foot. At the same time he heard the boom of the shot from the top of a wooded hill fifty yards away. He kicked his feet free of the stirrups and dived out of the saddle.

Even before he hit the ground, he yelled to Hawk, "Get down!"

His half-Absaroka son had the same sort of hair-trigger, lightning-fast reflexes Preacher did. He leaped from his pony and landed beside the trail just a split second after the mountain man did. A second shot from the hilltop kicked up dust at Hawk's side as he rolled.

Preacher had already come up on one knee. His long-barreled flintlock rifle was in his hand when he launched off the rangy gray stallion's back. Now, as he spotted a spurt of powder smoke at the top of the hill where the ambushers lurked, he brought the rifle to his shoulder in one smooth motion, earing back the hammer as he did so.

The weapon kicked hard against his shoulder as he fired.

Instinctively, he had aimed just above the gush of dark gray smoke. Without waiting to see the result of his shot, he powered to his feet and raced toward a shallow gully ten yards away. It wouldn't offer much protection, but it was better than nothing.

As he ran, he felt as much as heard another rifle ball pass close to his ear, disturbing the air. Those fellas up there on the hill weren't bad shots.

But anybody who had in mind ambushing him had ought to be a damned *good* shot, because trying to kill Preacher but leaving him alive was a hell of a bad mistake.

Before this ruckus was over, he intended to show those varmints just how bad a mistake it was.

From the corner of his eye, he saw Hawk sprinting into a clump of scrubby trees. That was the closest cover to the youngster. Hawk had his rifle, too, and as Preacher dived into the gully, he wasn't surprised to hear the long gun roar.

He rolled onto his side so he could get to his shot pouch and powder horn. Reloading wasn't easy without exposing himself to more gunfire from the hilltop, but this wasn't the first tight spot Preacher had been in.

When he had the flintlock loaded, primed, and ready to go, he wriggled like a snake to his left. The gully ran for twenty yards in that direction before it petered out. Preacher didn't want to stick his head up in the same place where he had gone to ground. He wanted the ambushers to have to watch for him.

That way, maybe they'd be looking somewhere else when he made his next move.

No more shots rang out while Preacher was crawling along the shallow depression in the earth. He didn't believe for a second that the men on the hill had given up, though. They were just waiting for him to show himself.

Over in the trees, Hawk fired again. A rifle blast answered him immediately. Preacher took that as a good time to make his play. He lifted himself onto his knees and spotted a flicker of movement in the trees atop the hill. More than likely, somebody up there was trying to reload.

Preacher put a stop to that by drilling the son of a buck. A rifle flew in the air and a man rolled out of the trees, thrashing and kicking. That commotion lasted only a couple of seconds before he went still . . . the stillness of death.

That luckless fella wasn't the only one. Preacher saw a motionless leg sticking out from some brush. That was the area where he had placed his first shot, he recalled. From the looks of that leg, he had scored with that one, too.

Were there any more would-be killers up there? No one shot at Preacher as he ducked down again. The mountain man reloaded once more, then called to Hawk, "You see any more of 'em movin' around up there, boy?"

"No," Hawk replied. Preacher recalled too late that he didn't much cotton to being called "boy." But he was near twenty years younger than Preacher and his son, to boot, so that was what he was going to be called from time to time.

"Well, lay low for a spell longer just in case they're playin' possum."

Now that Preacher had a chance to look around, he saw that his horse, the latest in a series of similar animals he called only Horse, had trotted off down the trail with Hawk's mount and the pack mule they had loaded down with beaver pelts. The big wolflike cur known as Dog was with them, standing guard, although that wasn't really necessary. If anybody other than Preacher or Hawk tried to corral him, Horse would kick them to pieces. But Horse and Dog were fast friends, and Dog wouldn't desert his trail partner unless ordered to do so.

That was what Preacher did now, whistling to get Dog's attention and then motioning for the cur to hunt. Dog took off like a gray streak, circling to get around behind the hill. He knew as well as Preacher did where the threat lay.

Preacher and Hawk stayed under cover for several minutes. Then Dog emerged from the trees on the hilltop and sat down with his pink tongue lolling out of his mouth. Preacher knew that meant no more danger lurked up there. He had bet his life on Dog's abilities too many times in the past to doubt them now.

"It's all right," he called to Hawk. "Let's go take a look at those skunks."

"Why?" Hawk asked as he stepped out of the trees. "They will not be anyone I know. I have never been in . . . what would you say? These parts? I have never been in these parts before."

"Well, they might be somebody *I* know," Preacher said. "I've made a few enemies in my time, you know."

Hawk snorted as if to say that was quite

an understatement.

"What about the horses?" he asked.

"Horse ain't goin' anywhere without me and Dog, and that pony of yours will stay with him. So will the mule."

Taking his usual long-legged strides, Preacher started toward the hill.

As he walked, he looked around for any other signs of impending trouble. The grassy landscape was wide open and apparently empty. Two hundred yards to the south, the Missouri River flowed eastward, flanked by plains and stretches of low, rolling hills. Preacher didn't see any birds or small animals moving around. The earlier gunfire had spooked them, and it would be a few more minutes before they resumed their normal routine. The animals were more wary than Preacher, probably because they didn't carry guns and couldn't fight back like the mountain man could.

"Since you ain't gonna recognize either of those carcasses, as you pointed out your own self, you keep an eye out while I check 'em."

Hawk responded with a curt nod. Preacher left him gazing around narrow-eyed and strode up the hill.

The man who had fallen down the slope and wound up in the open lay on his back.

His left arm was flung straight out. His right was at his side, and the fingers of that hand were still dug into the dirt from the spasms that had shaken him as he died. He wore buckskin trousers, a rough homespun shirt, and high-topped moccasins. His hair was long and greasy, his lean cheeks and jaw covered with dark stubble. There were thousands of men on the frontier who didn't look significantly different.

What set him apart was the big, bloody hole in his right side. Preacher could tell from the location of the wound that the ball had bored on into the man's lungs and torn them apart, so he had spent a few agonizing moments drowning in his own blood. Not as bad as being gut-shot, but still a rough way to go.

Remembering how close a couple of those shots had come to his head, and how the ambushers had almost killed his son, too, Preacher wasn't inclined to feel much sympathy for the dead man. As far as he could recall, he had never seen the fellow before.

The one lying in the brush under the trees at the top of the hill was stockier and had a short, rust-colored beard. Preacher's swiftly fired shot had caught him just below that beard, shattering his breastbone and probably severing his spine, too. He was dead as could be, like his partner.

But unlike the other man, Preacher had a feeling he had seen this one before. He couldn't say where or when, nor could he put a name to the round face, but maybe it would come to him later. St. Louis was a big town, one of the biggest Preacher had ever seen, and he had been there plenty of times over the years. Chances were he had run into Redbeard there.

Now that he had confirmed the two men were dead and no longer a threat, he looked around to see if they'd had any companions. His keen eyes picked up footprints left by both men, but no others. Preacher crossed the hilltop and found two horses tied to saplings on the opposite slope. He pulled the reins loose and led the animals back over the crest. Hawk stood at the bottom of the hill, peering around alertly.

Preacher took a good look at his son as he approached the young man. Hawk That Soars. That was what his mother had named him. She was called Bird in a Tree, a beautiful young Absaroka woman Preacher had spent a winter with, two decades earlier. Hawk was the result of the time Preacher and Birdie had shared, and even though Preacher had been unaware of the boy's existence until recently, he felt a surge of pride when he regarded his offspring.

With Preacher's own dark coloring, he hadn't passed along much to Hawk to signify that he was half-white. Most folks would take the young man for pure-blood Absaroka. He was a little taller than most warriors from that tribe, a little more leanly built. His long hair was the same raven black as his mother's had been.

One thing he *had* inherited from Preacher was fighting ability. They made a formidable pair. Months earlier, to avenge a massacre that had left Hawk and the old man called White Buffalo the only survivors from their band, father and son had gone to war against the Blackfeet — and the killing hadn't stopped until nearly all the warriors in that particular bunch were dead.

Since then, they had been trapping beaver with White Buffalo and a pair of novice frontiersmen, Charlie Todd and Aaron Buckley, they had met during the clash with the Blackfeet. During that time, Todd and Buckley had acquired the seasoning they needed to be able to survive on their own, and they had decided to stay in the mountains instead of returning to St. Louis with the load of pelts. Preacher, Hawk, and White Buffalo would take the furs back to sell.

Todd and Buckley had shares coming from that sale, and Preacher would see to it that they got them when he and Hawk made it back to the Rocky Mountains.

White Buffalo had surprised them by choosing to remain with a band of Crow they had befriended while they were trapping. Cousins to the Absaroka, the Crow had always gotten along well with Preacher and most white men. They had welcomed Preacher, Hawk, and White Buffalo to their village . . . and White Buffalo had felt so welcome he had married a young widow.

Preacher had warned the old-timer that the difference in age between him and his wife might cause trouble in the sleeping robes, but White Buffalo had informed him haughtily, "If she dies from exhaustion, I will find another widow to marry."

You couldn't argue with a fella like that. Preacher and Hawk had agreed to pick him up on their way back to the mountains, if he was still alive and kicking, and if he wanted to go.

That left just the two of them to transport the pelts downriver to St. Louis. Preacher figured they were now within two days' travel of that city on the big river, and so far they hadn't had any trouble.

Until today.

Hawk heard Preacher coming and turned to watch him descend the rest of the way.

"Two men," Hawk said as he looked at the horses Preacher led. "Both dead."

"Yep."

"Old enemies of yours?"

Preacher shook his head.

"Nope. One of them sort of looked familiar, like maybe I'd seen him in a tavern in the past year or two, but the other fella I didn't know from Adam."

"Then why did they try to kill us?"

Preacher pointed at the heavily laden pack mule standing with Horse and Hawk's pony and said, "Those pelts will fetch a nice price. Some men ask themselves why should they go all that way to the mountains, endure the hardships, and risk life and limb when they can wait around here and jump the fellas on their way back to St. Louis. I can't get my brain to come around to that way of thinkin' — if you want something, it's best just to go ahead and work for it, I say — but there are plenty of folks who feel different."

Hawk grunted. "Thieves. Lower than carrion."

"Well, that's all they're good for now."

Hawk nodded toward the horses and

asked, "What are you going to do with them?"

"Take them with us, I reckon. We can sell them in St. Louis."

"If those men have friends, they may recognize the animals and guess that we killed the men who rode them."

Preacher blew out a contemptuous breath. "Anybody who'd be friends with the likes of those ambushers don't worry me overmuch."

"And what about the dead men themselves?"

"Buzzards got to eat, too," Preacher said, "and so do the worms."

CHAPTER 2

Preacher's estimate was correct. Two more days on the trail found them approaching St. Louis. Above the point where the Missouri River flowed into the Mississippi, he and Hawk crossed the Big Muddy on a ferry run by a Frenchman named Louinet, a descendant of one of the trappers who had first come down the Father of Waters from Canada to this region a hundred years earlier.

Preacher saw the wiry, balding man eyeing the two extra horses and said, "Found these animals runnin' loose a couple days ago, back upstream. You have any idea who they might belong to?"

Louinet shook his head. "*Non.* Since you found them, I assume they are now yours."

"Reckon so. I just figured I'd get 'em back to whoever rightfully owned 'em, if I could."

"If those animals were running loose with saddles on them, then the men who rode them almost certainly have no further need for them."

"You're probably right about that," Preacher said with a grim smile.

He wasn't worried about who the two ambushers had been, but if Louinet had been able to give him some names, it might have helped him watch out for any friends or relatives of the dead men. But if they came after him and Hawk, so be it. They had only defended themselves and hadn't done anything wrong. Preacher was the sort who dealt with problems when they arose and didn't waste a second of time fretting about the future. It had a habit of taking care of itself.

That attitude was entirely different from being careless, though. Nobody could accuse Preacher of that, either.

Once they were on the other side of the river, Preacher and Hawk rode on, with Hawk leading the string that consisted of the pack mule and the extra mounts. They didn't reach St. Louis until dusk, and as they spotted the lights of the town, Hawk exclaimed softly in surprise and said, "They must have many campfires in this village called St. Louis."

"Those ain't campfires," Preacher said. "They're lights shinin' through windows.

Lamps and lanterns and candles. You'll see when we get there."

"Windows, like in the trading posts where we stopped from time to time?"

"Sort of, but a lot of these have glass in 'em." Hawk just shook his head in bafflement, so Preacher went on, "You'll see soon enough, when we get there."

More than likely, window glass wouldn't be the only thing Preacher would have to explain to his son before this visit was over. This was Hawk's first taste of so-called civilization, which held a lot of mysteries for someone accustomed to a simpler, more elemental life.

As they rode into the settlement sprawled along the west bank of the Mississippi, Hawk gazed in wonder at the buildings looming in the gathering shadows. He wrinkled his nose and said, "Ugh. It stinks."

"You're smellin' the docks and the area along the river," Preacher said. "It's a mite aromatic, all right. There are a lot of warehouses along there full of pelts, and not everybody's as careful about cleanin' and dryin' 'em as we are. They start to rot. Then you've got spoiled food and spilled beer and lots of folks who ain't exactly as fresh as daisies. It all mixes together until you get the smell you're experiencin' now."

Hawk shook his head. "The high country is better."

"You won't get any argument from me about that, boy . . . but this is where the money is."

"This thing you call money is worthless."

"Oh, it has its uses, as long as you don't get too attached to it. Your people trade with each other, and it's sort of the same thing."

"We trade things people can *use,*" Hawk said. "It is not the same thing at all."

"Just keep your eyes open," Preacher said. "You'll learn."

And the youngster probably would learn some things he'd just as soon he hadn't, the mountain man thought.

The pelts were the most important thing to deal with, so Preacher headed first for the local office of the American Fur Company. Founded by John Jacob Astor in the early part of the century, the enterprise had grown into a virtual monopoly controlling all the fur trade in the United States. In recent years, the company had declined in its influence and control, a trend not helped by Astor's departure from the company he had started. But it was still operating, led now by a man named Ramsay Crooks, and Preacher knew he wouldn't get a better price for the furs anywhere else.

Despite the fact that night was falling and some businesses were closing for the day, the office of the American Fur Company, located in a sturdy building with a sprawling warehouse behind it, was still brightly lit. Preacher reined Horse to a stop in front of it and swung down from the saddle.

"Tie up these animals and keep an eye on 'em," Preacher told Hawk. "I'll go inside and talk to Vernon Pritchard. He runs this office, unless somethin's happened to him since the last time I was here." He added, "Dog, you stay out here, too."

Preacher wasn't sure it was a good idea to leave Hawk alone on the streets of St. Louis, but the youngster had to start getting used to the place sooner or later. Besides, Dog wouldn't let anything happen to him or any of the horses. Preacher took the steps leading up to the porch on the front of the building in a couple of bounds, then glanced back at Hawk, who was peering around wide-eyed, one more time before going into the building.

A man in a dusty black coat sat on a high stool behind a desk, scratching away with a quill pen as he entered figures in a ledger book. He had a tuft of taffy-colored hair on the top of his head and matching tufts above each ear, otherwise was bald. A pair of pince-nez clung precariously to the end of his long nose. He looked over the spectacles at Preacher and grinned as he tried to straighten up. A back permanently hunched from bending over a desk made that difficult.

"Preacher!" he said. "I didn't know if we'd see you this season."

"You didn't think anything would've happened to me, did you, Henry?"

"Well, of course not," the clerk said. "You're indestructible, Preacher. I fully expect that forty or fifty years from now, you'll still be running around those mountains out there, getting into all sorts of trouble."

Preacher laughed. "I'm gonna do my best to prove you right." He jerked a thumb over his shoulder. "Right now, though, I've got a load of pelts out there. Vernon around to make me an offer on 'em?"

Henry's smile disappeared and was replaced by a look of concern. "You just left them out there?"

"Dog's guardin' 'em. And I told my boy to keep an eye on 'em, too."

"You have a partner now?"

"My son," Preacher said.

That news made the clerk look startled again. He hemmed and hawed for a moment and then evidently decided he didn't want to press Preacher for the details. Instead he said, "Mr. Pritchard is in the warehouse. You can go on around."

"Thanks." Preacher paused. "Henry, why'd you say that about me leavin' the pelts outside, like it wasn't a good idea?"

"St. Louis has gotten worse in the past year, Preacher. There are thieves and cutthroats everywhere. I hate to walk back to my house at night." Henry reached down to a shelf under the desk and picked up an ancient pistol with a barrel that flared out at the muzzle. He displayed the weapon to Preacher and went on, "That's why I carry this."

"Put that sawed-off blunderbuss away," Preacher said. "You're makin' me nervous."

"Preacher being nervous." Henry shook his head. "I'll never live to see the day."

Preacher lifted a hand in farewell and went back outside. Just as he stepped onto the porch, he heard a harsh voice say, "Damn it, Nix, Jenks, look at that. That's a redskin sittin' there with a nice big load o' pelts. Hey, Injun, where'd you steal them furs?"

Preacher paused and eased sideways, out of the light that spilled through the door. He drifted into a shadow thick and dark enough to keep him from being noticed easily. He wanted to see what was going to happen.

Hawk had dismounted long enough to tie the animals' reins to the hitch rail in front of the office, then swung back up onto his pony, which he rode with a saddle now rather than bareback or with only a blanket, the way he had when he was younger. He stared impassively at the three men who swaggered toward him, but didn't say anything.

They were big and roughly dressed. Preacher could tell that much in the gloom. He didn't need to see the details to know what sort of men they were. The clerk had warned him about the ruffians now making St. Louis a dangerous place, and Preacher knew he was looking at three examples of that.

"I'm talkin' to you, redskin," continued the man who had spoken earlier. "I want to know where you stole them furs. I know good an' well a lazy, good-for-nothin' Injun like you didn't work to trap 'em."

Hawk said something in the Absaroka tongue. The three men clearly didn't understand a word of it, but Preacher did. Hawk's words were a warning: "You should go away now, before I kill you."

One of the men laughed and said, "I guess he told you, Brice — although I ain't sure just what he told you."

Brice, the one who had spoken first, stepped forward enough so that the light from the doorway revealed the scowl on his face. He said, "Don't you jabber at me, boy." He waved an arm. "Go on, get outta here! You don't need them furs. Leave them here for white men, and those horses, too." He sneered. "You can keep that damn Injun pony. It probably ain't fit to carry a real man."

After spending months with Preacher, Charlie Todd, and Aaron Buckley, Hawk spoke English quite well. Only occasionally did he stumble over a word or have to search for the right one. So Preacher knew Hawk understood everything Brice said.

He also knew that Hawk had a short temper and probably wasn't going to put up with much more of this.

Brice came closer. "Are you not listenin' to me, boy? I said git! We're takin' those pelts."

"They are . . . my furs," Hawk said in English, slowly and awkwardly as if he wasn't what he was saying. "Please . . . do not . . . steal them."

In the shadows on the porch, Preacher

grinned. Other than that, he was motionless. Hawk was baiting those would-be thieves, and Preacher had a pretty good idea what the outcome was going to be. He wouldn't step in unless it was necessary.

"Don't you mouth off to me, redskin," Brice blustered. "Get outta here, or you're gonna get the beatin' of your life."

"Please," Hawk said. "Do not hurt me."

Brice grunted in contempt and reached up.

"You had your chance," he said. "Now I'm gonna teach you a lesson, you red ni—"

He closed his hands on Hawk's buckskin shirt to drag him off the pony.

Then, a split second later, he realized he might as well have grabbed hold of a mountain lion.

Hawk's leg shot out. The moccasin-shod heel cracked into Brice's head and jolted his head back. As Brice staggered a couple of steps away, Hawk swung his other leg over the pony's back and dived at the other two men.

They both let out startled yells when Hawk kicked their friend, and one of them clawed at a pistol stuck behind his belt. Before he could pull the weapon free, Hawk crashed into them and drove them both off their feet.

He hit the ground rolling and came upright as Brice recovered his balance from the kick and charged at Hawk with a shout of rage. The young man darted aside nimbly as Brice tried to catch him in a bear hug that would have crushed his ribs.

Hawk twisted, clubbed his hands together, and slammed them into the small of Brice's back as the man's momentum carried him past. Brice cried out in pain and arched his back, then stumbled and went down hard, face-first, plowing into the hard-packed dirt of the street.

Hawk whirled to face the other two men, who were struggling to get up. One of them he met with a straight, hard punch that landed squarely on the man's nose. Even from where Preacher stood on the porch, he heard bone and cartilage crunch. The man went back down a lot faster than he had gotten up and stayed down this time.

The third man had a chance to spring toward Hawk and managed to get his right arm around the youngster's neck from behind. He clamped down with the grip and used his heavier weight to force Hawk forward and down. His left hand grasped his right wrist to tighten the choke hold. He brought up his right knee and planted it in Hawk's back. That move proved the man was an experienced brawler, because now with one good heave, he could snap Hawk's neck.

CHAPTER 3

Preacher wasn't going to stand by and do nothing while his son was killed. He had two flintlock pistols shoved behind the broad leather belt around his waist. He reached for the guns, then realized that if he blew a hole in the man about to break Hawk's neck, there was a good chance the heavy lead balls would pass on through his body and into the youngster. Preacher couldn't risk that.

Instead he grabbed the tomahawk that was also stuck behind his belt. A perfect throw would lodge the sharp flint head in the back of the man's skull without endangering Hawk.

As it turned out, the mountain man didn't need any of his weapons. Hawk writhed like a snake, and his opponent couldn't hold him. Hawk worked his way out of the grip seemingly by magic and dropped to a crouch. His elbow drove back sharply into the man's groin, causing a startled, high-pitched yelp of pain. As the man began to double over, Hawk turned and lifted an uppercut with all the deceptive strength in his slim body. His fist crashed into the man's jaw and made his feet come off the ground as he flipped over backward, out cold.

A voice said, "That was as fine a display of pugilism as I've seen in a long time, lad!" A man with a thatch of gray hair and bushy side whiskers came toward Hawk. He must have been watching the fight from the corner of the building. "Who are you, my friend? Do you speak English?"

"I speak the white man's tongue," Hawk said. He pointed toward the porch. "And I travel with him."

Preacher chuckled and moved forward to the top of the steps. "You knew I was up here watchin' the whole time, didn't you, Hawk?"

"Of course. I am not blind as so many of your people seem to be."

The newcomer looked up at the porch and said, "Is that you, Preacher?"

"Howdy, Vernon," Preacher said by way of answer. "Good to see you again. The sprout over there" — he nodded toward Hawk — "is Hawk That Soars." Preacher paused. "My son."

"Is that so?" Vernon Pritchard said. He thrust out his hand toward the youngster. "I'm pleased to make your acquaintance, Hawk That Soars."

Hawk hesitated, still not entirely comfortable with the customs of the white men, but he gripped Pritchard's hand and shook it.

"I didn't know you had any children, Preacher," the trader went on.

Preacher scratched his jaw and said, "You and me both. But I've never been good at keepin' up with that sort of thing."

"I take it those are your pelts on that pack mule?"

"Mine and Hawk's and a couple of other fellas. You want to make us an offer on 'em?"

Pritchard went over to the mule, opened one of the packs enough to check the furs bundled inside it, then said, "All of them the same quality?"

"Yep."

With the keen eye of an experienced trader, Pritchard estimated the load's weight, then stated a figure.

"You can do a mite better than that," Preacher said.

Pritchard laughed. "You drive a hard bargain, my friend. I'll raise my offer by . . . ten percent."

"Twenty-five."

"Fifteen," Pritchard countered.

"Done," Preacher said.

"I'll have my men unload. What about the mule?"

Preacher pointed along the street and said, "We're gonna take the horses down to Fullerton's. If one of your boys can bring the mule along when you're done, I'll tell Fullerton to be lookin' for him."

"I can do that."

Preacher nodded toward the three men lying sprawled in the street. They were starting to come around, stirring a little and letting out an occasional moan. The bubbling noises coming from the one whose nose Hawk had broken sounded miserable.

"You know these varmints?" the mountain man asked.

"Not to speak of. There are dozens of crooked brutes just like them around now. Do you want me to send for the constable so you can have them arrested?"

"No, I reckon Hawk already dealt 'em out enough punishment for bein' stupid."

"I considered killing them," Hawk said, "but I thought the other white men might be upset and cause trouble for you, Preacher."

"Don't ever hold back on killin' somebody who needs it on account of me," Preacher advised. "If I worried overmuch about what other folks think, I never would've taken off for the tall and uncut when I was still just a younker."

With the deal for the furs settled, Preacher and Hawk walked toward the stable, leading the four horses. Dog padded alongside the mountain man.

After a minute or so, Hawk said, "I am pleased you did not try to help me back there. I can fight my own battles."

"Never doubted it," Preacher replied. He didn't say anything about how he'd been preparing to take action when Hawk got loose from the third man. His help hadn't been needed . . . but he had been ready if it was.

Full night had fallen by the time they reached Fullerton's Livery Stable. The proprietor, Ambrose Fullerton, was a short, round man with a white beard and a genius's touch with animals. Preacher wouldn't trust Horse to anybody else in St. Louis, and he knew Fullerton wouldn't mind if Dog stayed here, too.

Fullerton came out of the office as Preacher and Hawk led the four horses into the barn's broad center aisle. He shook hands with Preacher and patted Horse on the shoulder and Dog on the head. They wouldn't accept such familiarity from many people.

"And who's this?" Fullerton said as he smiled at Hawk.

"My son, Hawk," Preacher explained. "We've been doin' some trappin' together."

"It's good to meet you, Hawk. You'll find that your pa has a lot of friends here in Sant Looey."

Hawk nodded solemnly and said, "I am beginning to understand this. He likes to talk about how many enemies he has made, but I think he has made more friends."

"Not necessarily," Fullerton said. "Most of Preacher's enemies are dead."

Preacher ignored that and jerked a thumb toward the two extra horses. "Seen these mounts before?"

Fullerton looked the horses over, studying them for a couple of minutes before he said, "As a matter of fact, I think I have. I believe they were stabled here for a few nights, a week or so ago."

"Remember what their owners looked like?"

"One was a tall, dark-haired fella. Had a lean and hungry look about him, as Audie might say when he's spouting old Bill Shakespeare. The other one was shorter. Had a red beard, as I recall."

Preacher nodded. "That's them, all right."

Fullerton regarded Preacher intently for a second, then said, "I don't suppose they'll be needing those horses anymore."

"Nope, they sure won't."

"In that case, I can take them off your hands if you want. Give you a fair price."

Preacher didn't bother haggling this time. He took what Fullerton offered him, then said, "You don't happen to know the names of those two fellas, do you? Or if they had any family around here? If they did, the money for the horses should rightfully go to them."

Fullerton shook his head. "They didn't offer their names, and I didn't ask. They didn't act like they were from around here, though. Fact is, they rode into town with some other fellas. All of them were new to these parts, seems like."

"How many other men are we talkin' about?" Preacher asked.

"Fourteen or fifteen, I'd say. Some kept their horses here, some didn't. But they're all gone now. I didn't get names for any of them, either." Fullerton rubbed his chin. "I can tell you about one of them, though. Hard to forget him. He was even bigger than you, Preacher. Didn't have a beard, but he was sporting one of those long mustaches that curl up on the ends. Funny-lookin' thing. The way the others acted, he was sort of the leader of the bunch."

"But they're not around anymore, you say?"

Fullerton shook his head and said, "I haven't seen any of 'em for a few days. I reckon they took off for greener pastures, wherever that might be."

Greener pastures, thought Preacher. Like lurking around west of the settlement to rob and kill trappers on their way to St. Louis with a load of pelts. Well, two members of the gang wouldn't be doing that anymore.

As they left the stable, Hawk asked, "Where will we stay tonight? We should make camp before it gets much later."

"We won't have to sleep on the ground tonight," Preacher said. "A friend of mine has a place here in town. It's mostly a tavern, but he rents rooms, too, and we can get something to eat there. That's where we're headed now."

"Sleep . . . in one of these buildings?"

"You've slept in tepees your whole life."

"Those are different."

Preacher laughed. "We're gonna have this same conversation about everything when it comes to civilization, ain't we?"

"Sleeping in a building." Hawk shook his

head. "It seems wrong."

"Well, you'll just have to see if you like it. The place we're headed is called Red Mike's."

Preacher led the way to the tavern not far from the waterfront. He stopped here every time he visited St. Louis and considered the burly Irishman who ran the place to be a friend. More than once, Preacher had gotten into fights either inside Red Mike's or near the place, but that didn't stop him from returning.

The streets were busy, and now that night had fallen, it was likely there weren't too many innocents out and about. Preacher and Hawk passed a number of hard-looking men, but those fellows gave them a wide berth. Preacher supposed some of them recognized him and figured it wouldn't be a good idea to tangle with him. Others just instinctively gave him room.

He knew he had something of a lean and hungry look himself. He recognized the quote because he'd heard it often enough from his friend Audie, who had been a college professor many years ago, before giving up that life to come west and take up trapping.

There were also women in the windows of some of the buildings they passed, calling down coarse invitations to the men in the street and sometimes displaying their charms by lantern light. Preacher could tell Hawk was trying not to stare at them but only partially succeeding.

"There are too many people here," Hawk said with a scowl as they walked along.

"I hear tell there are even bigger, more crowded settlements back East, and I've even spent some time in one called New Orleans, down near the mouth of the Mississippi."

Hawk shook his head. "It cannot be. That many people would breathe up all the air."

"Sometimes I feel that way myself," Preacher agreed.

They came to an unimpressive-looking building which had no sign on it because everybody knew where Red Mike's was. Preacher opened the door and went inside. Hawk followed him but stopped short, making a face at the thick clouds of grayish-blue smoke that filled the air. At least half of the men in the tavern were puffing on pipes. Some of the serving wenches were, too. Adding to the miasma in the air were odors of spilled beer and whiskey, vomit, and human waste.

"How do you stand it?" Hawk asked when Preacher looked back to see what was keeping him.

"I'd say you get used to it, but I ain't sure if that's true or not, because I've never been here long enough for that. I spend a night or two now and then, but after that I'm on my way back to the mountains."

"That sounds like a good plan. Let us go now."

Preacher laughed and clapped a hand on his son's shoulder. "Come on. It ain't that bad. I'll introduce you to Mike."

Hawk allowed himself to be led reluctantly toward the bar at the side of the low-ceilinged room. On the other side of the tavern, stairs led up to the second floor, where those rooms for rent Preacher had mentioned were located.

The bar was crowded, but when Mike spotted Preacher, he bellowed, "Step aside there, step aside! Make room!"

"What the hell, Mike!" one of the drinkers protested. "We got as much right here as anybody else." The man glanced around to see who was going to displace them, then added with a frown, "More right than a damn Injun!"

"That's my son you're talkin' about, mister," Preacher said in a flat, hard voice.

"Then he's a dirty half-breed, and he shouldn't even be in here!"

Preacher stiffened. He was proud of his boy, and he wasn't going to let anybody insult Hawk that way. It was an insult to Bird in a Tree, too, and that was even more intolerable. He was about to throw a punch, despite the look he got from Mike that implored him not to start anything, when a voice like beautiful music from a bell cut through the hubbub in the room.

"Gentlemen, wouldn't you rather drink than fight?"

A bare arm, complete with smooth, creamy female flesh, was thrust in front of him, and the hand at the end of that arm held a foaming, brimming tankard of beer. He lifted his gaze to the prettiest pair of blue eyes he had seen in a long time, and behind him he heard Hawk exclaim softly in what sounded like awe.

CHAPTER 4

The girl stood there in a simple homespun dress from which the sleeves had been cut to leave her arms uncovered. Actually, the garment was a little ragged and worn, but on her it looked like an elegant gown as it hugged her generously curved figure. Long, straight fair hair framed a heart-shaped face. She was a mixture of innocence and worldly beauty, and the striking contrast made her even more appealing. Preacher was too old and had known too many women to ever be thrown for a loop by any of them, but even he had to admit this one was damned good-looking.

As for Hawk, he looked a little like he had been walloped between the eyes by an ax handle.

The man who had been complaining about being forced to make room for Preacher and Hawk at the bar was gawking, too. The girl offered the tankard of beer to him and went on, "Here, take this. It's on the house, isn't it, Mike?"

"It sure is," Mike said. A smirk lifted the corners of his mouth. "Why don't you take your beer over to one of the tables, mister? Maybe Chessie will bring you another one in a little while."

"I'd be happy to," the girl said. She pressed the tankard into the man's hand, turned him around, and steered him toward a table. He went willingly, with a stunned smile on his face.

"You showed up just in time, darlin'," Mike said to the girl he had referred to as Chessie. "Not that this would've been the first time a dandy little fracas got started in here, usually involving this woolly-lookin' spalpeen you see before you. Ain't that right, Preacher?"

Hawk found his voice and asked, "What did he say? I am confused."

Preacher ignored the youngster and smiled at the gal. "Mike makes me sound like a troublemaker," he said, "but when you come right down to it, I'm a peaceable man. They call me Preacher."

She held out a slim white hand and said, "Chessie Dayton."

Preacher clasped her hand, aware of how smooth her skin was against his rough, callused palm. "It's a plumb honor to meet you, Miss Chessie." He turned a little to nod at Hawk and added, "This here is my son, Hawk That Soars."

"What an inspiring name," she said, then glanced at Preacher. "He's not a . . . savage . . . is he?"

Instead of letting Preacher answer, Hawk said, "I am savage only to my enemies, and I never make war on women. You have nothing to fear from me."

"Oh! You speak English."

"I am half-white," Hawk said solemnly, "so I should know the white man's tongue."

"You speak it very well."

Mike laughed and said, "Better than most of the louts who come in here."

Preacher said, "I don't recollect seein' you before, Miss Chessie."

"That's because I haven't worked here for long," she said. "Mike was kind enough to give me a job after —"

She stopped short. Preacher saw something in her eyes. A flash of a painful memory, maybe. That was confirmed by Mike, who leaned both hands on the bar and said quietly, "Both of Chessie's folks died of a fever a while back. She was left to shift for herself, so I found a place for her here, servin' drinks." His voice hardened as he added, "And that's all she does."

Preacher knew what the Irishman meant by that. Mike was warning them that Chessie wouldn't be entertaining any men upstairs. He had a reputation for having iron-hard fists and a lump of flint for a heart, but Preacher knew Mike had a sentimental streak in him as well, like most sons of the Emerald Isle.

"Well, it's good to know you, miss," the mountain man said, "and I hope that life treats you a mite better in the future."

"Thank you. Can I get you anything?"

"I reckon Mike can take care of that."

"Indeed I can," Mike said. He filled another tankard with ale and placed it on the bar in front of Preacher, then looked at Hawk and raised his bushy red brows quizzically.

"I want nothing to drink," Hawk said rather curtly.

Since the youngster was half-white, Preacher didn't know if liquor would affect him as badly as it did most Indians. Of course, Preacher had seen plenty of drunken white men, too. But either way, Hawk's refusal of the drink wasn't a bad thing. Since he was in surroundings that were almost totally alien to him, it was probably best that he keep a clear head.

As for Preacher, alcohol had never muddled him any, so he picked up the tankard and took a long swallow. With a nod to Mike, he said, "Good as always. Really cuts the dust."

Some men at one of the tables were calling for service. Mike pointed them out to Chessie and handed her a bucket of beer. As she left to deliver the bucket, Mike said to Preacher and Hawk, "I appreciate you fellows holding your temper just now."

"We didn't come in here lookin' for a fight," Preacher said. "We're more interested in findin' a place to spend a night or two before we head back to the mountains."

"Did you bring in a load of pelts to sell?"

Preacher nodded. "Yeah. Made a deal for 'em with Vernon Pritchard over at the American Fur Company."

Mike frowned and asked, "Has he paid you yet?"

"No, we'll go by there tomorrow and pick up the money. Why do you want to know? I've got a few gold and silver pieces, I can pay for our rooms —"

Mike stopped the mountain man with a wave of his hand. "It's not that. I was just going to warn you that if you're carrying a very big sum, it'd be a good idea for you to get out of St. Louis as quickly as you can.

'Tis not as safe here as it once was. You'd be better off out on the trail."

"Yeah, I keep hearin' that," Preacher said, "but we were out on the trail when we got ambushed a couple of days ago."

"Ambushed!" Mike repeated. "What happened?"

Between sips of beer, Preacher explained to the tavern keeper about the two men who had taken potshots at him and Hawk.

"I put their horses down at Fullerton's along with our mounts," Preacher concluded. "Ol' Ambrose recognized 'em. Said he had them there in his stalls for a few nights, and that the men who were ridin' 'em came into town with a bunch of other hard-lookin' fellas. The boss seemed to be a big man with one of those fancy curlicue mustaches."

"Like this?" Mike pantomimed a mustache that curled up on the ends.

"That's what Fullerton said."

Mike leaned on the bar again, frowned darkly, and said, "Preacher, I've seen that fella in here. He's Hoyt Ryker."

Preacher was taking a drink as Mike spoke. He stopped, slowly lowered the tankard to the bar, and stiffened.

"Ryker?"

"None other."

"He didn't have a mustache like that the last time I saw him."

"No, I don't suppose he did," Mike said. "How long ago was it that the two of you had that run-in?"

Preacher rubbed his darkly beard-stubbled chin and frowned in thought as he tried to remember. After a moment he said, "Got to be three or four years. Maybe even longer."

"Yeah, Ryker's changed some since then. He's gotten bigger and meaner, if that's possible."

Preacher grunted. "Wouldn't have thought it was."

His mind went back to his previous encounter with Hoyt Ryker. The trouble hadn't happened here in Red Mike's but rather in another tavern, closer to the river and even more of a dive. A tall, brawny young man had come in and started boasting of his prowess at throwing a knife. Preacher had no use for braggarts, so he ignored the man as best he could.

Others in the tavern had egged him on, though, daring him to back up his boasts. All of them were drunk, including the young man, but that hadn't stopped him from grabbing one of the serving girls, shoving her up against the wall, and ordering her to stand there as he took out a long, heavy-bladed hunting knife. He'd claimed that he could stand across the room, throw the knife, and put it within six inches of the girl's ear.

Preacher figured the proprietor might put a stop to this dangerous tomfoolery, but the man didn't seem to care as long as his customers kept spending money. And if the man with the knife missed . . . what was one wench more or less in this world?

Finally, Preacher's disgust had forced him to his feet. The knife thrower was standing there with a big, drunken grin on his face as he drew back his arm and got ready. Other men shouted encouragement and furiously placed bets on whether or not the girl would survive.

On the other side of the room, the pale, terrified girl shook like she had the ague. The young man had warned her not to move, though, or else he'd give her a beating. And none of the riverfront scum in this place would stop him . . .

Except for one man whose home was the mountains.

The sleeves of the young man's homespun shirt were rather loose and hung down a little. Standing twenty feet away, Preacher drew his own knife and let fly without a lot of posing and posturing as he aimed. The blade flew true, pierced the man's shirt-sleeve without touching the flesh underneath, and pinned the garment to the wall behind the man, jerking him a step along with it. He let out a startled shout and dropped the knife.

Preacher had walked across the suddenly quiet room, kicked the fallen knife aside, and then turned to look at the girl and say, "Go on and get outta here, darlin', while you got the chance."

While he was doing that, the boastful young man, his face twisted with hate, reached up with his other hand, wrenched Preacher's knife free from the wall, and tried to plunge the blade into the mountain man's back.

Preacher had expected that. He turned, seemingly leisurely, and caught hold of the young man's wrist before the thrust could strike him. A twist hard enough to make bones grind together had sent the young man to his knees and brought a cry of pain to his lips. With his other hand, Preacher easily plucked the knife out of the man's suddenly nerveless fingers.

"A man who's truly good at somethin', whether it's knife-throwin' or anything else, don't have any need to show off about it, especially if it means puttin' somebody else in danger," Preacher had told him, the words clear in the still-hushed tavern. "You'd do well to remember that, son."

The young man stared up at him. His teeth were bared in a grimace as he said, "What did you just do . . . old man? Seemed like . . . showing off . . . to me."

"Nope," Preacher had said. "Just did what I had to to keep you from hurtin' that poor girl." Finally, he released the man's wrist and stepped back. The man slumped forward, cradling the throbbing arm against his body. Preacher said, "If I hear about you hurtin' her or anybody else, I'll be back to see you."

With an effort, the young man had lifted his head and said in obvious pain, "You don't scare me . . . mister. One of these days . . . you're gonna be sorry . . . you crossed Hoyt Ryker."

"That'd be you?"

"Damn right!"

Preacher grinned. "I never knew a man who referred to his own self by name that way to be worth a bucket of warm piss."

Then he had turned and walked out of the place. He'd had a hand near the butt of one of the flintlock pistols stuck behind his belt, just in case the young braggart's pride made him try something else. Preacher had been out of patience by that point, and if anything had happened, he would have gone ahead and killed the man.

But it hadn't happened, and Preacher hadn't seen hide nor hair of Hoyt Ryker since then. The story had gotten around the riverfront, though, about how Preacher had humiliated the young man. He figured Ryker had left town and gone someplace where nobody would have heard about the incident.

Now Preacher said, "So Ryker's back in these parts, is he?"

"That's right," Red Mike said. "He came in here with some other men a while back. I didn't recognize him at first, but somebody told me who he was. Then I could see it, even though that fancy mustache makes him look quite a bit different."

Hawk said to Preacher, "Another of those old enemies of yours that seem to be lurking under every rock?"

Preacher blew out a contemptuous breath. "I had one little scrape with him, that's all. Ain't hardly worth rememberin'."

"You can bet Ryker's never forgotten it," Mike said. "I haven't seen him around for a few days, though, so maybe he's moved on."

"It don't matter to me, one way or the other," Preacher said.

He wasn't surprised, though, to hear that the two would-be thieves he had killed had been affiliated with Hoyt Ryker. Most men were a mixture of good and bad, but some were just pure skunk and Ryker fell into that category. Preacher had heard rumors about various robberies and killings that might have involved Ryker. Under the circumstances, it made sense to assume that the men riding with him were the same sort.

Preacher didn't have much time to think about that, because just then another commotion caught his attention. He looked around and saw that another man had come into Red Mike's place. This newcomer was striding across the room, bumping men out of his way, and leaving behind some angry, profane muttering. He was well dressed in high-topped black boots, gray whipcord trousers, and a brown jacket over a fancy vest and white shirt. A black beaver hat sat on dark blond hair. Well-groomed and handsome, he didn't belong here in this rough frontier tavern. Anybody could see that.

Anybody could tell what he was after, too. He stalked straight toward Chessie Dayton with a determined expression on his face.

Chapter 5

Chessie had been moving around the room, talking to the tavern's customers and collecting empty mugs, while Preacher was talking to Red Mike. Preacher had been aware that Hawk was looking at the girl from time to time. Almost any young man would have a hard time keeping his eyes off a gal like her — and a sizable percentage of older gents would, too.

Still, Hawk seemed to be unusually fascinated by her, probably because of both her beauty and her novelty. He had never seen anyone like Chessie before.

She had noticed the fancy-dressed newcomer as well and turned to face him as he approached. Preacher noticed that she held the empty mugs and tankards she had collected in front of her, as if to defend herself with them if she needed to.

The young man stopped when he was still a few feet away from her and said, "I told you I'd be back to renew our acquaintance, Miss Dayton."

"Mr. Merton," she said. "Oliver . . . I . . . I didn't really think I'd ever see you again."

"I always keep my promises." He held out his right hand toward her. "If you'll come with me, I'd like to take you to dinner."

"Well, I . . . I don't know . . ."

A man at a nearby table spoke up, saying, "Hey, mister, can't you see that Chessie's workin'? You can't just waltz in here and steal her way from us."

"Yeah!" another of the tavern's customers added. "You don't reckon we come in here for the swill Mike serves, do you? It tastes a hell of a lot better when a pretty gal brings it to you!"

Over at the bar, Preacher asked quietly, "Who's the fancy pants, Mike?"

"Young fella's name is Oliver Merton," Mike replied. "He's been in here a few times lately. Seems mighty taken with Chessie, but of course, he ain't the only one. That's all I can tell you about him, 'cept that he dresses like he's got money."

Oliver Merton ignored the two men who had protested when he asked Chessie to leave the tavern and have dinner with him. He kept his hand extended toward her and moved slightly closer.

"It would be a true honor to share your company for the evening, my dear," he said. "Come back to the hotel with me, or we can go anywhere else you'd care to have dinner. The finest restaurant in St. Louis is none too good for you."

She shook her head and said, "It wouldn't be fittin' for me to go into a place like that." She gestured toward her dress. "Not wearing this. I look like a . . . a slattern —"

"Nonsense," Merton interrupted her. "Your natural beauty shines through and renders irrelevant any garment fortunate enough to be draped about your exquisite form."

Preacher had thought sort of the same thing when he first laid eyes on the girl, although he never would have phrased it in such flowery language.

The customer who had objected first got to his feet and said, "Damn it, mister, didn't you hear me? The likes o' you ain't welcome in here. You come in here thinkin' you're all better'n us and start botherin' this gal —"

Merton finally acknowledged the man, who was dressed like he labored on the Mississippi River docks. Merton gave his antagonist a contemptuous look and said, "First of all, it's up to Miss Dayton to decide whether or not I'm bothering her, and secondly, it's a matter of mere fact that I *am* better than all of you —"

That was as far as he got before the man threw a punch at him.

Merton leaned aside so that the knobby-knuckled fist shot past his ear. He snapped a sharp blow of his own into the man's face, landing it with enough force to make the fellow lurch back a step as blood spurted from his nose. Merton was about to follow up that right jab with a left cross when another man jumped on his back.

Chessie screamed.

As men leaped up from tables and scrambled to get out of the way, Merton staggered forward under the unexpected weight. The man on his back wrapped his arms around Merton's neck and locked his legs around the young man's waist.

"I got him, Everett!" the man cried. "I'll hold him, while you teach him a lesson!"

The man with the bloody nose had caught his balance. He shook his head, sending crimson droplets flying, and balled his fists. With a furious roar, he charged.

Merton was still stumbling around. He seemed to lose his balance and fall, but then the way he twisted his body made Preacher realize it was a deliberate move on the young man's part. The man on Merton's back hit first, crashing down on a table that broke under their combined weight. The impact knocked the man's grip loose as they both sprawled amid the table's wreckage.

Merton's right leg came up. His boot heel caught the charging Everett in the groin. The man howled in pain and doubled over, which brought his jaw within reach of Merton's left foot as the young man kicked upward again. Everett sailed backward.

With a fast roll, Merton came up on one knee. He was facing more enemies now as several other men jumped into the fray. Most folks didn't like an outsider to start with, and Merton had been asking for trouble with his arrogant attitude. As he tried to get the rest of the way to his feet, a hard fist slammed against his jaw. Men closed in around him, swinging punches and launching kicks.

Preacher figured that Merton was sort of getting what was coming to him, but at the same time, odds of five to one rankled the mountain man. Chessie had backed off. She wasn't screaming anymore, but she had her hands clapped to her face as she looked on in horror at the lopsided battle. Behind the bar, Mike scowled, obviously upset that this brawl had broken out, but he didn't show any signs of trying to stop it, and neither did anyone else.

That sort of left things up to Preacher.

Or so he thought, but then a second later he realized he was wrong about that. Whether Merton really deserved it or not, somebody was fixing to give him a hand.

Hawk charged into the fracas.

He tackled a man who was drawing back his leg to kick Merton in the head. The impact drove the man off his feet. As he landed on the rough floor, he writhed around and tried to punch Hawk. The young warrior ducked inside that looping blow and headbutted the man in the face. The man went limp and lay there stunned, out of the fight for the moment.

Hawk rolled, caught hold of another man around the knees, and with a quick yank upended him. The man banged his head hard against the floor when he landed, and he didn't seem to be in any hurry to get back into the fracas, either.

That improved the odds against Oliver Merton, and although he was still outnumbered three to one, Merton was able to struggle to his feet and start throwing punches again. The attitude he'd displayed earlier left a lot to be desired but at least he was a fighter. Preacher had to give him credit for that.

Merton knocked one man away from him, but he absorbed punches from the other two. His hat was long gone, knocked off during the fight, and his expensive clothes were rumpled and dirty. Blood from his own wounds and those of his opponents had spattered onto his frilly white shirt. He caught his balance, set his feet, and hooked a hard right into the belly of one of his attackers. An instant later, a fist exploded against his ear and sent him reeling.

Hawk was there to catch Merton and prop him up. Merton glanced at him. Preacher saw a look of distaste cross the young man's face. Merton must have just realized he had an ally — and that that ally was an Indian.

Prejudiced or not, Merton was still facing a superior number of foes. Practicality won out. He and Hawk stood back to back, trading punches with their attackers as four men closed in, two on each side. The spectators had fallen silent, so for a long moment there was no sound in Red Mike's tavern except harsh breathing from the combatants and the constant thudding of fists against flesh and bone.

Hawk and Merton each knocked down one of the men facing them. The remaining two, who hadn't been part of the battle originally, backed off and held up their hands, palms out in surrender. Now that the odds were even, they didn't want any more part in this ruckus.

"That's it," one of them panted. "We're done."

"That's right," the other man said. "We've had enough."

"Then get out of here," Merton snapped. "And take your scurvy friends with you."

Preacher could tell the young man was putting up a brave front. He was exhausted, and he had taken quite a pounding. As for Hawk, this was the second battle against superior odds he had fought in the past couple of hours, and that had taken a toll on him, as well. He and Merton both looked like they were about to collapse, but pride and grit kept them on their feet.

That was enough. The half-dozen men who had been mixed up in the fray on the opposite side struggled to their feet and stumbled out, moaning and cussing and leaking blood as they went.

Merton swayed and put a hand on the back of a chair to support himself as he turned to give Hawk a curt nod. That was his only expression of gratitude. Then he looked around, clearly searching for Chessie.

She was nowhere in sight. She must have

slipped out during the commotion, Preacher thought. Even he hadn't seen her go, and he didn't miss much.

Oliver Merton came over to the bar. He tried to stride imperiously across the room, but he was still too shaky to pull that off. He wound up having to lean on the hardwood with both hands when he got there.

"Where's Miss Dayton?" he demanded of Red Mike.

"I dunno," the Irishman said. "I didn't see her go, but she must've left while you and Hawk were brawling with those men."

"Hawk?" Merton repeated. "Is that the savage's name?"

"Hawk That Soars is my Absaroka name," the young man in question said as he came up beside Merton. "At least, that is how white men say it. And I am not a savage, except when the situation calls for it."

"I didn't ask for your help," Merton said sullenly.

"Those men would have killed you," Hawk said, "and there would have been blood all over the floor. My father's friend would have had to clean it up. This seemed unnecessary to me."

"And in case you ain't figured it out," Preacher drawled, "I'm Hawk's pa. They call me Preacher."

The name clearly meant nothing to Merton. He had no idea Preacher was the most famous mountain man since John Colter and Jim Bridger, at least in some circles. He turned back to Mike and asked, "Where does Miss Dayton live?"

"That's none of your business, mister," Mike replied.

"I'm making it my business. I intend to see her again while I'm in St. Louis." Merton reached inside his jacket, brought out a small leather pouch, and dropped it on the bar. Coins clinked inside it. "I'll pay well if you tell me where to find her."

Mike's face flushed angrily to almost match his hair. "No offense, Mr. Merton," he said, "but I think 'tis time for you to be leavin' my tavern." He poked a blunt fingertip against the pouch. "And you can take your filthy lucre with you."

"There's nothing filthy about money."

"Depends on where it comes from and what you use it for."

The two men glared at each other across the bar for a long moment while Preacher and Hawk looked on. Then Merton shrugged, picked up the pouch, and tossed it gently on the palm of his hand, making the contents clink again.

"It's your choice," he said.

"Damn right it is, because this is my place," Mike said.

Merton sneered, shoved the pouch back inside his jacket, and turned away. Preacher reached out and stopped him with a hand on his jacket sleeve.

"Hold on there," the mountain man said. "Are you headin' back to the hotel where you're stayin'?"

"What business is that of yours?"

"Some of those fellas you and Hawk licked just now might be waitin' around outside, just hopin' they'll get another chance to stomp you. Probably be a good idea if we walked along with you."

"You think I need the protection of a ruffian and a . . . a redskin?" Merton laughed. "Please. After the thrashing I gave them, those cowardly louts are long gone."

"You willin' to bet your life on that?" Preacher said.

"I'm armed," Merton said. He slipped a couple of fingers inside a pocket on his vest and brought out a single-shot derringer. "I don't have anything to fear."

The little pistol wasn't much bigger than something a man might carve out of wood for his kid. Probably not much more dangerous than that, too. But Preacher shrugged and said, "Suit yourself."

"I generally do," Merton snapped. He pointed a finger at Red Mike. "Tell Miss Dayton that I'll be back to see her."

"Keep wavin' that finger in my face and I'm liable to break it off," Mike said.

Merton snorted and stalked out of the place, steadier on his feet now.

"There goes a fella who's just naturally gonna get himself killed before he gets too much older," Mike said.

"You're probably right," Preacher said, "but I reckon I'll trail along after him and try to see to it that he lives through the night."

"Why would you do that?" Hawk asked. "He is an unpleasant man, and he was bothering the girl."

Hawk didn't care for the attention Oliver Merton had been paying to Chessie, and Preacher supposed he couldn't blame him for that. A girl like Chessie was going to leave a lot of jealous hombres in her wake.

But he told Hawk, "I've heard it said that the Good Lord looks after damned fools because somebody has to. I reckon tonight I'm standin' in for the Lord and doin' His work. That boy may be a dyed-in-the-wool son of a bitch, but he fought hard and he don't deserve to have his guts stomped out in an alley."

Hawk thought about that for a second, then shrugged and said, "We will go after him."

CHAPTER 6

St. Louis boasted a few oil-burning streetlamps, but not in the area where Red Mike's was located. The only lights there came from the buildings. A yellow glow spilled through a window here and there, making the illumination that greeted Preacher and Hawk as they set off after Oliver Merton haphazard.

Despite that, both men spotted Merton almost right away. He strode along as if he owned the street . . . which, in his mind, maybe he did.

By this time of the evening, most of those who were out and about were up to no good. Merton encountered several prostitutes who tried to entice him into nearby alleys. Preacher was glad to see that the young man passed them by without even a glance. If he had succumbed to temptation and followed one of them into the deeper darkness, likely he would have found the woman's male accomplice waiting for him, ready to club him over the head or cut his throat and then steal everything he had of value.

Even if he hadn't been robbed or killed, chances were that in a few days he would have been battling a maddening itch in his trousers, so either way he was better off walking on and ignoring the whores.

They hadn't gone very far, though, when Preacher spotted movement in the shadows behind Merton. He and Hawk were hanging back a good distance because they didn't want Merton to know they were following him and keeping an eye on him. Two men had moved into that gap like ghosts, and now they were the ones directly behind Merton.

"Come on," Preacher whispered to his son. They began moving in, gliding soundlessly through the gloom. Out in the mountains, the Blackfeet sometimes referred to Preacher as Ghost Killer because of his stealth and his deadliness. Hawk couldn't match that level of silent lethality yet, but he was learning.

Merton strode through a small patch of light. Full of confidence, he never even glanced behind him. If he had, he would have seen the two roughly dressed men following him. They were starting to close in when disaster fell on them from behind, striking without sound or warning.

Preacher's right forearm clamped like a bar of iron across the throat of one man. He grabbed that wrist with his left hand and dragged the would-be robber backward into the deeper shadows.

A few feet away, Hawk had tackled his target in the same manner, but the man outweighed him, and Hawk had more trouble handling him than Preacher did with the other one. The man's feet scrabbled against the hard-packed dirt of the street.

That made enough noise to prompt Oliver Merton to pause and half turn to look behind him and frown. The gloom hid Preacher, Hawk, and the two thieves. After a moment, Merton shrugged and went on.

The man Preacher had hold of flailed around some, but the mountain man must have caught him without much air in his lungs, because he passed out quickly. Preacher lowered the heavy, inert form to the ground and turned to see how Hawk was doing. Even in the thick darkness, Preacher's eyes were keen enough to make out what was going on.

Hawk's opponent was able to twist around and get a hand on the young man's throat.

He used his weight to shove Hawk against the wall of a building. The two of them swayed there as they tried to choke the life out of each other.

Preacher slipped the tomahawk from behind his belt, stepped up behind the man, and walloped him with the flat of the flint head. He could have split the man's skull just as easily, and to tell the truth, for a second he had been about to do that.

Then he remembered that he and Hawk didn't know for an absolute certainty the two men intended to rob and probably kill Oliver Merton. The chances of that being true were mighty high, of course, and if either of these varmints had wound up dead he wouldn't have lost any sleep over it, but under the circumstances it was enough to knock them out and keep them from attacking Merton.

The clout on the head made the man's knees buckle. His hand slipped off Hawk's throat as he collapsed.

"You all right?" Preacher whispered to his son.

"Fine," Hawk replied curtly. Preacher could tell that he was angry, probably because his pa had had to give him a hand. Hawk's pride was a powerful thing.

"We'd better catch up to Merton. He

might've gotten into mischief while we were dealin' with these two."

They cat-footed after the young man and caught sight of him again a few minutes later. Merton appeared to be unmolested. He strode along with the same self-assured gait as before.

It didn't take him long to reach St. Louis's best hotel. Preacher wasn't surprised that was where Merton was staying. Anything less than the best wouldn't be good enough for him.

That seemed to be true for beauty, as well. Preacher didn't see how there could be many gals in town prettier than Chessie Dayton — if, indeed, there were any.

Problem was, rich men had a habit of trifling with poor girls, getting what they wanted and then callously tossing their conquests aside. Preacher figured Chessie deserved better than that.

He and Hawk stopped outside the hotel, still out of the light, as Merton went inside. Hawk said, "He has no idea that we helped him again."

"And he'd likely just resent it if he did," Preacher said. "Well, I reckon we've done what we could. The young fella's on his own from here on out. Let's head back to Mike's and get some sleep. Tomorrow we'll collect what Pritchard owes us, pick up some supplies, and head out again. Ought to be back in the mountains in time to do some more trappin' before autumn gets here." As they started away from the hotel, Preacher went on, "What do you think of St. Louis so far?"

"It is big and crowded and it stinks," Hawk said. "And people want to fight all the time. Why would anyone want to live like this?"

Preacher thought about the magnificent high country he called home and said, "I've asked myself that same question, more than once."

No one accosted them on their way back to Red Mike's. The denizens of this neighborhood were as wary as animals, and none of them wanted to tangle with two fellas as obviously capable of protecting themselves as Preacher and Hawk.

They were almost back to the tavern when Preacher spotted a flash of fair hair up ahead. He put a hand on Hawk's shoulder to stop him, leaned close, and breathed, "Is that Miss Chessie up the street yonder?"

"I believe it is," Hawk replied, equally quietly. "Who is that with her?"

Two figures were visible in the shadows, walking toward Red Mike's. At least, they were visible to the sharp eyes of Preacher and Hawk. One was Chessie, easy to identify because of her long, pale hair.

The other person had to be a man, judging by the height and the way Chessie walked arm in arm with him.

"That ain't Merton," Preacher told Hawk. "I reckon he might've doubled back from the hotel and found her, although it ain't likely. But that fella's too tall to be him."

"She has another . . . what is the word? Suitor?"

"Yeah," Preacher said. "But who it is ain't any of our business. We don't need to be spyin' on 'em."

"Who she walks with is her affair," Hawk agreed . . . but Preacher thought he didn't sound all that happy, or even sincere, about it. Hawk had been smitten with Chessie as soon as he laid eyes on her.

Preacher remembered what it felt like to be young and experience the same thing. There had been a girl named Jennie who had meant the world to him. What was between them had been doomed from the start, as it turned out, but that didn't mean it was any less real.

The two of them stopped to give Chessie and her beau some privacy as they continued on toward the tavern. Preacher figured

Mike was letting the girl stay in one of the rooms upstairs, although he hadn't said as much. The two indistinct figures came to a halt at the corner of the building. They drew close to each other, merged into one for a long moment. Preacher knew there was some sparking going on up yonder. So did Hawk, judging by the breath that hissed sharply through his teeth.

Then the two shapes parted, and the taller one started walking back up the street toward the spot where Preacher and Hawk stood. With another flash of fair hair, Chessie opened the door and went into the tavern.

Preacher put his hand on Hawk's shoulder again and urged him back deeper into the shadows between buildings so they could let Chessie's suitor pass without noticing them. The man's long-legged stride carried him along quickly. His steps were confident.

He moved past them. Preacher caught a glimpse of the man's face, and his muscles suddenly tensed. It was a lean, rather wolfish countenance, with a thick mustache, oiled and curled up on the ends, dominating those features. Despite that major difference, the man still looked enough like he had several years earlier for Preacher to recognize him instantly.

Hoyt Ryker.

Preacher's jaw tightened. He had no interest in Chessie other than appreciating the fact that she was a pretty girl. But she had seemed sweet and a mite on the innocent side, and he didn't think she ought to be spending her time with a brutal scoundrel like Ryker. The mustache might have changed Ryker's appearance a little, but Preacher didn't believe for a second that the man's nature had changed.

The fact that those two varmints who had ambushed them west of the settlement were part of Ryker's bunch was proof enough of that, as far as Preacher was concerned. The man was no good.

Hawk must have noticed the distinctive facial hair and realized the same thing Preacher had. He gripped the mountain man's arm and whispered, "Ryker."

"Yeah, I know," Preacher said.

"Should we go after him?"

Preacher frowned, then shook his head in the darkness. "He ain't done nothin' to us."

"He is a bad man. An old enemy of yours. You said so yourself. He should not be with Miss Chessie."

"I reckon that's her decision to make," Preacher said, even though it pained him to do so. "Could be she don't know what sort of fella he really is, though, and she's got a right to."

"You are going to tell her?"

"I just might." One of the last things Preacher wanted to do was to get mixed up in some gal's love life, but he'd felt an instinctive liking for Chessie. She was young enough and probably inexperienced enough that she might be fooled by some big, handsome galoot like Hoyt Ryker and convince herself that she was in love with him.

She deserved better than that. Better than Oliver Merton, too.

Maybe she deserved somebody like Hawk?

Preacher grimaced and shoved that thought out of his head. Hawk was a fine young man, but he was half-Absaroka. That didn't mean a damned thing to Preacher — he didn't have a prejudiced bone in his body and judged everybody on the way they acted, that was all — but he was practical enough to know that not everybody in the world felt the same way. Hawk would always face trouble because of his mixed blood, whether he tried to live in the white world or the red. Any woman who became seriously involved with him would be a target for that trouble as well. He wasn't sure Chessie was strong enough to handle that.

Anyway, they had just met her this evening. It was much too soon to even be thinking about such things.

"I can follow Ryker and find out where he is staying," Hawk suggested. "If the rest of those men are still with him and they discover we killed two of their companions, they might prove dangerous."

Preacher shook his head. "We'll deal with that when and if the time comes," he said. "Let's go on in, claim one of Mike's upstairs rooms, and get some shut-eye."

Hawk didn't respond at first, but he fell in step beside Preacher as the mountain man started for the tavern. Then he said, "Those men attack us, and when we reach St. Louis we find they have been traveling with a man who hates you. Then we go to the tavern owned by your friend and discover the young woman who works there is involved with the same old enemy. What does this tell you, Preacher?"

"I don't know, but you sound like you've got it figured out. Why don't *you* tell *me* what it means?"

"It appears that the spirits are working to bring your path and that of Hoyt Ryker together again," Hawk said. "What will happen when those paths cross?"

Preacher didn't have an answer for his son, but he had a hunch that if he and Ryker butted heads again . . .

Blood would be spilled this time. Maybe a lot of it.

CHAPTER 7

The tavern was still busy. The broken table and the other signs of the struggle had been cleaned up, and men had gone back to their drinking as if the battle earlier in the evening had never happened.

Preacher didn't see Chessie when he and Hawk went inside, so he figured she had already gone upstairs. Mike confirmed that when they stopped at the bar.

"Poor girl was shaken up by what happened," he said as he mopped the bar with a rag. "I told her to get some rest. We can manage down here without her for the rest of the night."

Preacher and Hawk exchanged a glance but neither said anything. Preacher knew what his son was thinking, because the same thought was in his head. Chessie hadn't seemed all that upset when she was letting Hoyt Ryker kiss her.

But that was none of his business,

Preacher reminded himself. He slid one of his few remaining coins across the bar to pay for a night's lodging.

"This ain't a hotel, you know," Mike said, but he made the silver piece disappear anyway. "But go ahead. 'Tis better than sleeping in a stable, I suppose."

"Barely," Preacher replied with a grin.

The rest of the night passed quietly. The straw tick mattress on the bunk in the little upstairs room wasn't too infested with vermin. Preacher slept well, as he always did, and was rested when he went downstairs the next morning. The tavern was empty except for Mike, who stood behind the bar drinking a cup of coffee. He gestured to the pot sitting on the stove in the corner. Preacher took that as an invitation to help himself.

He did so and carried his cup over to the bar. Mike asked, "Hawk still asleep?"

"Yeah. Boy was up a little later than usual last night. Most times in the mountains or out on the trail, we'd turn in once it got dark. Here in a settlement, though, folks just keep goin' until they're wore out."

Mike grinned. "Which is good for fellas who own taverns, like me."

Preacher looked around and said, "Reckon that Chessie gal is still asleep, too."

"I suppose. I haven't seen her."

"You takin' an interest in her, Mike? Sort of like an uncle?"

A frown creased the Irishman's forehead under his tousled thatch of rusty hair. "What the hell do you mean by that, Preacher? You make it sound like you're askin' if I intend to take advantage of her!"

Preacher shook his head and said, "Nope. Just sayin' exactly what I mean, as usual. If you've got the girl's best interests at heart, there's somethin' you ought to know."

"Well, go ahead and tell me," Mike said, still glaring.

"When Hawk and I got back here last night after seein' to it that Merton made it to his hotel all right, we spotted Chessie outside. She was with a man, and she didn't seem upset. Fact is, the two of 'em were sparkin'." Preacher realized he was gossiping like an old woman. He didn't like the feeling. "We caught a glimpse of the fella as he left. It was Hoyt Ryker."

Mike stood up straight and stared at the mountain man. "Are you sure?"

"Yeah. He had that fancy mustache like we talked about, but I got a good enough look at his face to remember him from the last time we butted heads a few years ago, too. It was Ryker, all right. He ain't left town after all. I reckon he must've met Chessie one of the times he was in here recently."

"She's young enough she might fall for whatever he told her," Mike muttered. "Damn it! Somebody needs to talk to her and warn her about the varmint, but that ain't the kind of thing I'm good at."

"Well, since you've sort of appointed yourself her guardian, I reckon it's your responsibility."

"Yeah, but you're the one who actually saw 'em together!" Mike shook his head and sighed. "All right. I'll have a talk with her. I ain't promising it'll go all that well, though."

"Give it a try," Preacher said. "As for me and Hawk, we'll be headin' back to the mountains, where all we got to worry about is grizzly bears, catamounts, and Blackfeet!"

Vernon Pritchard had the payment for the pelts ready when Preacher and Hawk arrived at the American Fur Company later that morning. He set the leather pouch full of gold pieces on the desk in front of him and said, "There you go, Preacher. You can count it if you like."

"You never cheated me yet, Vernon, and I ain't expectin' you to start now," Preacher said as he scooped up the pouch. "Anyway, it'll get counted when Hawk and me head over to Fitzgerald's and stock up on supplies for our trip back to the mountains. We'll be spendin' most of these here coins, I expect."

"Fitzgerald's goods don't come cheap," Pritchard agreed. "They're of fine quality, though."

Preacher stowed the money away inside his shirt. "Pleasure doin' business with you," he told Pritchard. Hawk just grunted and gave the man a nod, then turned to follow Preacher out of the office.

Preacher said so long to Henry, the stooped clerk, and then led Hawk to the huge, sprawling general mercantile store a short distance away. The business occupied an entire block, with entrances and high loading docks on all four sides. Inside it was crammed with goods. Whether a trapper was an experienced frontiersman or a greenhorn, everything he might need for a trip to the Rocky Mountains could be found at Fitzgerald's. The store's customers also included many of the citizens of St. Louis, as well as those who lived on the growing number of farms in the surrounding area.

Those farms were a sign of civilization's inevitable encroachment, and Preacher sort of hated to see them sprouting up like weeds. They reminded him too much of his boyhood home. He had been eager to escape from there and head for more untamed lands. Now the sort of life he had left behind appeared to be catching up to him.

He took some small comfort in the fact that he spent most of his time hundreds of miles west of here in the mountains. Civilization would never make it *that* far, he told himself, at least not in his lifetime.

Despite the relatively early hour, the store was already busy, with wagons parked at the loading docks and horses tied up at the hitch racks. As Preacher and Hawk approached, the mountain man saw clerks wearing canvas aprons loading sacks and crates of supplies onto a pair of wagons. A tall man in woolen trousers and a buckskin shirt appeared to be supervising the loading. He also wore a felt hat with a high, rounded crown and an eagle feather stuck in the band. Something about that hat struck Preacher as familiar, and when the man turned so that Preacher could see his profile, he understood why. He had caught a glimpse of the hat the night before as its owner walked by after sparking with Chessie Dayton.

It was Hoyt Ryker standing there on the

loading dock telling the clerks how to load the supplies into the wagons.

Hawk had recognized Ryker, too. "There is the man with the mustache," he said as Preacher slowed and then stopped.

"Yeah," the mountain man said. He scratched his beard-stubbled jaw and frowned. Would Ryker recognize him, too, he wondered? Preacher was a little more grizzled now than he had been a few years earlier, but he still looked pretty much the same. And he didn't imagine Ryker would have forgotten their confrontation.

On the other hand, Preacher wasn't in the habit of letting anybody stop him from going where he wanted to go, and he sure as hell wasn't afraid of Hoyt Ryker. His mouth tightened into a grim line as he strode toward Fitzgerald's with Hawk beside him.

Ryker glanced in their direction, then looked at them again, more sharply this time. That answered the question of whether or not Ryker had recognized him, Preacher thought. Ryker wasn't paying any attention to what was going in the wagons anymore. He was watching Preacher, instead.

Preacher and Hawk went up the steps to the loading dock, which also doubled as a porch for the store. Ryker moved a little, not in any hurry, but Preacher noted that the shift put Ryker between them and the store's entrance. If they wanted to go inside, they had no choice but to come to a halt facing Ryker and tell him to step aside.

Ryker's mouth twisted in a smirk as Preacher and Hawk came up to him. He said, "Never thought you'd see me again, did you, Preacher?"

"Well, I was hopin'," the mountain man said. "We're goin' in the store, Ryker."

Ryker ignored that and nodded toward Hawk. "Who's the redskin?" he asked.

"I am Hawk That Soars," Hawk said. "Preacher is my father."

Ryker laughed and said, "Is that so? Spawned a whelp with some fat little squaw, did you, Preacher?"

Hawk took that badly, which came as no surprise. Ryker had meant to be offensive. Hawk started to step toward Ryker, but Preacher put a hand out to stop him.

"You know, you ain't any more pleasant to be around than you were the last time," Preacher said as his eyes narrowed in anger. "If you want to take up where we left off, you're makin' a good start on it."

Ryker lifted both hands, palms out. "Hold on, hold on," he said. "I'm not looking for trouble. I'm willing to forget all about what happened between us in the past. In fact, if you come right down to it, I'm grateful to you for what you did."

"Grateful?" Preacher repeated. He didn't believe for a second that Ryker was being sincere. "Why would you be grateful?"

"I was drunk that night," Ryker said, not telling Preacher anything he didn't already know. "Now, mind you, I was mighty good with a knife and I still am . . . but I *might* have missed because of all the whiskey I'd had, and that would've been terrible. I might not have had to answer to the law — she was just a tavern girl, after all — but I would've carried that guilt around with me for the rest of my life. So I owe you a debt, Preacher, for saving me from that."

Preacher didn't believe Ryker was capable of feeling guilt. He ignored what the man had said and told him, "We're goin' inside. You need to get out of the way."

"Before we've finished our talk?"

"We don't have anything to talk about," Preacher snapped. He took a step forward. He and Ryker were the same height. His chest was about to bump Ryker's chest when a heavy footstep sounded in the store's doorway. Ryker laughed and stepped aside.

Preacher saw that the entrance was still blocked, this time by a massive man who towered over both him and Ryker. A black beard jutted halfway down the man's chest, but the top of his head was bald as an egg, a fact revealed by his lack of a hat. Thick slabs of muscle on his arms, shoulders, and chest strained the homespun shirt he wore. He had a large, apparently heavy barrel perched on one shoulder like it didn't weigh anything at all.

"You want me to put this in the wagon, Hoyt?" he asked Ryker in a voice that rumbled like a rockslide.

"No, just set it to the side for now, Pidge," Ryker told him. "I want you to meet a couple of friends of mine. This is Preacher and his half-breed son, Hawk."

"We ain't your friends, Ryker," Preacher said coldly.

The huge man called Pidge ignored that and lowered the barrel to the loading dock, handling it easily. A grin wreathed his face under the bushy beard as he said, "Howdy, Preacher. Howdy, Hawk. I'm named after a bird, too, you know. Well, it ain't my Christian name, I reckon. I don't rightly remember what that was, but my ma always called me Pigeon when I was a boy, on account of I was so little and reminded her of a bird."

Preacher didn't see how Pidge could have ever been small enough to remind anybody of a bird, but he supposed anything was possible. He could tell that Pidge wasn't quite right in the head, so he said, "We'd be obliged if you'd step aside so we can go on in the store. We got to buy supplies."

Pidge didn't seem to hear him. He was fascinated by Hawk. He asked, "What kind of a Injun are you?"

"Absaroka," Hawk replied with a note of pride in his voice.

Pidge shook his head and said, "I don't know nothin' about them. Are they good Injuns or bad Injuns?"

"The Absaroka are an honorable people," Hawk said.

"Well, that's good, I reckon. We're gonna see a bunch of Injuns, Hoyt says. We're goin' west on a espy . . . exper . . ."

"Expedition," Ryker supplied.

"That's why you're loadin' up those wagons?" Preacher asked.

"That's right," Ryker said. "Although it's not really any business of yours, is it?"

It wasn't, but knowing that didn't stop Preacher from bristling at the man's tone. He was already inclined to dislike Ryker because of what had happened several years earlier, and seeing him with Chessie the night before hadn't helped matters. Preacher wasn't jealous, by any means, but he suspected that Ryker meant to trifle with Chessie's affections and he believed she deserved better than that. Maybe having him out of St. Louis, away from the girl, was a good idea.

"I don't care about your business, Ryker," Preacher said. "Just stay out of my way — that's all I want from you."

"So you're saying you don't want to be friends?" The sly smile that tugged at Ryker's lips told Preacher the man was up to something.

"Damn right I'm not your friend," Preacher said, repeating his declaration from a few minutes earlier.

Pidge frowned and reached out with a hamlike hand. He rested it on Preacher's chest as the mountain man tried to go around him.

"Wait just a doggone minute. How come you don't want to be friends with Hoyt? He's my friend."

"Well, I'm sorry about that," Preacher said, "because he's a no-good polecat and lower than a snake."

A thunderous roar came from Pidge as an angry frown darkened his face. "You can't talk that way about my friend!" he bellowed. He reached out and grabbed the front of Preacher's buckskin shirt.

Pidge heaved . . . and Preacher found himself flying wildly through the air.

CHAPTER 8

Preacher sailed off the loading dock and landed in the back of a wagon. His fall was cushioned by a pile of blankets stacked on top of some crates, but the impact was still enough to rattle his bones. He rolled off the goods and fell to his knees in the wagon bed.

Up on the dock, Hawk had moved in and was hammering punches to Pidge's head while Hoyt Ryker stood off to one side with a satisfied smirk on his face. Unfortunately, Pidge didn't seem to even feel Hawk's fists. With another roar, he swung an arm the size of the trunk of a young tree. The backhanded blow swept Hawk off his feet and sent him sliding along the planks.

Preacher pulled himself up, planted a foot on the wagon's top sideboard, and shoved off in a leap that carried him onto the loading dock again. He charged Pidge.

"Look out!" Ryker shouted to his man.

Pidge turned lumberingly toward Preacher and threw a roundhouse punch that might have taken the mountain man's head off his shoulders if it had landed. Instead, Preacher ducked under it and drove ahead with all the strength in his powerful legs. He lowered his shoulder and rammed it into Pidge's ample belly.

It was a little like tackling a redwood tree, but Preacher packed a lot of power in his lean frame. He was gratified when Pidge staggered backward. Pidge's back slammed into the wall of the store, which shivered from the impact. Pidge's head bounced off the wood.

That would have been enough to knock most men out of the fight. Pidge was far from a normal man, though. He ignored the punches Preacher began hooking into his belly and reached down to grab him by the right arm and left thigh. Pidge's hands were big enough to go all the way around Preacher's arm and almost all the way around his leg.

Preacher let out an alarmed shout as Pidge lifted him. Suddenly Preacher found himself above the behemoth's head, poised so that Pidge could heave him again, like a doll being cast away by a giant child. Pidge stomped toward the edge of the loading dock. A toss from there would carry Preacher into the street and might well result in some broken bones.

Before Pidge could do that, Hawk hit him from behind, low, at the knees. Pidge wasn't prepared for that. His knees buckled, and as he sagged, he couldn't hold Preacher up anymore. All three men fell in a tangled heap on the loading dock.

Preacher and Hawk scrambled free before their bigger but slower opponent did. Hawk lunged at Pidge and swung his legs to lock them around the big man's neck in a wrestling hold that cut off Pidge's air. At the same time, Preacher rammed both knees into the man's belly and kept them there as he crashed his fists into Pidge's face.

Pidge's eyes began to roll up in their sockets. Preacher knew the man was about to pass out. He stopped punching and was ready to signal Hawk to let off on the pressure on Pidge's throat. They didn't want to kill the big varmint, but rather just make sure he was no longer a threat.

From the corner of his eye, Preacher saw Hoyt Ryker slip a knife from its sheath at his waist and draw his arm back. Ryker was going to take advantage of this chance to plant the blade in him, Preacher realized. His hand flashed to the butt of one of the pistols stuck behind his belt. He pulled the gun, leveled it, and eared back the hammer before Ryker could make his throw. Ryker might have gotten away with it if he had hurried more, but clearly he hadn't expected such a swift reaction from Preacher.

"That arm of yours moves even a fraction of an inch, this pistol ball's goin' right between your eyes, Ryker," Preacher warned. "Drop that knife."

Ryker's lips drew back from his teeth in a hate-filled grimace that was visible even through the thick mustache. He didn't respond immediately to Preacher's command, but after a couple of heartbeats, Ryker's fingers opened and the knife dropped onto the loading dock just behind him, landing point first so that it stuck there, upright and quivering.

"Step away from it," Preacher went on.

"You're going to be sorry you ever laid eyes on me again," Ryker said.

"I already am. Now move."

Ryker took a couple of steps to his left. Preacher could tell he was seething with rage, but as long as the mountain man's pistol was pointed at his head, there wasn't anything he could do about it. Not without getting killed, anyway.

The clerks who had been on the loading

dock when the fight began had all drawn back out of the way, but they were still standing near the building, waiting to see what was going to happen. More people, customers and employees alike, peered through the open double doors. The ruckus had drawn a crowd of spectators in the street, too.

"Hawk, are you all right?" Preacher asked without taking his eyes off Ryker.

"Yes. The man Pidge has passed out."

"You didn't choke him to death, did you?"

"There was no need to kill him," Hawk replied with a touch of disdain in his voice. Like Preacher, he didn't hesitate to take a life when it was necessary, but he didn't believe in wanton slaughter, either.

The crowd in the street suddenly parted as a man said in a loud, commanding voice, "Let me through. Step aside, blast it. Out of the way."

The words had a haughty, imperious tone, as if the speaker was accustomed to being obeyed instantly and without question. The man went on, "Ryker, what the devil is going on here?"

Ryker still looked angry, but he hid the out-and-out rage his expression had displayed a moment earlier. He said, "I'm glad you're here, Mr. Merton. These fellas attacked us for no reason, and now that one's threatening to kill me. I reckon you should summon the law."

Merton?

Despite the fact that Preacher didn't trust Ryker, when he heard that name he had to glance toward the newcomer. Instead of Oliver Merton, he saw a stocky, middle-aged man with dark hair and a florid face. He was well-dressed, though, like Chessie's suitor of the night before, and wore an expensive silk hat, the new fashion that was bringing down the price people were willing to pay for furs. That right there was enough for Preacher to be not too fond of the gent.

The man went on, "You were supposed to be buying supplies for our journey, not getting into brawls. I was hoping we'd be able to make our departure today."

"We will, we will, don't worry about that," Ryker said. "These fellas ought to be locked up, though, after they jumped us like they did."

"That's not the way it happened and you know it," Preacher said coldly. "I reckon there are plenty of folks around who'd be willin' to speak up and verify that, too."

"Will you stop pointing that pistol at my man?" Merton said, visibly annoyed. "I see no need to involve the authorities in this matter, sir, unless you persist in your stubborn assault."

"Ryker works for you?"

Merton sniffed. "Indeed he does."

"I'm sorry to hear that . . . sorry for you. He's a dangerous son of a bitch and ain't to be trusted."

"I'll allow no such talk about one of my employees. Now put that gun down!"

A couple of feet away, Pidge groaned and shook his head as consciousness began to come back to him. At the same time, another voice spoke up from the crowd in the street, asking, "Father, what's going on here?"

Preacher glanced over again as he recognized the voice. He saw Oliver Merton pushing his way through the press of spectators. As the young man broke out into the open and saw Preacher and Hawk on the loading dock, he stopped short.

"You two again!" he exclaimed.

The elder Merton frowned and said, "You know these troublemakers?"

"I met them last night," Oliver replied, "but they weren't making trouble then. In fact, the Indian helped me out of some."

Preacher was glad the young man had told the truth. Oliver hadn't acted very grateful at the time, but he seemed to understand that Hawk had pulled his fat out of the fire.

"Ryker claims they attacked him and Pidge for no reason," Merton said.

Oliver cocked his head to the side and said, "I'm not sure I believe that. Who would go out of his way to attack such a gargantuan foe as Pidge?"

Gargantuan sounded like a word Audie would have used, Preacher thought. He himself would have just said *big.*

This had gone on long enough. Preacher told Hawk, "Circle around there and get Ryker's knife."

"You can't steal my knife!" Ryker protested.

"We ain't stealin' it. Hawk, toss it in one of those wagons, out of Ryker's reach. Then we can talk without me havin' to worry about gettin' cold steel in my gizzard."

Hawk did as Preacher said, staying well away from Ryker as he pulled the knife from the plank where it was stuck. Instead of just tossing the knife into one of the wagons, Hawk made an expert throw of his own that stuck the blade's point into the side of a crate. Hawk was showing off a little, but under the circumstances, Preacher didn't blame him.

With that threat taken care of for the moment, Preacher lowered the pistol's hammer but kept the weapon in his hand. He held it at his side as he got to his feet.

Pidge pushed himself up into a sitting position and shook his head ponderously. He looked around. His eyes didn't focus at first, but then they locked on Preacher and a growl sounded deep in his throat.

"Better call him off, Ryker," the mountain man said. "I don't want to see the big fella get hurt."

Merton added, "We don't want any more trouble."

Ryker nodded and said, "Pidge, come on over here."

Pidge climbed slowly to his feet and trudged over to Ryker's side like a dog called by its master. He stood there with his head hanging as he glowered at Preacher and Hawk.

"I'm Edgar Merton," the stocky man introduced himself. "Is it true what my son said, that you two men befriended him last night?"

It would be stretching the truth to say that they were friends with Oliver, Preacher thought. Especially Hawk, who hadn't liked the attention that Oliver paid to Chessie Dayton. But Preacher didn't see any point in going into all that, so he just shrugged.

Merton went on, "I'm going to assume

that this trouble between you and my men is just a misunderstanding and let it go at that. Is that agreeable to you?"

"There ain't no misunderstandin'," Preacher said. "Ryker and me don't like each other, and the feelin' goes back a ways. But I'm willin' to let it go, like you say. Whatever you've got in mind, though, I ain't sure it's a good idea for you to hire a skunk like Ryker."

"That's none of your business," Edgar Merton said. "But as it happens, Mr. Ryker and his friends were highly recommended to me. They're going to serve as guides and hunters on an expedition I'm leading to the Rocky Mountains."

"What sort of expedition?"

Merton's response was curt. "I've said enough. Good day, sir." He turned to Ryker. "Finish loading the supplies. Then we'll all assemble at the hotel and set out from there. Understood?"

"Sure," Ryker said. "There won't be any more trouble."

"There had better not be."

Merton turned, went down the steps, and strode through the crowd as if he expected it to open up before him — which it did. His son Oliver cast an unreadable glance at Preacher and Hawk and then followed.

Ryker snapped at Fitzgerald's clerks and got them started putting supplies in the wagons again. Pidge picked up the barrel and loaded it, then went into the store to get more. Preacher and Hawk stood off to one side, keeping an eye on things until the task was finished.

Then Ryker took the reins of one team and Pidge the other. As they drove the wagons along the street toward the hotel where the Mertons were staying, Hawk watched them go and said quietly, "They plan to take those two fools out into the wilderness, kill them, and steal everything of value."

"I know," Preacher said, "but we've done been told it ain't any of our business." He jerked his head toward the store's entrance. "Come on. We got supplies of our own to buy."

CHAPTER 9

Thomas Fitzgerald was a jowly, canny Scotsman who had been selling supplies to trappers for a long time. Preacher had known him for quite a few years, so after he'd introduced Hawk and while Fitzgerald's clerks were putting together the order, the mountain man asked, "What can you tell me about that fella Merton, Tom?"

Fitzgerald had a pipe clenched between his teeth. He took it out and said, "You wouldn't be holdin' a grudge agin the man because o' wha' happened out there on th' loadin' dock, would ye, Preacher?"

"Nope. Just curious, that's all. I don't know if you heard or not, but Hawk and me ran into Merton's boy last night over at Red Mike's."

"Did this encounter involve yet another brawl?"

"Well . . ." Preacher said with a smile, "it might have. Fact is, it did."

" 'Tis no surprise to me. Trouble seems to follow ye around, man. And don't go talkin' about how peace-lovin' ye are. Both of us know better."

"What about Merton?"

Fitzgerald set his pipe aside and leaned both hands on the counter. "He come in here a couple o' days ago with that fella Ryker. Had a big order for me to fill. Enough supplies t' last a dozen or more men several months. Wherever he's goin', he plans to stay there for a while."

"But he didn't say where that is?"

Fitzgerald shook his head. "He dinna drop even a hint."

Hawk spoke up, saying, "They go to trap beaver."

"Now, that's what ye'd think. An' truth t' tell, Merton bought a few traps. But not enough for a group that size. Not if they intend to take enough pelts t' make th' trip worthwhile."

Preacher rubbed his chin and said, "That's interestin'. What other reason could there be for traipsin' all the way out yonder, other than goin' after furs?"

"I've supplied a few expeditions of natural scientists, artists, and the like."

Preacher grunted. He had run into more than one expedition like that himself, and every time, the results had been violent. Scientists and artists always brought trouble along with them, it seemed like.

Edgar Merton hadn't struck him as being either of those things. Merton looked and acted like a businessman.

"Do you know who recommended that he hire Hoyt Ryker?"

"Can't help you there, either," Fitzgerald said. "I remember Ryker. Never heard anything good about the scoundrel, either. But he hasn't been around for a while. Maybe he's changed his ways."

Preacher knew better. He had seen enough of Ryker to know that the man hadn't changed. He was still as dangerous as ever.

Hawk said, "Ryker could have paid someone to suggest that Merton hire him."

"What would be the purpose o' that?" Fitzgerald asked. "Unless . . ."

He stopped, and Preacher nodded knowingly. If Ryker had pulled a scheme like that, then he had to be up to no good. But Preacher had known that already.

"Somebody ought to have a talk with Merton," Fitzgerald went on after a moment.

"You reckon it'd do any good? I tried, but he didn't seem to want to listen to me."

"Well . . . I can't say I'm surprised,"

Fitzgerald replied. "A fella like Merton, he's got t' be right all th' time. Once he's made up his mind about somethin', he's not likely t' change it, because that would mean admittin' he was wrong."

Preacher nodded and said, "That's the way I've got it figured, too. I already told him that throwin' in with Ryker wasn't very smart, and he didn't pay no attention. I reckon what happens from here on ain't any o' my lookout."

"True," Fitzgerald agreed, nodding solemnly. "Still, I hate to see a man go off willingly to what might be his own doom."

"Folks do it all the time," Preacher said. "We're gonna go collect our horses and pack mule from Fullerton. You suppose our packs'll be ready by the time we get back?"

"I'll see to it," Fitzgerald promised.

As they left the store, Hawk said quietly, "Despite what you said in there, you are not going to allow Merton and his son to leave with Ryker, are you?"

"I don't see how I can stop 'em," Preacher said.

"Then you are going to do nothing."

Preacher laughed humorlessly and replied, "I didn't say that, neither."

Dog and Horse were glad to see Preacher.

The mule, as always, showed no reaction whatever. Preacher settled up with Ambrose Fullerton, then he and Hawk led the animals back to Fitzgerald's store, where they fastened the packs containing their supplies to the mule.

"Let's stop by Red Mike's and say so long," Preacher suggested. An idea was stirring in the back of his mind, and he thought paying a visit to the tavern might help bring it into focus.

"That will mean going out of our way," Hawk said.

"Not that far. And we don't have to be anywhere at any particular time, do we? That's one mighty good thing about livin' the way we do."

Hawk just shrugged. What Preacher wanted to do might make no sense to him, but he was willing to go along with it.

Even though it wasn't the middle of the day yet, men had started to drift into Red Mike's for a drink, either stealing a few minutes away from their work or getting a late start on it. The Irishman was staying busy pouring cups of coffee and filling mugs of beer. Nobody was drinking whiskey much this early except for the most devoted sots.

"I figured you fellas would be pullin' out for the mountains by now," Mike greeted

Preacher and Hawk.

"We're on our way," Preacher told him. "Our outfit's outside with Dog watchin' over it." Preacher looked around the tavern. "Appears you could use some help this mornin'."

Mike blew out a disgusted-sounding breath. "Yeah, I could, but you don't see anybody pitchin' in, do you? It's too early for most o' my other girls to show up, and Chessie seems to be gone!"

"Gone!" Hawk repeated with a look of alarm on his face. "Where would she go?"

"Beats me, friend," Mike said with a shake of his head. "I figured she was still asleep, but when I went to her room a while ago and knocked on the door, she didn't answer. I looked inside, and she wasn't there. Looked like her bed had been slept in, but she was gone and so were her things."

"She has run away," Hawk said. He sounded as if he couldn't believe it.

"Yeah. Sure took me by surprise, too. She had told me how grateful she was for me helpin' her out, and I believe she meant it. But I reckon something came along that she wanted to do more than staying here working in a tavern." Mike chuckled wryly. "Can't say as I really blame her for that. I hope she's all right, though."

"I expect she is," Preacher said, although he wasn't really sure of that at all. "Young women have minds of their own, I reckon."

Mike snorted. "Yeah, and they never grow out of it, either. You two want some more coffee before you head out?"

"No, the mountains are callin' us." Preacher stuck his hand across the bar. "So long, Mike. See you next time."

"And you'll be bringing trouble along with you when you do," Red Mike said as he shook hands with Preacher and then Hawk. "I'd bet one of those brand-new silk hats on that!"

They left the tavern and walked west toward the edge of town. Their route took them past the hotel where the Mertons had been staying. Preacher looked for the wagons that had been at Fitzgerald's earlier, but the vehicles weren't there.

It appeared that the "expedition," whatever it was really after, was already on its way.

"Where could the girl have gone?" Hawk asked as a frown creased his face. Preacher had been able to tell that his son had been chewing over that question ever since they'd left Red Mike's.

"Well, hell, haven't you figured it out?" he

said. "She went with the Mertons and Ryker."

Hawk drew in a sharp breath. "You believe this to be true, Preacher?"

"Like Mike said, I'd bet a hat on it. Think about it. Oliver Merton comes to St. Louis with his pa, who's puttin' together an expedition to the mountains. He meets Chessie at Red Mike's and decides that he's sweet on her. But she's already mixed up with Ryker, who tells her to string Oliver along once he finds out what Oliver's pa is doin'. There's a good chance Chessie's the one who first said something about Merton hirin' Ryker and his bunch to go along on the trip."

Hawk's expression had darkened while Preacher was talking. He said, "Oliver's father would not take the word of a tavern girl about who he should hire."

"No, he wouldn't," Preacher agreed. "But she could have sold Oliver on the idea without any trouble, and he could've brought it up with his pa. And, Ryker could've bribed somebody — say, one of the local officials — to vouch for him with Merton. You got to admit, Hawk, it could've played out that way."

"It could have," Hawk said with obvious

reluctance, "but that does not mean that it did."

"Come up with a better explanation for everything that's happened, and I'll listen to it."

Hawk didn't respond to that. He couldn't, because Preacher's theory made sense.

After they had walked along for a few more moments, though, Hawk said, "Why do you think Chessie went with them?"

"You heard what Mike said about her. Her folks are dead, and she don't have any other family around here. She's got nothin' to hold her in St. Louis."

"The mountains are dangerous."

"They sure are, but she'll be travelin' with a large, well-armed group of men who are pretty rough around the edges. She's got to figure that if there's any trouble along the way, they'll be able to handle it. Plus, if she's fallen for Ryker, she'll be around him."

"You said she has been making Oliver believe she cares for him."

"Well," Preacher said with a smile, "she wouldn't be the first gal to play two fellas against each other, would she?"

Hawk shook his head and said curtly, "I know nothing about such foolish games."

"You will, if you live long enough. In the meantime, we'll find out soon enough if I'm right about Chessie goin' with Oliver and his pa and their expedition."

"What makes you say that?"

"We're gonna follow 'em," Preacher said. "Right now, they're headed the same direction we are, so I don't see any reason we can't stay on their trail for a ways."

Chapter 10

Preacher and Hawk walked, leading the horses and the pack mule, until they reached the outskirts of St. Louis. Dog bounded ahead of them and then ran back, happy to be traveling again instead of stuck in a barn. Horse had some extra spirit in his step as well, as if he sensed that another long trail lay before him, and he was eager to get to it. Hawk's pony displayed some of the same excitement and anticipation.

Once they were at the edge of town, they swung up into their saddles and set off at an easy pace. Hawk asked, "How long do you think it will take us to catch up to the expedition?"

"Shouldn't take long," Preacher replied. "They've got at least two wagons with 'em. For all we know, they have more than that. Those wagons'll have to move slower than we do on horseback. We should be within sight of them before nightfall."

Hawk nodded. Preacher knew he was anxious to confirm that Chessie Dayton actually was traveling with the Mertons. Of course, what Hawk would do once they found out about that, Preacher didn't know. Chessie was old enough to make up her own mind about where she went — and who with — so it was none of Hawk's business. The question was whether he would abide by that.

The day had warmed considerably by noon. Preacher and Hawk didn't push the horses. Even so, around midafternoon Preacher spotted some dust hanging in the air half a mile ahead of them. He pointed it out to Hawk and said, "They're headed for Louinet's ferry. That's where I figured we'd catch up with them."

"They will not allow us to join their group," Hawk said. "Ryker would not stand for that, and I do not believe Oliver Merton would like it, either."

"Never said we were gonna join up with 'em. I figure we'll hang back far enough they won't notice us, but close enough we can get a look and make sure Chessie's travelin' with 'em."

"And if she is?" Hawk asked.

Preacher frowned. "That'll complicate things," he admitted. "I don't trust Ryker and his bunch as far as I could throw that big varmint Pidge. They're dangerous, and Oliver and his pa were fools to throw in with 'em, no doubt about it. But I don't like to mix in another fella's affairs. If Chessie's with 'em, though . . . she's gonna be in danger sooner or later, and I ain't the sort to ride off and leave a gal in a bad spot."

"So we will follow them without them knowing about it and try to protect her."

"That's sorta what I had in mind," Preacher said. He shrugged and added, "And I guess while we're at it, we can keep an eye on Oliver and his pa, too, and try to keep them from gettin' killed if it ain't too much trouble."

After some more riding, they reached the crest of a long, tree-covered ridge where they were able to look down at the broad Missouri River flowing at its stately pace toward the Mississippi. Louinet's ferry was in sight, crossing the river on its heavy ropes drawn by a team of oxen plodding in circles around a big capstan on the southern bank.

Preacher was pretty sure the wagon that was on the ferry at the moment was one of the vehicles that had been at Fitzgerald's, being loaded with supplies. The other wagon of that pair was parked not far from the ferry landing, waiting its turn to cross.

Another wagon was there as well, this one lighter and smaller, with an arched canvas cover over its back. From where Preacher and Hawk were, they couldn't see whoever was handling the reins, but Preacher wondered if it might not be one of the Mertons.

In addition, a dozen men stood around holding horses. Those would be Hoyt Ryker's men. Ryker himself, identifiable by the tall hat with the feather in its band, stood beside the smaller wagon, talking to whoever was on the driver's seat.

The ferry reached the landing on the other side of the river. The man handling that wagon drove off onto the bank, then climbed down from the box and waved an arm over his head to signal that he was all clear. From the size of him, Preacher thought it was Pidge over there on the far bank. Another man was with him. The two of them would stay there and keep an eye on the wagon and its contents while the rest of the party made the crossing.

Preacher and Hawk watched this from the top of the ridge. Hawk said, "I do not see Miss Chessie anywhere."

"She could be inside that covered wagon, or up on its box," Preacher said. "We can't see that good from up here. We get any closer, though, and they're liable to spot us."

"Oliver and his father are stupid," Hawk said in a voice made sullen by jealousy. "They deserve whatever happens to them."

Preacher couldn't really disagree with that sentiment. On the other hand, everybody had to learn one way or another how to survive on the frontier. He himself had had several mentors when he'd first come out here as not much more than a kid, plus he'd had the hard-won benefits of some bitter experiences. He hadn't been impressed with Edgar Merton, but Oliver had shown that he was a fighter and that was a good start toward being a frontiersman. Oliver might not be such a greenhorn one of these days . . . if he lived long enough.

When the ferry returned to the south landing, one of the men drove the second supply wagon onto it, and the crossing resumed. Preacher and Hawk dismounted and spent the next hour in the trees atop the ridge, watching as the second wagon and all the horsemen crossed, with the exception of Ryker, who was staying close to the smaller wagon.

The reason for Ryker's actions became clear when the time came for someone to drive that wagon onto the ferry. Two people climbed down from the seat, with the first one turning to help the second. Preacher believed the man was Oliver Merton; long, fair hair, shining in the sun, was clear evidence the second person was Chessie Dayton. Edgar Merton was probably inside the wagon, Preacher thought as Ryker stepped up to the driver's seat to handle the team of mules hitched to the wagon.

Preacher noted the way Hawk stiffened at the sight of Chessie. "If Oliver truly cares for her," Hawk muttered, "how can he take her along on such a dangerous journey?"

"Fella like that is used to gettin' his own way. Oliver thinks about what he wants and not much else. He's still got a heap of growin' up to do."

"He will get himself killed, and her, too!"

"Could be," Preacher said. "But we'll do what we can to keep that from happenin'."

Hoyt Ryker drove the smaller wagon out onto the ferry. Oliver and Chessie followed and stood next to the vehicle. As Louinet led the oxen around in their circle, the ferry lurched into motion. Chessie held on to Oliver's arm as if the ferry's movement made her nervous.

She didn't really have anything to worry about. The Missouri's current was powerful but slow. Even if the ferry had broken loose, it would have just drifted downstream until it grounded on one side or the other. But it wasn't going to break loose, because the Frenchman did a good job of maintaining his operation.

When the ferry reached the landing on the far side of the river, Ryker drove the wagon off and then hopped down from the seat to wave his hat over his head. Louinet returned the wave. He would have settled the fare with Edgar Merton before the crossing ever began, so his business dealings were over. He brought the ferry back across the river, then walked toward the little cabin near the landing on this side, where he lived.

Across the river, Ryker had swung up onto one of the saddle horses. The other men were mounted as well. Oliver helped Chessie onto the seat of the covered wagon, then pulled himself up after her. From the looks of things, he was doing the driving. That raised him a little more in Preacher's estimation. Not everybody could handle a team of mules. It wasn't easy work at times.

The expedition got moving, angling away from the river but following its general course.

"We should go," Hawk said. "They will get ahead of us."

"Not so far ahead that we won't know

right where to find 'em," Preacher said. "Let's give 'em a chance to get out of sight first."

Hawk's impatience grew as they waited, but Preacher ignored that. When the wagons and riders were out of sight and he judged that enough time had passed, he whistled for Dog and told Hawk, "All right, let's go."

They rode down the slope toward the landing. Louinet must have heard the horses approaching, because he came out to greet them.

"A most busy and profitable day," the Frenchman commented as he raised a hand.

"You've had some other customers?" Preacher asked, as if he and Hawk had no idea about the expedition that had just crossed the Missouri.

"*Oui.* Three wagons and a group of men on horseback." Louinet waved vaguely toward the other side of the river. "They are not very far ahead of you. Perhaps you could catch up and join their party, if you wish."

"Hawk and me tend to travel alone. These folks say who they were and where they're goin'?"

"I did not ask. My only business is transporting people across the river. I could tell that the man who seemed to be in charge, the one I dealt with regarding the fare, was not from . . . how do you say? Not from these parts. And he was a canny bargainer, as well."

"You mean cheap," Preacher said.

Louinet laughed. "He was not going to part with any more coins than was absolutely necessary, this is true."

"How about the others in the bunch?"

Evidently, Louinet regarded the mountain man's questions as the sort of casual gossip that most people on the frontier indulged in. Life out here was pretty tedious most of the time, so anything that might break up the monotony was welcome.

A smile appeared on the Frenchman's face. "There was one whose presence was a bit surprising but most welcome. A very beautiful young mademoiselle, with hair almost as pale as the mist that hangs over the river in the mornings." Louinet's smile disappeared. "But as for the rest . . . bah. Men not to be trusted, to my way of thinking. The man from the East and a younger one — his son, I think — as well as the girl, I would worry about them, if it was any of my business to do so."

Preacher nodded slowly. "Sounds like it might be shapin' up to be trouble for somebody. That's a good reason for me and

Hawk to avoid 'em, since we're so peace-lovin' and all."

Louinet snorted to show how seriously he took that statement. "You wish to cross?" he asked.

"We do," Preacher said.

The Frenchman named a price. Preacher paid it, then he and Hawk led their horses and the pack mule onto the ferry. Preacher had to call Dog a couple of times to get him to jump from the dock at the landing to the floating craft. The big cur lay down, rested his chin on his front paws, and didn't look happy about venturing out onto the river.

Louinet went to the oxen, grabbed the harness on one of the massive animals, and urged it into motion. Hitched into the spokes of the wheel-like capstan, the others had no choice but to plod along, too.

The ferry jerked and started to move out onto the water. Once they had ridden away from the landing on the other side of the river, they would have put the last outpost of civilization for hundreds of miles behind them. Up ahead were vast plains, soaring, snow-capped peaks . . . and plenty of ways for a fella to wind up dead.

CHAPTER 11

Preacher set an easy pace the rest of that day as he and Hawk rode west by northwest along the river, following the tracks left by the wagons and the hoofprints of the horses. Occasionally, from the top of a rise, they caught a glimpse of the wagons ahead of them. As the day drew to a close and twilight shadows began to gather, Preacher and Hawk kept moving until they spotted the glow of a campfire.

"With a fire like that, they tell the whole world where they are," Hawk grumbled.

"They've got enough men and guns that I reckon they ain't worried," Preacher said. "Besides, they're only one day out of St. Louis. It ain't likely they'll run into any trouble this close to a big settlement like that."

"Do none of the hostile tribes ever raid this far east?"

"The Pawnee sometimes do," Preacher

replied. "But if there's a ruckus, we're close enough to hear the shootin', and we'll go give 'em a hand."

Hawk seemed to accept that. A few minutes later, they found a good spot to make camp and settled down for the night.

This close to civilization, as Preacher had pointed out to Hawk, and with the keen senses of Dog and Hawk to warn them if any trouble came sniffing around, it wasn't necessary to stand guard during the night. Both men were able to roll in their buffalo robes and sleep soundly until morning.

They followed that same general pattern for the next few days, although the farther west they traveled, the more wary and watchful they became. Now there was more danger of running into a Pawnee hunting party. If that happened, the Pawnee might decide that two men traveling by themselves was too tempting a target to pass up, especially since they had a pack mule loaded with supplies with them.

Because of that possibility, Preacher and Hawk took turns standing guard at night, and as they rode during the day they kept a close eye on the distant hills and ridges for any riders who might be keeping an eye on *them.*

They were almost a week out of St. Louis

when Hawk reined in and pointed at the wagon tracks. "Look! They have turned north."

Preacher frowned as he brought Horse to a stop. He studied the tracks as well and said, "Yeah, they have. Not due north, but more that direction than west now."

"They are not following the river anymore. Where can they be going?"

Preacher shook his head. "Don't know. Remember how Fitzgerald said they didn't really outfit themselves like they was plannin' to do a lot of trappin'?"

"What else is there to do?"

"Some rich folks come out here to hunt. Oliver and his pa didn't really strike me as the sort to do that, though, and they ain't artists, neither. At least, they sure didn't act like it. From what we know of him, Edgar Merton seems more like a fella who wouldn't do anything unless he thought there'd be some profit in it."

"What is in that direction?" Hawk asked, nodding toward the north.

"More plains, a few mountains, a range of hills the Sioux think of as sacred, and then, if you go far enough, Canada."

"Are we going to follow them?"

Preacher directed his gaze more westward, seeing in his mind the trails that ran along the Missouri, the Yellowstone, and the Big Horn.

"Charlie and Aaron and White Buffalo are waitin' for us out yonder," he said, knowing Hawk would understand what he meant. "If we head north after this bunch, there ain't no tellin' how long it'll take us to get back to where we were headed."

"But there are many hostiles north of here?"

"Like I said, the Sioux are up there. So are the Cheyenne and some other tribes, and even a few Blackfeet might wander that direction now and then."

"Then the danger will grow worse the farther they go."

Hawk didn't make it sound like a question, but Preacher nodded anyway as he said, "More than likely."

"I think we should go after them," Hawk stated flatly. "No matter how long it takes us to return to our friends."

"You only feel that way because of the girl."

"You said yourself you would not want to ride off and leave her in danger."

Preacher grunted and then grinned wryly. "I did say that, didn't I? Well, I guess you've got a point. Besides, I'm a mite curious just what they're after."

"Then we are following the wagons?"

Preacher nudged Horse into motion again and said, "For now, anyway."

The terrain through which they rode flattened out more as they put the river many miles behind them. The grass still grew thickly, but it wasn't as tall nor as green as it was along the stream. Without the vantage points of hills and ridges, Preacher and Hawk could no longer see the wagons, but it was easy enough to follow the wheel tracks and the hoofprints and know they were still on the expedition's trail.

At night, they could see the orange winking eye of the campfire a mile ahead of them. A fire like that was bound to draw attention sooner or later. East of the Mississippi, Hoyt Ryker might be a dangerous outlaw, but out here he was just another greenhorn making mistakes that might get him killed.

Preacher and Hawk always stopped early each day and built a small fire from buffalo chips that smoked hardly at all. They cooked their supper and boiled coffee over those flames, then put the fire out before darkness fell and rode on for a short time.

They had seen no other human beings since taking the ferry across the Missouri.

Several times, they had spotted large, dark masses in the distance that Preacher knew were buffalo herds. Now and then they saw a wolf loping along, staying well away from them. Prairie chickens and rabbits abounded. A couple of eagles had soared high overhead one day. Other than the wildlife, though, they might have been all alone in this vast wilderness.

Preacher knew that their seeming isolation was deceptive. More than once, he believed he felt eyes watching him, but he was never able to spot whoever it was. Then, finally, as they got into slightly rougher terrain broken up by shallow ridges and bluffs, one day as they rode along Hawk said, "To your left, about five flights of an arrow."

"Yep, I saw him a few minutes ago," Preacher replied quietly. "Just one fella on a pony. But where there's one, there are bound to be more not too far away."

"He has not moved. He just sits there watching us."

"Yeah, and I'd be willin' to bet he watched those wagons and riders go past earlier, too."

Hawk tensed in his saddle. "Are they going to attack the expedition?"

"No tellin'," Preacher replied with a slight shake of his head. "It all depends on what sort of mood they're in. And there's never no predictin' that when it comes to . . ."

"Redskins?" Hawk snapped. "Is that what you were about to say, Preacher?"

"Don't get your fur in an uproar, son. You know as well as anybody that I don't care if a fella's white, red, brown, or purple. He's either a friend or he ain't, and that's all that matters to me. You got to admit, though, Indians are plumb notional at times. That's just a fact."

"That one watching us . . . he is Sioux?"

"Or Cheyenne. Could be either, in these parts. I wouldn't say there's no difference between 'em, but for the most part they get along all right and even partner up sometimes to go to war against other tribes. They've fought on the same side against white folks, too."

"So they *are* going to attack the wagons."

"They might," Preacher admitted.

"We should warn them."

"Wouldn't be a bad idea."

Preacher dug his heels into Horse's flanks and urged the stallion to a swifter pace. Beside him, Hawk pushed his pony into a trot. Behind them, at the end of the lead rope fastened to Hawk's saddle, the pack mule labored to keep up. Preacher wasn't going to cut the animal loose, though. With Indians around, that would be the last they ever saw of the mule and their supplies.

They had ridden only a few hundred yards when Preacher spotted movement to the right from the corner of his eye. When he looked in that direction, he saw several Indians mounted on ponies, galloping to intercept them. At the same time, Hawk called, "Preacher!"

"I see 'em," Preacher replied over the drumming hoofbeats. He veered Horse to the left, and Hawk followed suit on his pony.

It wasn't going to be enough, he realized mere seconds later. The Indians had too much of an angle on them. Preacher hadn't seen them until they were close, so he knew that as he and Hawk had made their approach, the warriors must have been hidden in one of the dry washes that crisscrossed the area.

"Looks like we're gonna have to make a fight of it!" he told Hawk.

"There are five or six of them!"

"More targets for us to aim at," Preacher said with a grin. The Indians were within rifle range now, so he hauled back on the reins and brought the stallion to a skidding, dust-raising halt. As Horse planted his hooves and steadied, Preacher lifted the long-barreled flintlock to his shoulder. The rifle was already loaded and primed. All he had to do was ear back the hammer and settle the sight on one of the charging warriors. He pressed the trigger.

With a loud *boom,* gray smoke gushed from the rifle's muzzle as the brass-plated butt kicked back against Preacher's shoulder. The mountain man squinted through the smoke and saw the Indian he had aimed at go flying backward off the galloping pony underneath him. The warrior's arms were flung wide. He landed on his back and didn't move again.

A heartbeat after Preacher's shot, Hawk's rifle roared as well. Another of the Indians slewed around under the lead ball's impact and almost toppled off his pony. A desperate grab at the animal's mane was all that kept him from being unseated. But the pony slowed and then stopped, and from the way its rider was hunched over in obvious pain, he was probably out of the fight as well.

Preacher slung his empty rifle on the saddle and turned Horse back toward the enemy. Guiding the stallion with his knees, he charged toward the onrushing Indians. He reached down to his waist and pulled both pistols from behind his belt.

Preacher let out a defiant, ear-splitting yell as the gap between him and the Indians closed in a matter of seconds. There were four of the attackers left, and he headed straight through the middle of them. Arrows cut the air around his head. He thrust the pistols out to right and left and pulled the triggers. The shots blended in a thunderous roar.

The pistols were double-shotted and heavily charged with powder. At this close range, when both balls from the right-hand pistol struck the warrior on that side in the head, they practically decapitated him. Not much of his skull was left as he flopped off his pony.

One of the balls from Preacher's left-hand pistol missed entirely, but the other bored through the lungs of an Indian and caused blood to explode from his mouth and nose. He fell under the flashing hooves of his companion's pony but never felt the thudding impacts. That caused the pony's legs to tangle, though, and with a scream the animal went down, plunging headfirst to the ground. The rider was launched into the air and landed in a wild, out-of-control sprawl.

Dog was waiting for him. No sooner had the Indian stopped rolling than the big cur was on him, teeth slashing and tearing. Dog ripped the warrior's throat out in a spray of blood before the man knew what was happening.

That left only one of the attackers still mounted and able-bodied. He screeched and flung a lance at Preacher, who batted it aside with the empty pistol in his right hand. The Indian lunged his pony toward Preacher, but the animal had gone only a couple of strides when Hawk's rifle boomed again. The remaining warrior threw his arms in the air, swayed sideways, and fell in a limp heap. The pony came to a stop, unsure what to do without a rider urging it on.

Preacher glanced around, saw no more immediate threats, and started reloading his pistols with swift, efficient movements that testified to the thousands of times he had performed this task. In the distance, the wounded Indian trotted away, leaning forward over his pony's neck to make himself a smaller target in case either Preacher or Hawk decided to take a potshot at him.

Preacher was content to let the wounded man go. The Indians already knew about him and Hawk being here, so killing the man wouldn't serve any purpose.

Preacher shoved the reloaded pistols behind his belt and started pouring powder down the rifle's barrel. Hawk rode up and asked, "You are all right?"

"Yeah," Preacher said. He used the ramrod to seat ball, patch, and wadding in the rifle's breech.

"Then why did you let that Indian go?" Hawk demanded.

"From the way he was ridin', his shoulder's busted. He ain't gonna be much of a threat anymore. And he can't tell any of his friends we're here, because they already know that."

Hawk swung down and rested his rifle's barrel across the pony's saddle to steady it. He nestled his cheek against the smooth, polished wood of the stock as he drew a deep breath, held it, and aimed. Then he squeezed the trigger.

In the distance, the last of the attackers lurched and then fell off his horse as the echo of Hawk's shot rolled across the prairie.

"He still had one good arm," Hawk said as he stepped back from his pony. "That was all he needed to slit an enemy's throat. Maybe your throat, Preacher . . . or Miss Chessie's."

Preacher couldn't dispute that point. But there was no time to argue anyway, because a sudden flurry of gunfire in the distance told him that the wagons were under attack.

CHAPTER 12

A glance at the decorations and markings on the buckskin clothing worn by the dead Indians had told Preacher they were Sioux. Some of the fiercest fighters came from that tribe, so he knew the expedition was in deadly danger. He called, "Come on!" to Hawk and Dog and heeled Horse into a run.

The rangy gray stallion had power and speed to spare. Hawk's pony was swift but didn't have Horse's long, ground-eating stride. Hawk also had the pack mule to deal with. Preacher quickly left them behind. Dog ran hard and managed to stay not too far behind the mountain man.

Preacher spotted the thin gray haze of powder smoke in the air before he saw the wagons themselves. The vehicles had come to a stop right where they were when the attack began, lined up one behind the other. There hadn't been enough time to try to pull them into a circle. With only three wagons that would have been difficult anyway.

The covered wagon was in the lead with the two supply wagons behind it. Men had taken cover underneath all three wagons. From there they fired at the Sioux warriors on horseback, who raced back and forth, sending a storm of arrows at them. Preacher estimated that there were at least two dozen Indians in the war party.

Ryker's men had thrown themselves from their horses and scrambled to reach the shelter of the wagons when the assault began. Preacher could tell that from the way the mounts had scattered across the broad, open ground between two shallow ridges. The Sioux had been hidden up there on both sides, he figured, and when the expedition was between them, they had attacked.

None of the horses were down, but one man was. He lay on his face with two arrows sticking up from his back. He wasn't moving and never would again.

Preacher spotted a couple of riderless Indian ponies dashing around, spooked by all the gunfire and commotion. He didn't see the bodies of those ponies' riders, but he assumed two of the Sioux were done for, as well. Despite that, the war party still far outnumbered the expedition.

The only advantage the defenders had was the greater range of their rifles. The lead balls whistling around the heads of the Sioux made them pull back after a few moments of furious fighting.

Preacher slowed Horse and considered his options. He saw a little hummock of ground off to his left. If he could take cover there, he might be able to pick off several of the Indians before they realized what was going on. Then they would have to split their force to deal with him. By that time, Hawk would be arriving and could create some additional havoc among the Sioux.

It was a decent plan, but just as Preacher was about to implement it, an arrow with its tip blazing brightly arched through the air and landed on the canvas cover stretched over the supplies in the back of the third wagon. Flames began to leap up as the canvas caught fire.

Preacher heard shouts from the defenders. He couldn't make out the words, but it must have been someone issuing orders, because a figure crawled out from under the wagon and started trying to tear the burning canvas cover away before the supplies or the vehicle itself caught fire. From the size of the man working at that task, Preacher knew it had to be Pidge — unless the expedition had *two* giants in its midst.

One of the Sioux had another flaming arrow ready to go. Preacher spotted him as the warrior drew back his bowstring and aimed at the other wagons. Trusting to instinct and years of experience to guide his shot, Preacher brought the rifle to his shoulder and fired without seeming to aim.

The Indian had wrapped cloth soaked in pitch around the arrowhead and had dismounted to strike a spark with flint and steel and set it ablaze. He stumbled forward just as he released the shaft. That caused the arrow to fly into the sky at a much steeper angle than the warrior had intended. It landed well short of the expedition's wagons.

The Sioux staggered and fell forward on his face. Preacher knew his rifle ball had found its target.

Over at the wagons, Pidge had succeeded in ripping the burning canvas off the supplies, but as he did so, one of the mounted Indians dashed closer and loosed an arrow. The missile struck Pidge in the upper left arm. Preacher knew the wound had to be painful, because Pidge bellowed like a bull.

The Sioux underestimated the big man, however. He charged closer and lifted a coup stick, intending to hit Pidge with it.

Getting close enough to strike an enemy like that in battle was the greatest honor a warrior could achieve, since it was a powerful demonstration of his courage.

Pidge reached up and caught hold of the Sioux's wrist. He jerked the warrior right off his pony and swung him through the air. When Pidge let go, the Sioux flew at least twenty feet before crashing to earth with bone-breaking force. A second later, more shots rang out from underneath the wagons and several rifle balls thudded into the luckless man's body.

More arrows flew around Pidge as he stomped out the burning canvas, but none of the Sioux rode within reach of him. One of the arrows skewered his leg, which made him stumble but didn't knock him off his feet.

While that was going on, Preacher and Dog struck the Indians from behind. Since his hastily formed plan to pick off some of them before they knew what was going on hadn't panned out, the best course of action was to hit the enemy hard and fast while he still had surprise on his side. He blew two of the Sioux off their ponies with his pistols, then stuck the empty weapons behind his belt and yanked out his tomahawk.

Preacher understood the Indian concept of counting coup, but it had always seemed foolish to him. If you were going to get close enough to your enemy to tap him with a stick, why not just go ahead and kill him so you didn't have to take the time and trouble to do it later?

To that end, when he struck with the tomahawk it was with deadly intent. He leaned over in his saddle and crashed the weapon's flint head against the skull of a warrior as he rode past the man. Bone splintered under the impact. Preacher didn't look back to see if the Sioux fell off his pony, but he knew the blow was fatal.

He rode close to another man and whipped the tomahawk back the other way. The warrior got an arm up to block it, but the bones in his forearm snapped. Doing that didn't save him, either. As he howled in pain from the broken arm, Preacher crowded in and backhanded the tomahawk across the man's face, shattering his jaw and ripping it halfway off. The scream died in a bubbling gurgle as the maimed warrior toppled from his pony.

Dog was among the Sioux as well. The big cur leaped and knocked one of the warriors off his horse. Dog landed on the man's chest, closed his powerful jaws around his throat, and ripped it out in a bloody spray.

With a drumbeat of hooves, Hawk galloped up to the battle. He had an arrow nocked and drawn. Without slowing his pony, he loosed the shaft and planted it in the middle of a Sioux warrior's chest.

Fully a third of the attackers were down now, and as more shots roared from the wagons, another Sioux fell, riddled by rifle balls. That was enough to convince the others that continuing the assault wasn't a good idea. Yipping in frustrated rage, they yanked their ponies around and raced toward one of the bluffs in the distance.

Preacher reined in and hit the ground almost before Horse had stopped moving. He hurried from body to body, checking to see if any of the fallen Sioux were still alive. None of them were.

He turned and strode toward the wagons, where the defenders were starting to emerge. Preacher saw Edgar and Oliver Merton, both apparently unharmed but very pale and shaken. Oliver turned back and helped Chessie from underneath the covered wagon where he and his father had been. Preacher was glad to see that she seemed to be all right, too.

Pidge leaned against the supply wagon he had saved from burning. Blood leaked around both arrows embedded in his flesh, but he seemed steady enough. He gave Preacher a curt nod, but clearly that was as far as he was willing to go to express his gratitude.

Hoyt Ryker didn't even do that much. He crawled out from under the second wagon, stood up, and started toward the closest Sioux corpse, pulling a long-bladed hunting knife from his belt as he did so.

"What are you doin', Ryker?" Preacher asked in a sharp voice.

Ryker pointed the knife at the bodies and said, "I'm going to scalp all those redskins, if it's any of your damned business."

"Seein' as I just helped save all of y'all's bacon, I'm makin' it my business," Preacher snapped. "You need to get your people gathered up and start these wagons rollin' again. Tend to Pidge and anybody else who's wounded. Hawk and me will round up your saddle mounts."

Ryker sneered at him. "Who the hell are you to give orders like that?"

"Somebody who don't want you massacred. Those Sioux may be gone now, but that don't mean they won't come back, and they might bring more friends with 'em next time. Leave those bodies where they lay without mutilatin' 'em, and the Sioux might decide they've had enough and won't follow you. Scalp 'em and the rest of the bunch will track you to the ends o' the earth to square that debt."

Edgar Merton came up in time to hear Preacher's words. The man glared at him and said, "You presume too much, sir. I'm in charge of this expedition, and Mr. Ryker is our head guide. We'll decide the best course of action."

"Suit yourselves," Preacher said. "Just be sure to save one shot each for your son, Miss Dayton, and yourself. Better a pistol ball through the head than what the Sioux will do to you if they capture you."

Chessie looked a little sick at that warning. Oliver put an arm around her shoulders and squeezed as if to reassure her, but he looked pretty worried himself.

After a moment, Merton cleared his throat and said, "Mr. Ryker, perhaps we should listen to this, ah, gentleman. There's no need to aggravate the situation."

"You've got to teach those damned heathens their place," Ryker insisted.

"Not at the cost of our lives. I want to get moving again as soon as possible."

Ryker obviously didn't like it, but he nodded and said, "You're the boss."

Preacher whistled for Horse and swung

up into the saddle. He and Hawk rode off to round up the expedition's mounts.

That took a while. Preacher kept a sharp eye out while they were doing it, just in case the Sioux decided to double back and attack again.

That didn't happen, and less than half an hour later the wagons lurched into motion again, heading north with the rest of the party on horseback. They left the sprawled corpses behind them, untouched.

The only body they took with them was that of the lone member of the expedition who had been killed in the opening minutes of the attack. He was wrapped in a blanket in the back of one of the supply wagons and would be buried when they made camp that night.

Pidge rode in the back of the same wagon, next to the corpse. He had been driving it while Ryker handled the team hitched to the other supply wagon, but with an arrow in his arm Pidge couldn't be expected to wrestle mules into line, so one of the other men had been forced to take over. The wounds in Pidge's left arm and right leg had crude bandages wrapped around them, but the arrows were still in place.

Preacher rode alongside the wagon and told the giant, "We'll get those arrows out of you later, once we've stopped for the night. A fella's got to know what he's doing, or else he's liable to cause even more damage tryin' to get 'em out."

"Nobody asked for your help, mister," Pidge rumbled.

"Maybe not," Preacher said with a smile, "but you'd all be in piss-poor shape without it right now, wouldn't you?"

Pidge didn't have any answer for that, so he just scowled. Preacher nudged Horse on and rode up alongside the covered wagon in the lead. Hawk was already there.

Both Mertons were on the driver's seat, with Chessie peering out from under the arched canvas cover over the wagon bed. Edgar Merton frowned at the mountain man and said, "You haven't been invited to accompany us, you know."

"Not only that," Oliver said, "but just how did you happen to be close enough to come galloping up like that?" His voice had a suspicious edge as he added, "Have you been following us?"

"We're just headed back out to the frontier," Preacher said. That was true as far as it went, but it certainly wasn't the whole story. He and Hawk *had* been following the expedition. However, he didn't see any point in admitting that.

"You shouldn't act like that, Oliver," Chessie put in from her position behind the father and son. "If not for Preacher and Hawk, there's no telling what might have happened. We might all be dead now." She paused, then went on, "Although I'm sure Mr. Ryker would have thought of some way to save us."

Preacher knew better than that, and Chessie probably did, too. But there was some connection between her and Ryker, Preacher recalled, so she had to remain loyal to him . . . without being *too* conspicuous about it, because she had Oliver Merton wrapped around her little finger and wanted to keep him there.

Of course, that was true of Hawk as well. He couldn't seem to take his eyes off Chessie.

Edgar Merton appeared to be deep in thought as the wagon rocked along. Finally he said, "I suppose it would be all right if you rode along with us for a while, until the danger from the Sioux is past. That is, if we wouldn't be keeping you from anything else."

"We can trail along with you for a spell," Preacher said. Now that circumstances had forced him and Hawk to reveal their presence, there was no reason to follow at a distance anymore. "But I've got a hunch Ryker ain't gonna like that idea."

Merton sniffed and said, "You leave Mr. Ryker to me."

If Merton actually believed that he could handle Ryker, he was sure wrong about that.

Preacher intended to see to it that Merton didn't turn out *dead* wrong.

Chapter 13

The expedition pushed on for several more miles that day. Preacher and Hawk ranged out ahead on either side, not only scouting the route but looking for signs of potential trouble. Preacher wouldn't be surprised if the Sioux tried to ambush the wagons again.

The Indians weren't the only possible source of problems. Late in the afternoon, when Preacher had started keeping an eye out for a good place to camp, he heard hoofbeats behind him and reined in. Dog was close by, and he growled as the mountain man twisted in his saddle to see who was coming.

He recognized Hoyt Ryker by the man's tall hat. Preacher rested his right hand on a pistol butt as Ryker approached. Dog growled again. The hair on the back of the cur's neck was standing up like stiff bristles.

"Take it easy," Preacher told him quietly. "Don't worry, old son, if I need to turn you loose, I will."

Ryker hadn't come a-shootin'. He looked more like he wanted to talk. Preacher supposed he ought to hear him out, even though he didn't trust Ryker one little bit.

Ryker lifted his right hand in greeting as he reined in with his left. Neither hand drifted toward the pistol or knife at his waist. If Ryker made a move for either of the weapons, Preacher was confident that he could draw and fire first.

"I'm not looking for trouble," Ryker said.

"I hear that a lot. Sometimes I even say it myself. Funny how it hardly ever works out that way, though."

Ryker grinned. "Did you ever think maybe that's because you attract trouble like a lodestone draws iron filings?"

"I never spent that much time ponderin' it. What do you want, Ryker?"

Ryker moved his hands now, but only to rest them both on the saddle and lean forward. "There's bad blood between the two of us, Preacher. No point in denying it."

"Didn't know that I had."

Ryker went on as if he hadn't heard Preacher's response. "But just because there's bad blood doesn't mean we have to let that cause problems. We're out here in the middle of the wilderness, with hundreds of hostiles maybe just waiting for a chance to jump us. We may need each other to survive. We're both smart men, so there's no reason we can't set any hard feelings aside and make sure we both live to see another day."

Preacher used his left hand to scratch at his beard-stubbled jaw. "I sort of thought me and Hawk were doin' that when we pulled your fat out of the fire earlier today."

Ryker stiffened a little. He didn't seem to like being reminded of that incident. He said, "We would have been all right without your help."

"No way of knowin', either way, is there?" Preacher responded with a shrug.

Ryker shook his head. "That's not what I wanted to talk to you about. Mr. Merton's very grateful to you, even though he may not show it much. Let's just leave it at that. I want to talk about the rest of the trip." His voice hardened. "I'm not going to let you lord it over me all the way to where we're going."

"Where's that?" Preacher asked.

The sharp question made Ryker's frown deepen. He said, "I don't rightly know . . . yet. Merton's the one who's telling us which way to go. I don't know if he's got a map, or if he's been over this route before."

The latter possibility seemed unlikely to Preacher. Edgar Merton hadn't struck him as a man who had spent a lot of time — or *any* time, really — on the frontier. He would have bet that this was Merton's first trip out here.

"Merton's a stubborn man," Ryker continued. "He's promised to tell me more about our destination later. For now my job is to find the best trail that takes us in the right general direction and to keep him and his son safe until we get there."

"And Miss Dayton," Preacher said.

Ryker's mouth twisted in a smirk. "I wasn't really counting on her coming along," he said, "but she insisted. And since I wouldn't have even known about Merton's expedition without her, I couldn't really tell her no."

Of course he could have. He had brought Chessie along because he wanted to. Preacher still believed that Ryker intended to double-cross Edgar Merton at some point, and when that happened, Ryker would kill Merton and Oliver, steal whatever they were after, and take Chessie with him, too.

But he couldn't do that as long as Merton kept playing his cards so close to the vest.

Maybe the easterner wasn't quite as big a fool as Preacher had taken him for at first.

"What is it you want from me?" Preacher asked. "Why'd you ride out to find me?"

"I just want things understood. You and that half-breed — I mean, your son — can come along with us, but you're not members of this expedition. Don't be expecting to claim a share of whatever it is when everything is said and done."

"I wasn't," Preacher said honestly. His only interest was in keeping Ryker and the others from murdering Merton, Oliver, and Chessie.

And if he satisfied his curiosity about Merton's mysterious destination at the same time, then so much the better.

"I have your word on that?" Ryker asked as he lifted his reins.

"You do."

Ryker cocked his head to the side. "Everybody knows that Preacher is an honest man. I suppose I can take your word for it." He started to turn his horse away, then paused. "One other thing. Don't get any ideas about Chessie."

"Why would I? She's Oliver's girl, ain't she?"

Preacher didn't let on that he had seen

Chessie and Ryker embracing outside Red Mike's.

"We'll see about that," Ryker said. "But the situation doesn't need any more complications."

"Won't be any from me," Preacher declared.

"Good."

This time Ryker pulled his horse's head around and urged the animal into a lope back toward the wagons, which had come into sight about a quarter of a mile away.

Preacher had no intention whatsoever of getting mixed up in a romantic tangle that already included Chessie, Oliver, and Ryker.

Now, *Hawk,* on the other hand . . . Preacher couldn't speak for the boy.

Preacher had been through these parts before, although several years had passed since then. Once the mountain man had been somewhere, he never forgot its physical features. He knew they were nearing an area where several rocky humps reared up from the prairie, so he rode back to the wagons and told Edgar Merton it would be smart to keep going until they reached those knobs. That would be a good place to camp.

Merton's agreement brought a scowl to Hoyt Ryker's face, but Ryker didn't say anything. Probably his pride was hurt, but Preacher had promised not to try to cut himself in on whatever game Ryker was playing, so he was willing to go along with it.

Preacher figured he could honor that pledge and still do his best to keep the Mertons and Chessie safe.

They reached the knobs a little before dusk. Preacher directed the men handling the wagon teams to drive to the top of one of them. The slope wasn't too much for the wagons to handle, and trees grew thickly enough up there to provide cover. The lower slopes were clear of trees, giving anyone on top a good field of fire in case of an attack. As long as they had food, water, and ammunition, the expedition could hold off an army from up here.

Preacher didn't expect things to get that bad. His hunch was that the surviving members of that Sioux war party wouldn't come after them. But it never hurt to be prepared for trouble.

When some of the men began to build the usual large campfire, Preacher didn't try to stop them. The damage had been done already. The time for stealth had been when half the countryside didn't know the wagons and riders were there.

Besides, he would need good light for tending to Pidge's injuries.

Preacher told Hawk to keep an eye on their surroundings, then went over to the wagon where Pidge now sat on the lowered tailgate. The big man was pale and sweating in the firelight. The shape he was in didn't do anything to improve his mood. He glared at Preacher as the mountain man approached.

"We got to get those arrows out of you," Preacher said. "They've been in there too long already. The wounds may be startin' to fester. But there wasn't a chance to tend to 'em until now."

Pidge reached up with his right hand and grasped the shaft of the arrow stuck in his left arm. "I can yank the damn thing out anytime," he said.

"Hold on! If you do that, you'll rip out a big chunk of meat along with it. The way that would bleed, along with all the blood you've already lost, might be enough to do you in. You'll be better off in the long run if we push it on through first."

Pidge's eyes widened. "What the hell!" he roared. "Push it on through? You're crazy! Mr. Ryker!"

Chessie and Oliver walked over, drawn by

the commotion. Oliver asked, "What's this about?"

Pidge pointed at Preacher. "He says he's gonna push this arrow right on through my arm!"

"It's the best way to handle a wound like this," Preacher explained. "I'll push the arrowhead out the other side, then cut it off so I can pull the shaft back out on this side without doin' any more damage. I've done it a heap of times, seen it done even more, and pushed a few arrows through my own carcass to get 'em out. I'll need some whiskey, though, to clean the wound when I'm done."

"How about a bottle of brandy?" Oliver asked. "We brought some along for medicinal purposes."

"If that's what you've got, it'll have to do."

"Gimme a drink of it first," Pidge said, scowling. "I ain't gonna let you touch me otherwise."

Preacher grinned. "I reckon that'd be all right. Just don't guzzle it all down. You're gonna need it outside as well as inside."

Oliver went back to his wagon to fetch the brandy. Chessie stayed to comfort Pidge, patting him on the shoulder and telling him that everything was going to be all right. That attention from such a pretty girl made him perk up a mite, as it would most men.

Ryker was with Oliver when he came back with the bottle. With a suspicious frown, Ryker asked, "Just what is it you're planning to do here?"

Preacher explained the process again, then took the bottle from Oliver, pulled the cork from its neck, and handed it to Pidge. The giant tipped the bottle up but had taken only one swallow when Preacher pulled it away from him.

"Hey!" Pidge protested. "I need more than that."

"This is what you need," Preacher said. He unwound the bloody bandages from Pidge's arm, ripped the stained shirtsleeve away, and poured a little of the brandy on the wound. Pidge yelled at the liquor's fiery bite.

"Damn it, you need to warn me before you do anything else, mister."

"I will," Preacher promised as he got a firm grip on the arrow. "I'll tell you in plenty of time —"

While he was still talking, he shoved on the arrow as hard as he could. The flint head emerged from the back of Pidge's arm. Pidge howled again and tried to stand up.

"Hold him down!" Preacher called to Ryker, Oliver, and the other men who were standing around watching.

If Pidge had really wanted to stand up, Preacher doubted if they could have stopped him. But the big man calmed down a little when they grabbed him. Preacher pulled out his knife, held the shaft with his other hand to steady the arrow, and quickly sawed the head off.

Then he said, "This is gonna hurt, too," and pulled the shaft back through the wound. It came out cleanly. "I need a piece of clean cloth."

Chessie reached down, pulled up the hem of her dress, and tore off a piece of petticoat. Preacher told her to soak it with the brandy. Then he wrapped the cloth around the ramrod from his rifle and ran it through the wound, too, to clean it out. Pidge yelled some more but didn't try to get up.

With that done, all that remained on this injury was to bandage it, which Chessie accomplished in short order, using more strips from her petticoat.

"What about the arrow in his leg?" Ryker asked.

"The way it's lined up, I don't think I can push it on through without the bone gettin' in the way," Preacher said. "Also, it ain't as deep to start with. I reckon I can cut it out."

"Cut it out!" Pidge roared. He made a

grab for the brandy. "Gimme that bottle!"

Preacher let him glug down another swallow before taking it back. Judging by Pidge's slightly unfocused gaze, he didn't have much of a tolerance for liquor, which was surprising, considering his great size.

Preacher had him lie back on the tailgate. He cut away the trousers and long underwear to be able to get at the wound better. Then he said again, "Hold him down. And I mean it this time. Hang on tight."

The other men did so. Preacher made a couple of swift but deep incisions around the wound and then got his fingers in there to hold the flesh open as he carefully worked the arrowhead loose with his other hand. Pidge groaned and tried to buck, but the men held him. Preacher heard Chessie gasp as more blood flowed. The arrowhead came free.

He tossed the arrow aside, grabbed the brandy, and splashed the liquor into the wound. Pidge bellowed. Preacher said, "Is there a needle and thread in those supplies?"

"There should be," Oliver said.

"Fetch 'em, quick as you can." Preacher put a folded piece of cloth over the wound and leaned on it. "Should've had 'em ready, but I didn't think of it. I ain't no doctor."

"Probably the closest thing to it out here," Chessie said as Oliver hurried away.

"Naw, there's plenty of folks who can patch up bullet, knife, and arrow wounds. If my pard Audie was here, he would've done a better job than me. But Pidge ought to be all right if we can get that hole in his leg sewed up."

Another quarter of an hour saw that task accomplished. Preacher let Pidge drink more while he was busy putting in the stitches, and the big man was half-asleep by the time Preacher finished. When Preacher finally stepped back from the lowered tailgate, Oliver said, "He would have died without what you did, wouldn't he?"

"He might yet," Preacher said. "He lost a lot of blood, and he's probably gonna run a fever for a day or two. But if he rests and somebody keeps him cool and gets him to drink plenty o' water, he's got a good chance."

"I can do that," Chessie said. "I've taken care of sick people before."

"That'll be fine," Preacher told her.

He noticed that some of the men were looking at him with friendlier expressions now. They appreciated not only his help in driving off the Sioux but also what he had done for Pidge.

Hoyt Ryker didn't look too happy, though. He might be worried that his leadership of the group was going to be challenged.

He didn't have to be concerned about that. Preacher had no interest in bossing a gang of cutthroats, and that's what they still were, even if they weren't as suspicious of him as they had been.

Sooner or later, there would still be a showdown.

Chapter 14

By morning, Pidge was muttering in feverish delirium as he lay in the back of the wagon in a space cleared from the supplies. At least he didn't have to share the wagon bed with a corpse any longer. The man who had been killed in the Sioux ambush had been laid to rest the night before, after Preacher had carried out the crude surgery on Pidge.

Chessie rode in the wagon, too. She had a bucket of water and a cloth that she soaked and used to bathe Pidge's face in an effort to keep his temperature down. She also used a small tin cup to dribble water past the big man's lips and down his throat fairly often.

Overall, Preacher still didn't fully trust the girl because of her connection to Ryker, but as he rode alongside the wagon for a few moments and watched her, he had to admit that she was doing a good job of nursing Pidge back to health.

Preacher and Hawk resumed scouting ahead and to the sides of the expedition. At midday, Preacher told Hawk to drop back and see if anyone was following them. The young warrior nodded curtly and slowed his pony to let the wagons and riders pull ahead of him.

Preacher knew that scouting their back trail like that could be dangerous, but he had full confidence in Hawk's ability to take care of himself. Even so, as the hours went on with no sign of his son, the mountain man began to worry.

Then Dog barked and Preacher looked back to see a distant figure on horseback coming toward them. The rider was just a dark, moving dot at first, but as Preacher reined Horse to a stop and waited, he began to make out enough details to know that Hawk was catching up to them.

A few minutes later, as Hawk rode up and reined in, Preacher noted that his pony was sweaty and winded. Hawk had been pushing the mount hard. That could mean only one thing.

"Trouble back there?" Preacher asked.

"I saw dust in the distance behind us," Hawk reported. "I thought at first it might be from a hunting party crossing our route, but it remained directly to the south and came closer. Whoever they are, it is likely they are following us."

Preacher grunted. "Sioux. Could you tell how big a party?"

"Large," Hawk said with grim brevity.

"Well, we knew there was a good chance of that. Those wagons can't turn back without runnin' right into that bunch, and if they keep goin' the direction they are now, the Sioux will overtake 'em in a few days. The country to the east is too open. Only chance is to cut west into more rugged terrain and try to give 'em the slip."

"These are Sioux hunting grounds," Hawk pointed out. "They know this land better than anyone else. What are the chances of that working?"

Preacher's smile was cold as he replied, "Not very good. But what else is there to try?"

Hawk didn't have an answer for that. After a moment, he nodded and nudged his pony up alongside Horse as Preacher rode toward the wagons.

They drew even with the wagon carrying Pidge first. Preacher slowed Horse to a walk and asked Chessie, "How's he doin'?"

"He's still running a fever, but I'm not sure it's as high as it was earlier," the girl said. "I changed his bandages a little while ago. The wounds don't look too bad."

Preacher nodded. "It would've been better if we'd had some moss to pack in there, but there ain't any of the right kind out here. When we get to where there is some, if he's still havin' trouble we'll try it then."

Pidge's eyes had been closed when Preacher and Hawk rode up, but now they opened and the big man peered around, his gaze bleary and unfocused. He looked in Preacher's direction and said, "Ma? Ma, is that you? Don't you know me? It's your little pigeon."

"You just rest, Pidge," Preacher told him. "You'll be better after a while."

"You sure sound funny, Ma. I never knew your voice was so gravelly." Pidge sighed. "But I reckon if you want me to rest, I will."

He closed his eyes and settled back against the sack of flour that was propped behind his head and shoulders.

"Do you need help with him?" Hawk asked Chessie, his voice quiet so as not to disturb Pidge again.

She smiled and said, "No, I'm fine. He's really not much trouble, as long as he doesn't go out of his head from the fever or anything."

"If you need me, I will be happy to give you a hand."

"Thank you, Hawk." Her smile was dazzling, and Preacher could tell that it affected Hawk. The young man practically had to tear himself away to follow Preacher toward the lead wagon.

"You did not say anything to her about how the Sioux are pursuing us," Hawk said quietly. "She should know that soon we may be running for our lives."

"What good would it do to tell her?" Preacher said. "The Sioux will either catch us or they won't, and if they do, we'll fight. It's pretty simple. Anyway, if we change direction, she'll probably figure out what's goin' on."

Hoyt Ryker rode beside the lead wagon at the moment. Oliver Merton was at the reins with his father on the seat beside him. All of them turned to look at Preacher and Hawk as they rode up.

Oliver was observant enough to notice their expressions. "Trouble?" he asked.

"Looks like an even bigger bunch of Sioux is comin' up behind us," Preacher said. "I knew there was a chance those varmints might go and fetch their friends."

"How do you know for sure they're back there?" Ryker asked. "Did either of you see them?"

"I saw their dust," Hawk said.

Ryker snorted disdainfully. "You saw dust," he said. "That could have come from anything. A herd of buffalo, maybe, or some other Indians on their way somewhere else."

Hawk shook his head and said, "The dust I saw stayed directly behind us and moved quickly in this direction. They are pursuing us. No other answer is possible."

"What do you think we should do, Mr. Ryker?" Merton asked.

"We routed those red devils once," Ryker blustered. "We can damn sure do it again."

"You defeated a small force," Hawk said. "There could be a hundred men in the war party coming after us now. Perhaps even more."

"Our guns make us more than a match for any bunch of savages," Ryker insisted.

"I wouldn't be so sure about that," Preacher said. "Anyway, just because that first batch didn't have any rifles don't mean this war party won't. There could be plenty of them with guns. We just don't know."

"We don't *know* anything. This is all just pure supposition." Ryker turned toward the wagon and went on, "I think we should continue the way we're going, Mr. Merton —"

"You do that and they'll overtake us and wipe us out," Preacher broke in. "What we need is a place to fort up, and the closest one is several miles west of here."

"I hate to deviate from our course," Merton said with a frown.

"Anyway," Ryker went on, "even if there *are* Sioux chasing us, they're a long way back. There's a good chance they'll give up and turn around before they ever spot us. You know how shiftless those heathens are, Mr. Merton —"

Again, Preacher interrupted him. "If they've gone to the trouble of comin' after us, they ain't gonna give up. They'll stay on our trail until they catch us. The only thing that'll make them change their minds is to spill enough of their blood to make 'em believe it ain't worthwhile to keep fightin'."

"Can we *do* that?" Edgar Merton asked with obvious doubt.

"Maybe. If we've got some high ground to hold."

"Where are we going to find high ground?" Ryker wanted to know. "Except for those little hills back there, this country is flat as a table!"

"Not to the west. There are some badlands over in that direction. We get amongst 'em, we can put the wagons in a little canyon where the Sioux can't get to us except one way. We can put riflemen up high, too, to pick some of 'em off."

Oliver spoke up, saying, "If there's only one way *in* to the canyon you're talking about, that means there's only one way *out,* too. We'd be trapped in there as long as they wanted to keep us bottled up."

Preacher nodded. "That's why we'll have to kill enough of 'em to make 'em decide to go back where they came from." He shrugged. "It's a gamble, ain't no two ways about it. But goin' on the way we're headed and tryin' to outrun 'em . . . that's certain death."

A moment of silence followed that grim declaration. Finally, Edgar Merton said, "Well . . . if you're sure . . ."

"I am," Preacher said flatly.

"Then I suppose we should head west, as you suggest." Merton raised a hand to silence Ryker when the man opened his mouth to protest. "Do we need to hide our trail, so there'll be a chance they won't find us?"

"We can try," Preacher said. "It probably won't do any good, but as long as it don't slow us down, it won't hurt anything, either."

"Turn west, Oliver," Merton ordered his son. "Follow Preacher. Mr. Ryker, pass along the change in plan to the other drivers and the rest of your men."

"Sure, boss," Ryker said, even though his jaw was clenched tightly in anger. He jerked his horse's head around and rode back to the other wagons. As he did, he waved an arm to call in all the outriders.

Oliver Merton hauled on the reins and swung the team of mules around until they were plodding westward. Preacher caught Hawk's eye and leaned his head toward the other wagons. He wanted Hawk to fall back again and keep an eye out behind them. Hawk nodded to show that he understood and turned his pony.

"You believe an attack to be inevitable, Preacher?" Edgar Merton asked.

"I do," the mountain man replied.

"Realistically speaking . . . what are our chances of surviving?"

"Well, it ain't like tryin' to figure the odds in a poker game. Unless somebody's cheatin', there's only fifty-two cards in a deck. We're talkin' about a hundred or more Injuns, plus the fellas in our bunch. That's a lot to predict."

Merton smiled faintly. "Is that your way of saying that we don't stand much of a chance of making it out alive?"

"Nope. Just sayin' we'll get ready to fight, and then we'll see what happens."

Oliver kept slapping the reins against the backs of the mules, urging them on to greater speed. Trying to, anyway. The stubborn brutes didn't want to cooperate. With a note of frustration in his voice, Oliver said, "Since it's starting to look like we may never reach our destination, Father, don't you think it's time you tell me just where we were headed and what you intended to do there?"

Preacher cocked an eyebrow when he heard that. So Oliver didn't know what they were after, either. That was interesting.

"That's enough, Oliver," Merton snapped. "You know your grandfather swore me to secrecy and said that I shouldn't tell anyone until it was absolutely necessary."

"It's not necessary, now that we're facing a great likelihood of death?"

"It won't change anything for you to know," Merton said stubbornly. "If it would, I would tell you." He looked at Preacher. "I trust I can count on your discretion, sir?"

"The only thing on my mind right now is findin' a good place to kill us some Sioux," Preacher replied honestly.

Within an hour's time, Preacher was able to make out the rising column of dust behind them. He had never doubted Hawk's word, not for a second, but now he had visual confirmation of the pursuit.

But he could also see a low, lumpy dark line along the western horizon and knew that was the badlands, a mostly arid region of rocky draws and canyons, razor-sharp ridges, and an occasional sandstone spire towering over all of it. In many places, the ground and the rocks had red casts to them, so that when the sun washed over them at certain angles, it looked like some giant butcher had splashed buckets of blood over everything.

By tomorrow morning, it might look like that for real, Preacher mused.

The bleak assessment didn't show on his face as he pointed out where they were going to Edgar and Oliver Merton.

"Been a good while since I spent much time in that region," Preacher said, "but I'm pretty sure we won't have to go too deep into it before we find one o' those canyons like I was talkin' about. I hope that's true, because it's hard to get wagons in and out o' there. It'll be slow goin'."

"We have to find a good place," Oliver said. "I . . . I don't think I could stand it if something were to happen to Chessie . . . I mean, Miss Dayton."

"*That's* what you're worried about?" his

father responded sharply. "Honestly, Oliver, she's just a common tavern wench. There are hundreds like her in any city. We shouldn't have brought her along in the first place. You and Ryker are both too smitten with her."

Oliver showed his irritation with Merton by slapping the reins harder against the mules' backs. "Common?" he repeated. "Have you not taken a good look at her, Father? Chessie is far from common."

Merton waved a hand. "She's attractive, I'll grant you that. But again, there are a multitude of attractive women in the world. You should know that. You've dallied with enough of them who were only interested in your money . . . just like your Miss Dayton."

Oliver's face flushed a dark red. He looked like he wanted to turn on the seat and punch his father. Instead he controlled his anger with a visible effort and said to Preacher, "Those tall rocks are very striking. Is that where you plan to put men to fire on the savages?"

"Yep," Preacher said. "They'll have to carry food and water up with them, along with powder and shot, because it's liable to be a while before they're able to climb down again. Best part about a perch like that is that it's hard to fire an arrow that high."

"I don't think I'd care for being posted there. If that's all right with you."

"My son is scared of heights," Merton said.

"It's not that . . . I'd rather stay closer to Miss Dayton, so I can be sure she's protected." Oliver sneered at his father. "Surely you can understand *that* . . . or have all the shreds of chivalry inside you dried up?"

"Chivalry never paid a bill," Merton muttered.

Preacher found their wrangling tiresome. He said, "You know where you're goin', Oliver. Just keep headin' in that direction." He pointed. "See them two spires settin' sort of close together? Aim for them, and don't slow down for nothin'."

"I can do that, Preacher. What are you going to do?"

"Might be a good idea to scout around a little." The mountain man turned in the saddle, caught Hawk's eye, and waved him forward. "Hawk and I will be back when we've found a good place to fort up. Don't worry, we'll be here before you get to the badlands."

Hawk loped up on his pony. He had a frown on his face, probably because he didn't want to leave Chessie. That gal bewitched young men like some sort of . . .

witch . . . Preacher thought.

"We're gonna take a look around up yonder," Preacher told his son, then nudged Horse into a run. Hawk galloped after him toward the badlands.

Chapter 15

Preacher had led the wagons over the stoniest ground he could find in the race to the badlands. He hadn't really expected that to do much good in hiding their trail, and obviously it hadn't because the Sioux were still back there, closing in on them.

When you couldn't avoid a fight, the thing to do was be in the best position to hurt your enemy while minimizing your own chances of getting hurt. The badlands offered a chance at that . . . the only real chance the expedition had.

Preacher and Hawk slowed their mounts as they entered the rocky, broken ground. Dog bounded ahead, leaping from boulder to boulder. Preacher tilted his head back to look up at the spires he had pointed out to Oliver Merton. There was a trail of sorts running between them. It would be rough going for the wagons, but Preacher thought they could make it.

"They look like gates," Hawk said. "Or sentinels standing guard."

"Reckon you can climb one of them?"

Hawk shrugged. "I would rather stay with the wagons."

Like Oliver, Hawk wanted to stay close to Chessie so he could protect her. Preacher knew that, but he couldn't allow sentiment to color his judgment. He said, "We need good shots up there."

"Fine," Hawk replied with a sullen tone in his voice. "But not yet. We must find a place for the rest of the expedition to take cover."

The two of them rode between the spires and followed the trail a quarter of a mile into the badlands before it twisted sharply and sandstone walls heaved up on both sides. The way the walls leaned toward each other, it was almost like riding into a tunnel that was a hundred yards long.

At the far end, the landscape opened into a rough bowl, and on the far side was a narrow canyon cut into the rocky upthrusts surrounding the bowl. Preacher pointed to it and said, "That's where we'll put the wagons. We can make our first stand here at this gap, and if we can't hold it, we'll fall back to the canyon."

"Do you still want riflemen on the spires?"

Preacher thought about it and then nodded. "The men up there can let the Sioux go on past, then start droppin' 'em from behind when they try to attack through the gap. They'll think they're bottlin' us up, but actually we'll have them caught between two fires."

"That could work," Hawk said with a speculative frown. "There will be too many of them for us to wipe out, though."

"I ain't figurin' on wipin' 'em out. I just want to hurt 'em bad enough to make 'em light a shuck and leave us alone."

"We may be able to do that," Hawk said.

Preacher nudged Horse into motion again. "Let's go take a look at that canyon and make sure it'll work for what we need."

They rode toward the opening. Dog ran ahead and disappeared into the canyon. The mouth of it was fifty feet wide, and the rough walls rose eighty feet to irregular rimrocks. As they entered the canyon, Preacher looked up and then pointed out several ledges.

"If we could get fellas up there, too, they'd have a good field of fire. If we put up just enough of a fight to draw the whole war party into the gap, then with riflemen on the high ground on both ends, we could trap them there."

"And if they try to break out either end,

we will be ready for them." Hawk nodded. "Yes, that could work."

Preacher looked around the canyon and asked, "Where'd Dog go?" The big cur was nowhere in sight, so Preacher supposed he had wandered off around a bend farther up the canyon. He whistled, but Dog still didn't return.

A moment later, though, they heard a series of growls and snarling barks from the other side of that bend, followed by a sharp yelp that made Preacher stiffen in alarm. "What the hell!" he blurted. "Dog!"

He heeled Horse into a run. Hawk followed closely behind. They pounded along the canyon and around the bend. As they did, Preacher spotted Dog sprawled on the rocky canyon floor with a grotesque figure looming over him. It was human but red as a devil, with a shaven head and a wiry body that was nude except for a cloth twisted around its loins. The creature clutched a tomahawk and had it poised to finish off Dog, who was moving around feebly and whining.

Preacher shouted incoherently in rage as he whipped his rifle to his shoulder and fired. The red creature's arm jerked violently as the rifle ball shattered its elbow. The tomahawk flew out of its fingers. Howling in pain, the creature whirled around and raced away.

Preacher galloped up to Dog and threw himself out of the saddle as Hawk rode on past in pursuit. The big cur was struggling to stand up. Preacher put his arms around his old friend and helped him. He saw a bloody patch on Dog's head, between the ears, but the wound didn't appear to be deep. Preacher figured the creature had struck at Dog with the tomahawk but landed only a glancing blow, stunning him.

Dog shook himself and growled as he looked along the canyon where Hawk and his quarry had disappeared. Preacher could tell now that Dog wasn't badly hurt, and that fact made relief flood through him.

"Lucky for you that ol' skull bone o' yours is hard as rock," he told the cur.

Somewhere along the canyon, another gunshot blasted. Preacher's head jerked up at the sound.

Dog took off running, already throwing off the effects of his injury in his excitement. Preacher swung into the saddle and charged after him.

As they rounded the bend, Preacher saw Hawk on the ground, fighting with several more of the bizarre red creatures. He gripped the barrel of his rifle and slashed back and forth with it, trying to hold them off as they darted in and hacked at him with tomahawks.

Dog reached the melee first and hit one of the attackers from behind, driving the creature off its feet and tearing at the screeching thing with sharp teeth. Preacher rode down another one. Horse's hooves snapped bones and pulped flesh as he trampled the creature. Preacher wheeled the stallion and yanked both pistols from behind his belt. They blasted, sending thunderous echoes cascading through the canyon, and two more of the red devils went down.

The others broke off the attack and fled, seeming to vanish into the rocky canyon wall. Preacher knew there had to be cracks and crevices there that served as escape routes.

Blood oozed from a cut on Hawk's forehead, Preacher saw as he dismounted. The young warrior wasn't too steady on his feet. Preacher knew that Hawk, like Dog, must have been clipped by a tomahawk, probably thrown at him from ambush. He gripped his son's arm to brace him and said, "Are you all right, Hawk?"

Hawk didn't answer the question directly. Instead he asked in a stunned voice, "What . . . what *were* those things?"

"Indians," Preacher said. "Outcasts, some call 'em. They're fellas who are so bad in one way or another that the rest of their tribes don't want nothin' to do with 'em. They've gathered up here, I reckon, and made their own little tribe."

"Their skin was so red . . ."

"They crush and grind red sandstone into a powder and then plaster it all over themselves. I used to hear about 'em, but I figured they were just stories that squaws used to scare their young 'uns. Then some fellas I trust told me they had seen the critters with their own eyes, a good ways north of here, so I decided they were real after all. I reckon they've drifted down this way since then."

"They looked insane," Hawk said in a hollow voice. "Their eyes were like the eyes of snakes, but somehow worse."

"Because they're men," Preacher said. "It ain't comfortin' to think that fellas like us could somehow wind up so twisted and evil."

Hawk shook his head. "We cannot take refuge from the Sioux here. Not with these . . . demons . . . lurking close by, ready to attack."

"We don't have any choice," Preacher said. "Maybe they'll leave us alone, now that we've killed a few of 'em."

"Do you actually believe this?"

A grim, humorless smile tugged at Preacher's mouth under the salt-and-pepper mustache. "Nope. But when you've got enemies on all sides, the only thing you can do is fight."

Preacher sent Hawk back to guide the wagons into the badlands while he dragged the bodies of the dead Indians into a crevice where they would be out of sight. Hawk didn't want to leave his father there by himself when it was possible the deadly outcasts could return, but Preacher had Dog with him and knew he could count on the cur to warn him if any of the creatures came near.

"He's got their scent now," Preacher explained, "and he don't like it. He'll let me know if they're anywhere around."

Hawk went, reluctantly. Preacher completed the grim task of disposing of the bodies, then explored the canyon further. It ran for about half a mile before narrowing down and ending in a wall of blank stone. The tiny chimneys the outcasts had used to escape were so small it didn't seem possible that anything human could have writhed through them. Preacher considered the possibility that the creatures would return to attack the expedition and decided that guards would have to be posted to watch the back of the canyon, not just the direction the Sioux would come from.

Talk about being caught between a rock and a hard place . . .

He hadn't expected to run into such danger here in the badlands, but even if he had known about the outcasts moving into this region, he would have had to lead the expedition here. It was the only place they could put up a fight against their pursuers.

How bad did a fella have to be for his own tribe to cast him out? Preacher had heard that some folks back East believed all Indians were noble and peaceful and just wanted to get along with everybody. That was pure foolishness. Life on the frontier was hard and mean and bred hard and mean people, red and white alike. Most tribes tortured their enemies at some point. There was more than enough casual brutality to go around. Cannibalism was uncommon but certainly not unheard of. Preacher didn't want to speculate too much about what those varmints might have done to make their own people turn on them. He recalled Audie quoting something old Bill Shakespeare wrote about how hell was empty and all the devils were here.

Today, that seemed to be true in these badlands.

He mounted up and rode back to where the twin spires towered over the prairie's edge. From here he could see the wagons approaching, less than half a mile distant now.

But no more than two miles behind them, the thick dust cloud that marked the war party's location rose toward the cloudless sky. They couldn't have cut it much closer than this, Preacher thought. As it was, they would barely have time to prepare before the Sioux arrived.

He rode out and waved the expedition on between the spires. As the wagons rolled past, he saw that both Edgar and Oliver Merton looked pale and frightened now. They had seen the dust and realized that Preacher was right about the deadly danger on their trail. In the supply wagon with the wounded Pidge, Chessie Dayton looked scared, too. Preacher gave her an encouraging nod but didn't know if it did any good.

Hoyt Ryker rode up and reined in. With obvious reluctance, he said to Preacher, "You were right. That's a big bunch, and they're after us."

"That ain't all," Preacher said. "Some

renegade Injuns are sort of squattin' in these badlands, and they ain't happy about us bargin' in on 'em."

Ryker cursed bitterly at that news. "*More* Indians? What are we going to do?"

"Only thing we *can* do. Keep an eye out for them while we're fightin' off the Sioux." Quickly, Preacher explained the layout of the canyon. He didn't like or trust Ryker, but for the moment they were allies against overwhelming odds and had to rely on each other. "Put men with rifles up on those ledges just inside the canyon. Since Pidge is hurt, he'll be a good one to keep watch for those crazy Injuns. Give him a couple of pistols and plenty of powder and shot."

Ryker nodded in understanding. "You want the rest of us to put up a fight and draw the Sioux through the gap after us?" he asked, showing that he had a quick grasp of the tactics Preacher had in mind.

"Yep. We're gonna pin 'em down in there and whip 'em bad enough that after a while they'll be happy to head back south and leave us alone."

"Might work," Ryker said. He turned his horse to see about setting up the defense.

Hawk came trotting up on foot, carrying a rifle. He had two powder horns and two shot pouches slung over his shoulder. One of Ryker's men, equipped in the same way, was with him. This man was reed thin, with a lantern jaw and a thatch of dark hair under his hat.

"This is Simon Bishop," Hawk introduced his companion. "He has volunteered to climb up onto the other spire."

Preacher nodded and said, "Appreciate that, Bishop. Be careful. It'll be a long fall if you slip."

" 'Tain't likely I'll slip," Bishop drawled. "I grew up in the Appalachians, so I been climbin' rocks as far back as I can remember."

Preacher had to grin at that. He wished Hawk and Bishop luck, added, "Stay out of sight up there until the war party's gone on past." Then he turned and rode quickly to the canyon to see how things were going there.

The wagons were inside the canyon. Preacher pointed and told the drivers to line them up across the opening so they would form a barricade. "Get the teams unhitched and move them back," he ordered briskly. No one objected that he had taken command in this situation, not even Hoyt Ryker. The threat was too great for any pettiness now.

Pidge was sitting on a rock with a couple

of pistols beside him. He still looked pale and shaky, but his eyes were clear and alert as he said to Preacher, "Hoyt told me to keep an eye out for some other redskins who might be in here."

"That's right," Preacher said. "And these redskins are as red as they can be. You'll know 'em if you see 'em, that's for sure."

"Are they . . . monsters?"

"No, they're human," Preacher assured the big man. "They'll bleed like anybody else if you shoot 'em."

"Well, that's good, then." Pidge nodded. "I'll watch for them."

Preacher clapped a hand on his shoulder and said, "Good man. Where's Chessie?"

"I dunno. Mr. Oliver Merton came and got her a few minutes ago."

Preacher went to look for them and found them at the covered wagon. Oliver and his father were checking their guns. They looked terrified, but they were holding their fear in check, at least for the moment. Chessie was inside the wagon, peering out from the opening at the front of the canvas cover.

"You stay low in there, miss," Preacher told her. "You have a gun?"

"Yes, Oliver gave me a pistol," she said.

Preacher started to tell her to save the last

ball for herself, but then decided not to. She already knew that.

"You two stay close to the wagon and defend Miss Dayton," he said to the Mertons.

Edgar Merton said, "We're all going to die in this godforsaken place, aren't we?"

"We've got a good chance of makin' it out of here," Preacher said. "If you have to shoot, make every shot count." He turned to Hoyt Ryker and went on, "Send another man to help Pidge watch our backs. The rest of us are gonna head for the other end of that gap to be the first line of defense."

"You sound like a military man, Preacher," Oliver said.

The mountain man shook his head. "Nope. The only army I've ever been part of was the one Andy Jackson gathered up to fight the British down in New Orleans, way back a long time ago. But it seems like I've been fightin' my whole life, one way or another."

"If we do have a chance, it's because of you."

Ryker glared at Oliver's words of praise. Preacher saw that but ignored it. He motioned with his head toward the gap and said, "Come on."

Nine men moved into the gap on foot:

Preacher, Ryker, and seven of Ryker's companions. It was a pitifully small force to take on a hundred or more angry Sioux. Preacher knew that. Everything would have to break just right for any of them to survive . . .

At the far end of the gap, he dispersed his forces behind rocks near the opening and told them, "Open fire whenever the Sioux are in rifle range. It's more important that we lead 'em into this trap, but every one you kill startin' out makes the odds against us better. When I give the word, we'll pull back through the gap and head for the canyon. Ryker, I'll need a couple of men to climb up on those ledges just inside the canyon mouth. You got two more men who can climb?"

Ryker looked around and said, "Plemmons, how about you and Watson?"

The two men nodded their agreement.

"I guess everybody knows what they need to do, then," Preacher said, then added as he glanced between the spires, "and not a minute too soon, because here they come!"

CHAPTER 16

The members of the Sioux war party had begun to be distinguishable as individual figures at the base of the dust cloud their horses kicked up. They couldn't have been galloping those ponies full speed the entire time they'd been chasing the wagons, or else the poor animals would have collapsed by now. But they had been pushing their mounts pretty fast, Preacher knew.

Now the warriors began to slow as they approached the edge of the badlands. They had to know that was where their quarry had gone, and they weren't just about to give up the hunt for vengeance.

But a wariness seemed to seize them now, and Preacher couldn't have that. He nestled the rifle's butt against his shoulder, rested his cheek against the smooth wood of its stock, and drew a bead on one of the riders in the lead, a warrior with a big feathered headdress.

Preacher squeezed the trigger.

The rifle boomed and kicked against his shoulder. Through the gush of powder smoke, he saw the rider throw his arms in the air and fall off his pony. Preacher heard the shrill whoops of rage that greeted the results of his shot and saw the war party surge forward again.

Ryker and the other men followed Preacher's example. A ragged volley of shots rang out. The war party was big enough that it was difficult to miss. As Preacher was reloading, he saw several more men fall. A couple of Indian ponies went down, too, causing others to stumble and fall, and in seconds there was a wild pileup that blunted the attack and caused it to falter.

The delay was brief, however. The Sioux regrouped in a matter of seconds and charged again. The new casualties left them even more maddened with hate and rage than they had been. Preacher and the other defenders had reloaded by now, and another hail of lead scythed into the war party's front ranks.

Preacher knew they couldn't manage more than another volley or two, so he called to Plemmons and Watson, the two men who were going to climb to the ledges just inside the canyon mouth, and told them to fall back and get to those posts. The men took off at a run through the shadowy gap.

"Let's slow 'em down again!" Preacher called to his companions.

More shots blasted, more Indians fell. Preacher saw puffs of smoke coming from scattered places along the line of charging Sioux and knew some of them had rifles, just as he expected. Most of the firearms were probably old trade muskets that were wildly inaccurate, but a stray bullet could kill a man just as dead as a perfectly aimed one.

"Fall back!" he ordered. "Get to the canyon and fort up behind the wagons!"

Preacher glanced up at the spires. He didn't see any sign of Hawk or Simon Bishop on the stone pillars, but that was good. If he couldn't spot them, the Sioux couldn't, either.

He finished reloading as the other men peeled away from the rocks where they had taken cover and raced between the looming walls of the gap. He had just lined his sights on the war party and taken another shot when he heard a matching report from a nearby rifle. A glance to his left revealed that Hoyt Ryker was still there, kneeling behind a boulder.

"Ryker, I said pull back!"

"Not until you do!" Ryker responded as he started to reload. "I'm damned if I'll let you be the last one to retreat and grab all the glory!"

"A damned fool, that's what you are!" Preacher reached for his powder horn. The Sioux were almost on top of them. He didn't know if he had time to reload for one more shot.

"I'll go when you do!" Ryker shouted over the rumble of charging hoofbeats.

Preacher let his powder horn drop on its strap and grabbed a pistol from behind his belt instead. The Indians were within range of the pistol now. He pointed it at the war party and fired, then yelled, "Let's get outta here!"

He turned and dashed toward the gap. Arrows flew around his head. From the corner of his eye, he saw Ryker pounding alongside him. They raced into the gloom of the tunnel-like passage. Their swift footsteps echoed from the walls. Arrows whipped through the air around them.

When they reached the far end, Preacher glanced over his shoulder and saw that the first members of the Sioux war party had entered the passage's far end. The charge had narrowed down so that they were riding four or five abreast. All of the Indians would fit in the gap.

And once they were in there, Preacher didn't intend to let them out again, at least for a while.

As he and Ryker emerged into the bowl and legged it toward the canyon mouth, he saw the other men scrambling behind the wagons and getting ready to fight again. He looked up toward the ledges on each side of the opening, where Plemmons and Watson were pulling themselves into place. They needed to hurry. It wouldn't be long before those fighting-mad Sioux came boiling out into the open.

Ryker was huffing and blowing by the time they reached the wagons. Preacher wasn't out of breath, but his heart was beating pretty fast. Ryker ducked through the narrow gap between the two supply wagons and Preacher followed him. The other men had arranged themselves behind the wagons as Preacher had ordered, and they had their rifles aimed at the gap.

Preacher heard a whoop and looked around to see several Sioux warriors breaking out into the open. A shot blasted from somewhere above the mountain man's head. One of the Indians went over backward.

"Open fire!" Preacher shouted to the men

behind the wagons. "Pour some lead in there!"

A wave of gunfire slammed out. The echoes bounced around the high walls of the bowl and combined into a thunderous roar that shook the very earth beneath Preacher's feet. Sioux warriors and ponies went down in a welter of flesh and began to pile up in front of the opening. The Indians had the advantage of numbers, however, and as more of them emerged from the opening, they leaped their ponies over and around the chaos and continued the attack.

Preacher fired and knocked one of the Sioux off his pony. While he was reloading, the mountain man glanced to his left and right and saw that the defenders seemed calm as they went about their business, which was good. Keeping a cool head in battle greatly increased a man's chances of coming out alive.

Even Edgar and Oliver Merton were putting up a good fight. Edgar stood at the back of the covered wagon while Oliver had posted himself at the front. They reloaded somewhat clumsily between shots, but they didn't appear to be getting flustered.

Preacher hoped Chessie was hunkered down low in the wagon bed, with as many trunks and crates piled around her as she could get. If circumstances had been different, Preacher would have sent her to hide in the rocks somewhere deeper in the canyon, probably with Pidge to watch over her. But with the threat of those grotesque outcasts looming back there, he had decided she might be safer here.

When you came right down to it, nobody in this canyon today was really safe, on either side, wherever they were. They all had to take their chances . . .

Plemmons and Watson were doing a good job of choosing their targets, picking off the attackers who made it too close to the wagons. But they could load and fire only so fast, and it was inevitable that one of the Sioux would get through.

That happened a moment later. One of the warriors drove his pony into the canyon mouth, so close to the wagons that he was able to leap from the animal's back, clear with a bound the wagon tongue that blocked his path, and slash at the nearest defender with a tomahawk.

Preacher was behind the Indian. He yanked the pistol that was still loaded from behind his belt and fired at close range. The ball struck the Sioux in the back of the head and blew his skull apart in a grisly spray of blood, brain matter, and bone shards. His lifeless body flopped forward.

A shout made Preacher turn back in the other direction. He saw that another warrior had breached the barrier formed by the wagons. This man was struggling with Edgar Merton. He had a knife in his upraised hand and had been about to strike Merton with it when the easterner caught hold of the Sioux's wrist with both hands. Merton was hanging on for dear life while the warrior pummeled him with his other hand. Preacher knew Merton wouldn't be able to hold on for much longer, and all it would take was one slip for the Indian to plunge the blade into his body.

Oliver was closer and came to his father's aid before Preacher could. He lunged in and reached over Merton's shoulder to ram the brass butt plate of his rifle into the Sioux's face. The Indian fell back, tripped, and sprawled on the ground as Edgar Merton let go of him. While the warrior was still stunned, Oliver slammed the rifle butt into his face three more times with all the strength he could muster. Each time he struck, Oliver yelled in incoherent anger, so caught up in the heat of battle he might not even have realized what he was doing.

The Indian's shattered, bloody face didn't much resemble anything human by the time

Oliver came to himself and stepped back with the rifle hanging loosely in his hands. The butt was smeared with gore. Oliver looked at it in distaste and tried to wipe it off on the ground.

While he was doing that, another Sioux leaped to the driver's box on the wagon and aimed an arrow at Oliver's back.

Preacher's rifle came up smoothly and boomed. The Indian flew backward off the wagon before he could loose the shaft.

Inside the wagon, Chessie screamed. That sound cut through Oliver's half stupor. Another Sioux was trying to clamber over the tailgate into the wagon. Oliver dropped the rifle, grabbed the man, and flung him to the ground. The Sioux was able to pull Oliver down with him, and an instant later they were rolling around, locked in a desperate struggle.

Preacher didn't have time to go to Oliver's aid or even to watch and see how the fight turned out. Another Sioux had reached the wagons and managed to get between them. This one had an old musket and was lining it up on Preacher when the mountain man spotted him from the corner of his eye. Preacher dived to the ground as the weapon boomed. The ball hummed over his head. He rolled and came up with his tomahawk in hand. The flint head flashed out and buried itself between the warrior's eyes as Preacher struck. The blow was so powerful it almost cleaved the man's head in two. He dropped bonelessly to the ground as Preacher wrenched the tomahawk free.

Shrill cries came from the Indians and cut through the continuing din of gunfire. Preacher whipped around and saw that the Sioux had had enough, at least for now. They whipped their ponies as they retreated toward the gap. Two more of them fell as the defenders behind the wagons kept firing until the last of the warriors disappeared into the shadowy passage.

More than likely, they intended to ride on through the gap and regroup outside to plan another attack on the expedition. A grim smile tugged at Preacher's lips as he heard rifle shots crack in the distance. That would be Hawk and Simon Bishop picking off the first of the Sioux to emerge from the gap. The shots were followed by confused, angry cries. Preacher couldn't see the surviving members of the war party milling around in there, but he could imagine it easily enough. The Sioux had no way of knowing how many rifles were waiting for them on the other side. If they rode out blindly, they might all be slaughtered. In time they would probably figure it out, but for now they would be cautious.

That was exactly the way Preacher wanted them.

He walked over to the covered wagon, where Edgar and Oliver Merton leaned against the sideboards and breathed heavily. Both men were pale and drawn. Preacher asked, "Either of you fellas hurt?"

"I . . . I don't think so," Oliver said. He looked down at the Indian sprawled at his feet. The bone handle of a knife stuck up from the warrior's chest. Glassy eyes stared sightlessly up at the sky. "I killed that man," Oliver went on hoarsely. His eyes flicked toward another, even more gruesome corpse, the man whose face he had battered in. "And that one. And maybe more when I was shooting at them . . ."

From the back of the wagon, where she was climbing over the tailgate, Chessie said, "You saved my life, Oliver. If that savage had gotten in here, he would have killed me. I know he would."

As soon as her feet hit the ground, she ran over to Oliver and threw her arms around him. He swallowed, still looking a little dazed, and raised a hand to pat her awkwardly on the back as she embraced him.

Edgar Merton said, "They're not gone, are they?"

"No, but we've got 'em bottled up inside that gap," Preacher said, "just like I explained earlier." The shooting from the spires had stopped now, so he knew the Sioux weren't venturing out. "We want to hurt 'em so bad that when they do light a shuck outta here, they won't want to come after us again."

"Do you believe that's possible?"

Preacher looked at the bodies of the Sioux scattered around the wagons and said, "I reckon we ain't far from that point now."

CHAPTER 17

Preacher left Edgar Merton mopping his sweating forehead with a handkerchief while Chessie and Oliver comforted each other. The mountain man walked over to see if Hoyt Ryker or any of the other men had been hurt in the battle.

"We're fine," Ryker said. "A couple of the Sioux reached the wagons, but we were able to shoot them down before they did any damage. Added to the ones you took care of and the ones we downed when they first came out of that gap, we must have killed nearly half of the red-skinned bastards!"

"You're overcountin' by a long ways," Preacher told him. "There are fifteen or sixteen bodies where we can see 'em, and we may have wounded a few more bad enough that they're done for. But we've killed a fifth of 'em, at most."

"That's still a lot of men to lose."

Preacher nodded. "It all just depends on

how many warriors they think their revenge is worth. With every one of 'em we kill, the blood debt gets higher, but there'll come a time when they have to say enough is enough."

"We'll keep killing them until it is," Ryker said, a sneer curling his lip.

Preacher wasn't happy about fate putting him on the same side as a man like Ryker, at least for the time being, but there was nothing he could do about it.

"Haul these carcasses back away from the wagons," he said. "Wouldn't want anybody trippin' on a body durin' a fight."

Ryker looked like he wanted to make some comment, probably about Preacher issuing orders that way, but he didn't. He just nodded curtly and turned away to appoint men to that grim task.

Preacher walked back to the rocks where Pidge and another man were keeping an eye out for the crimson-daubed renegades who had attacked Preacher and Hawk earlier. "Any sign of trouble?" he asked Pidge.

The wounded giant shook his head. "No, but it sure was hard stayin' back here while all that fightin' was goin' on. There's hardly ever a fight that I ain't right in the middle of."

"You're doin' the job I asked you to do,"

Preacher assured him. "And it's a mighty important one. I don't want us to have to tangle with those other Injuns unless we have to."

Pidge nodded and said, "We won't let 'em sneak up on you. I give you my word on that, Preacher."

Pidge looked on him now with almost the same sort of doglike devotion that he afforded to Hoyt Ryker, Preacher noted. That probably had something to do with Preacher being the one who had cut those arrows out of him. Pidge might not be very smart, but it could have soaked in on his brain that without Preacher, he likely would have died.

Preacher clapped a hand on the shoulder of the big man's uninjured arm and nodded. "We all appreciate that, Pidge. Keep up the good work."

As he had been talking to the others in the aftermath of the battle, he'd heard an occasional shot and figured Hawk and Bishop were picking off some of the Sioux who continued trying to make a run for it out the other end of the passage. Now as he turned back to the wagons, three shots blasted out in quick succession. The two sentries on the towers had turned back a bigger push for freedom.

"Throw some lead into that gap!"

Preacher called. "We want to keep 'em hunkered down."

Gunshots pounded the ears and powder smoke stung the eyes and noses of the men as they followed Preacher's order and opened fire. They couldn't see the Sioux, who had withdrawn deeply into the shadowed gorge, so they were shooting blind. Still, in those circumstances some of their shots had to find a target.

Finally, Preacher shouted for them to hold their fire. Not much wind made it into this enclosed bowl, which was why the heat had been growing oppressive, so it took a while for the clouds of powder smoke to dissipate. When they did, Preacher peered into the shadows inside the gap and wished he could tell what was going on in there.

If the Sioux ever stopped to think about it for very long, they would realize the men on the rock spires couldn't reload fast enough to stop them from breaking out that way. Preacher was counting on their bloodlust to keep them focused on the defenders inside the canyon until they had suffered enough to give up. If they retreated now, they might regroup and decide to take up the chase again. The next time, the expedition might be out in the open and not have a chance to fort up like this.

Suddenly, Preacher rested a hand on a wagon and leaned forward as he listened intently. A sound drifted faintly to his ears from the gap. A sound he had heard before . . .

"What in the world is that?" Edgar Merton asked. He had heard it, too. "It sounds like some of them are . . . chanting."

"That's what they consider singin'," Preacher said, "and every song has a reason for it. That one there" — he nodded toward the gap — "that one's a death song."

"My God," Merton breathed. "Whose death, theirs or ours?"

Preacher shook his head. "Right now, I don't reckon it really matters much to them."

After hearing the song from the gap, Preacher knew that another attack was inevitable, and it probably wouldn't be very long in coming. If any of the medicine men who had ridden along with the war party were still alive, they would be in there egging on the others, telling them that their medicine was strong and that the spirits would protect them as they punished the white invaders for daring to venture into land the spirits had given to the People. That was the way nearly every tribe thought of itself: only they were the True People. Anyone else was somehow inferior.

Preacher's hunch was right. Not much time had passed before shrill whoops rang through the afternoon air and the Sioux charged out of the gap again. Their strategy was different with this attack. The first dozen riders were armed with muskets, and they fired more or less simultaneously. Most of the shots went high, but some of them slammed into the wagons. None of them struck any of the defenders.

But that hadn't been the point, Preacher realized a second later. That thunderous volley had been enough to make the members of the expedition duck lower. That took their eyes off the charge for a moment. During that time, the Indians armed with muskets had peeled to the sides to let men with bows and arrows dash past them. Those archers loosed their shafts, and again the defenders had to crouch lower as arrows whistled around them and thudded into the wagons' sideboards.

This time when the archers split, as the warriors with muskets had done before them, the next rank of attackers was close enough that a few lunging strides from their ponies would allow them to reach the wagons.

"Fire!" Preacher yelled.

The defenders did, but the shots were rushed because the Sioux were almost on top of them. At that range, some of the rifle balls had to find their targets and blow warriors off their ponies, but half a dozen attackers got through and made it to the wagons. They leaped off their mounts and engaged the defenders in hand-to-hand combat, which tied them up and allowed more warriors to gallop in and join the battle.

Preacher knew they were on the verge of being overrun, and if that happened it would lead to an inevitable slaughter. He was everywhere seemingly at once, dashing here and there, firing his pistols at point-blank range, hammering at skulls with the empty weapons, then dropping them and filling his hands with tomahawk and knife. The blade licked out and sunk in flesh again and again, while the tomahawk shattered bone and sent enemies flying. Blood sprayed in the air until it was like a crimson rain around Preacher. The sleeves of his buckskin shirt were smeared with gore to the elbows.

He fought with such a frenzy that he almost single-handedly broke the back of the Sioux assault. The Blackfeet had learned to fear the mountain man as an almost supernatural force, and now the Sioux were learning the same grim lesson. Preacher was everywhere at once, and death rode on his shoulder.

With a bellow like that of an angry grizzly, a figure almost as big as a grizzly appeared beside Preacher. Pidge didn't even seem to feel the wounds in his arm and leg as he grabbed one of the Sioux, raised the warrior over his head, and threw the man into several other Indians, scattering them like ninepins. Bounding forward amidst the chaos he had created, Pidge struck right and left, his mallet-like fists hammering into flesh and bone. He picked up one of the senseless warriors, spun around, and flung the man into the side of a wagon with bone-shattering force.

Preacher and Pidge were both like forces of nature, spreading devastation through the attackers, and abruptly, the Sioux had had enough of it. Those of them on foot broke and ran. Some of them were picked up by their friends who were still mounted. Preacher shouted, "Reload!" Shots began to ring out, hurrying along the fleeing Indians and knocking a few of them off their feet.

Preacher stood there, splattered with blood from head to toe, and watched the retreat. He knew what a near thing the battle had been. They had all been within a whisker of dying.

The Sioux dead were heaped high. He hoped that would be enough to convince the survivors to leave and never come back. More than likely, they could wipe out the white men if they kept attacking — but it would cost the lives of nearly all of them in the process. Would victory be worth that price?

There would always be more white men coming along to kill. The Sioux had to have figured that out by now.

Preacher shoved his bleak thoughts aside and looked around. Among the welter of Sioux bodies lay two of Ryker's men, obviously dead. All the other defenders still appeared to be on their feet, although most of them were banged up and bloody from what looked like minor wounds.

He turned and stiffened as he saw both Edgar and Oliver Merton lying facedown on the ground. Preacher sprang to Oliver's side and knelt there, setting his weapons aside to grasp the young man's shoulders and roll him onto his back.

Oliver was alive, Preacher saw immediately. His chest rose and fell. But he was unconscious, and a bloody gash on the side of his head where he'd been hit showed the reason why. Other than that, he didn't appear to be injured.

Hoyt Ryker had noticed that the Mertons were down, too. He ran over to Edgar Merton and said, "Damn it, he can't be dead! If he is, we'll never know what we came out here after!"

Preacher was worried about more than that. He went around to Merton's other side and turned the older man onto his back, as he had with Oliver. Merton had the same sort of wound on his head where he had been knocked out. He was still breathing, too.

That left just one person unaccounted for, and as Preacher hurried to the back of the covered wagon and yanked aside the canvas flap that covered the opening, he had a pretty strong hunch what he was going to find.

Chessie was gone.

Preacher's keen eyes searched the inside of the wagon for blood. He didn't spot any, or any other signs of violence, but that didn't really relieve his mind. *Something* had happened to Chessie, and under the circumstances, he didn't see any way it could be anything good.

He ran over to Pidge and caught hold of the big man's uninjured arm. "You were supposed to stand guard back there behind us," he said.

"I know, Preacher." Pidge hung his head. "I'm sorry. I just never have been able to stay out of a ruckus for very long. I can't help myself. If there's a fight, I got to be in the middle of it."

"What about the fella with you?"

"Clark? He said he'd stay there."

Preacher bit back a curse as he ran deeper into the canyon to the cluster of boulders where he had left Pidge and the other man. He stopped short at the sight of a pair of legs protruding limply from behind a rock. Another couple of steps revealed Clark lying there, the upper half of his body bearing so many wounds it looked like someone had tried to hack him to pieces. They'd come close to doing it, too.

Preacher looked up at the canyon walls, heaved a sigh, and then went back to the wagons. When he got there, he found Oliver and Edgar Merton sitting up, leaning against the vehicle's wheels. Both men looked sick and dazed, but Oliver had recovered his wits enough to look up and ask with a note of hysteria in his voice, "Where's Chessie?"

Preacher spotted something on the wagon's tailgate he hadn't seen before. He reached over and wiped his finger across it. A smear of fine red powder was visible on his fingertip.

"Chessie's gone," he said, "and the outcasts have got her."

CHAPTER 18

Another burst of gunfire from the direction of the rock spires made Preacher turn his head toward the sound. Whoops echoed back through the gap. He knew the Sioux were trying to break out the other end. They might be determined enough to make it this time. If so, good riddance to them. Preacher had other things to worry about at the moment.

One of them was Oliver Merton, who had clambered to his feet. He wasn't too steady yet, but he managed to reach out and grab the front of Preacher's buckskin shirt with both hands.

"Gone!" he said. "What do you mean, she's gone? And who are these outcasts?"

"You're still a mite dizzy from that wallop on the head," Preacher said coldly. "You best sit down again."

Oliver glared at him for a second, then let go of his shirt and braced himself on the wagon wheel instead.

"I'm all right," he insisted. "I just want to know what happened to Chessie."

Preacher asked a question of his own. "What do you remember about what happened durin' the battle?"

"I . . . Nothing . . . I mean, I remember shooting at the Indians . . . and it was loud and . . . frightening. But then . . ." Oliver frowned. "Something made me glance around. I had a feeling that must be what people are talking about when they say it feels like someone is walking on their grave. Like death is so near." His pallor grew even deeper. "I looked over and just caught a glimpse of . . . something. For a split second I thought it was some sort of animal, but then I realized it was . . . human . . . and something hit me." Oliver shook his head and then winced at the movement. "That's all I remember."

"That's more than I recall," Edgar Merton said. "I was shooting at the Indians, and then I was waking up a few minutes ago. Nothing in between."

"What *was* that creature?" Oliver asked. "Was it really . . . a man?"

"Used to be, anyway," Preacher said. He realized no one had said anything to either of the Mertons about the outcasts. "There's a band of Injuns that's moved in here since the last time I've been through these parts. They ain't all from the same tribe. In fact, they probably hate each other. The only folks they hate more . . . are everybody else. They've been forced out of their own tribes, so they've made their own."

"Forced out?" Merton repeated. "Why?"

"Because they're too evil and twisted for the rest of the tribe to put up with."

Oliver's eyes widened with horror. "Good Lord!" he gasped. "And these . . . these creatures have Chessie?"

"Everything says they do. Some of 'em slipped up here while the fightin' was goin' on, walloped you and your pa, and grabbed Chessie. With all the commotion, she could've screamed without anybody hearin' her."

Pidge, Ryker, and the other men had gathered around to listen, and now Pidge let out a wail of dismay.

"I was supposed to be watchin' for those red fellas," he said. "It's my fault they got Miss Chessie!"

Oliver turned hotly to Pidge and said, "You let this happen, you mindless brute —"

"Take it easy," Ryker snapped. "Pidge didn't mean to not do his job. He just gets distracted easy, like a little kid."

Pidge covered his face with his massive hands and breathed raggedly, shaking as if he was sobbing.

"This ain't doin' any of us any good," Preacher said. "We'll go after those bastards who took Chessie, find 'em, and get her back —"

"Somebody's coming!" one of Ryker's men called excitedly.

Preacher turned to look and saw that Hawk had emerged from the gap and was trotting toward them, carrying his rifle.

Hawk didn't appear to be injured at all, Preacher noted. He wasn't surprised. The top of one of those spires was just about the safest place around here today. He stepped over a wagon tongue and strode out to meet his son.

"The Sioux are gone," Hawk reported without preamble. "Bishop and I could not hold them, and after the sounds of battle we heard coming from in here, we thought it might not be necessary to do so any longer."

"Yeah, let 'em run," Preacher said. He leaned his head toward the heaps of corpses. "We hurt 'em plenty bad. Chances are they'll head for home and spend a good long time lickin' their wounds."

"Bishop stayed on the other spire to watch them and make sure they do not double back. If they do, he will fire a warning shot. But by the time I had climbed down, they were out of sight, although I could still see their dust." A grim smile touched Hawk's lips for a second. "It was fading."

"Well, all the news ain't good. Three of Ryker's men were killed."

"Considering the odds, it is a miracle not more of them were lost."

"And Chessie is gone," Preacher said.

Hawk's eyes widened. "Miss Dayton?" he said sharply. "What do you mean, gone? Killed?"

Preacher shook his head and said, "It looks like those outcast Injuns slipped up behind us while we were dealin' with the Sioux and grabbed her. They took her with 'em, somewhere back in the badlands."

Hawk started to take a quick step past Preacher. "We must find her —"

The mountain man took hold of his arm. "We're goin' to. You and me will go after 'em." He lowered his voice. "I don't like leavin' Oliver and his pa at Ryker's mercy, but I'll be damned if I'll let those creatures do whatever unholy thing it is they've got in mind for Chessie. She's been playin' Oliver and Ryker against each other for a while now, seems like, but even so she don't deserve a fate like that."

Hawk's jaw was so tight it made a little muscle jump below his ear. "We will save her even if it means having to kill every one of that evil brood."

"Maybe it won't come to that," Preacher said, although he wouldn't be surprised if it did. "Come on."

He gathered the others around and told them, "Hawk and I are goin' after the Injuns who took Miss Chessie."

"I'm coming with you," Pidge said. "I'm the one who let those ugly varmints capture her."

Preacher shook his head. "No, you ain't, Pidge. You're still wounded, even though you fought those Sioux like a plumb crazy man. You'd slow us down, and we got to move quick-like. We'll take Dog, because with his nose he's the best tracker among us."

Dog's muzzle was speckled with blood. He had taken part in the battle with the Sioux, too. He gave a little growl deep in his throat as Preacher reached down and scratched behind his ears for a second. The big cur seemed to realize that a pursuit was about to begin, and he would be leading the way.

"I'm coming," Oliver Merton announced.

His father said, "Oliver, don't be insane —"

"You and I were supposed to be protecting Chessie, Father," Oliver snapped. "We let her down, and now her life is in danger because of that."

"We had no chance against those red devils —"

"Nothing you can say will change my mind." Oliver faced Preacher again. "I'm coming."

"If I tell you that you ain't, what are you gonna do?"

"Follow you anyway," Oliver said simply.

"Yeah, that's what I figured. I reckon I'd rather have you where I can keep my eyes on you. I'm warnin' you, though. Slow us down and we'll leave you. Get in our way and we'll go over you."

"Fair enough," Oliver said. "Now, why are we wasting time standing around here talking?"

Edgar Merton fretted and argued but couldn't persuade Oliver not to accompany Preacher and Hawk on the search for Chessie.

Hawk wasn't happy about the situation, either. He said quietly to Preacher as they were gathering their gear and some supplies, "We should not take him with us. His presence will just make things more dangerous for us as well as Chessie once we have rescued her."

"Could be you just don't want the gal feelin' grateful to him," Preacher observed.

Hawk made a disgusted sound but didn't say anything else.

Preacher went over to Ryker and said, "Pick up Bishop on your way out and then head north. There's a little range of hills about five miles from here. You ought to be able to find a good place to camp there. There's decent water and graze for the animals, and the trees will give you some cover if those Sioux decide to come back — which I don't believe they will. You can wait there for us to rejoin the expedition with Miss Chessie."

"Shouldn't that be Merton's decision, since he's paying for everything?" Ryker wanted to know.

"You don't really figure he'll say to go off and leave Oliver, do you?"

"Well, I suppose not," Ryker admitted. "But when you say for us to make camp and wait for you there, how long are you talking about? We can't just wait forever, Preacher, you know that. And there's a chance none of you will be coming back."

Ryker wouldn't mind a bit if things worked out that way, Preacher thought, although he might be a little disappointed if he didn't get to have his way with Chessie. But there were lots of pretty gals in the world, and Ryker seemed to believe that whatever Edgar Merton was after, it was going to wind up being worth a heap of money. For a moment, Preacher considered changing the plan and telling Hawk to stay with the rest of the expedition while he and Oliver went after Chessie, but then he discarded the idea. For one thing, he knew Hawk would never go along with it.

For another, if he was going up against those outcasts, he wanted his son at his side for what might be one hell of a fight.

Ryker was still waiting for an answer to his question. Preacher said, "If we ain't back in a week, I reckon you can move on. We can catch up to you later, if we're still alive."

"That's a deal," Ryker said with a nod, but he didn't offer to shake hands on it. Preacher wouldn't have believed him, even if he had. The best they could do under the circumstances was to hope that Ryker wouldn't attempt some sort of double-cross.

A short time later, Preacher got one of Chessie's dresses from the back of the covered wagon and held it so that Dog could take a good long sniff and learn her scent. Then he tossed the dress back into the wagon and said sharply, "Dog, find!"

The big cur took off up the canyon in a loping run.

Preacher looked at Hawk and Oliver Merton. Oliver had tied a rag around his head to serve as a bandage for the wound the outcasts had given him, which was still seeping blood. His face wore a determined expression, but Preacher could see doubt and fear in his eyes.

"You fellas ready to go?" Preacher asked.

Hawk didn't bother to answer. He just gave his father a look of disdain that said he was *always* ready. Oliver tightened his grip on the rifle in his hand and nodded.

"I'm ready," he said. He glanced over at Edgar Merton. "Good-bye, Father."

"Please . . . be careful," Merton said. "You don't want to lose your life over a —" He stopped himself before he could say whatever he'd been about to. Considering the angry look that flashed across Oliver's face, that was probably a good thing.

Oliver just nodded curtly to his father and strode away after Dog. He glanced back over his shoulder at Preacher and Hawk and added, "Well? Come on."

Hawk made a noise low in his throat but didn't say anything. Preacher just grinned for a second, despite the grim circumstances. Then the two of them started after Oliver.

Behind them, Horse blew out a breath. He didn't like being left behind, along with Hawk's pony. But where they might have to go in the badlands, horses couldn't follow. The two mounts would go with Merton, Ryker, and the others, to be reclaimed when Preacher and Hawk caught up with the expedition.

Oliver averted his eyes when they passed the spot where the man called Clark had been butchered. His body still lay there. Ryker would recover it and take it to the hills, along with the other two men who had been slain, and all of them would be buried there.

The Sioux, callous though it was, would be left for the scavengers.

Within minutes the three searchers were around the bend in the canyon and out of sight of the rest of the expedition. Preacher's keen ears could still hear the men calling to one another as they got ready to move out, but that faded quickly, as well.

Then they were on their own, with the canyon walls looming redly around them.

Preacher heard a faint whistling sound and knew it was the wind moving through the spires and crannies of the badlands.

He wasn't the only one to notice it. Oliver Merton said, "That sounds like the wailing of lost souls."

"I reckon there are probably some in here, all right," Preacher said, "but they can't make no noise anymore. Best keep your voice down, Oliver. We don't want to tell those varmints where we are."

"They are probably watching us already," Hawk said. "Like lizards, hidden in the rocks."

Oliver swallowed hard, clearly not liking that thought very much.

Dog had slowed ahead of them but continued moving steadily deeper into the canyon. Preacher knew he was still on the scent. Now and then the cur paused and lifted his shaggy head. Whenever he did that, he whined. He sensed the outcasts, Preacher knew . . . and he didn't like the smell of them, or anything about them, really. Preacher understood that, because he felt the same way.

They passed the spot where he and Hawk had battled with the crimson-daubed creatures before. Preacher pointed out the little cracks in the rock wall where they had fled.

"No one could possibly get through those openings," Oliver said. "They're too small."

"I reckon those varmints can twist themselves up more than you'd think they could. From what I've heard about 'em, they're pretty twisted inside. I suppose that extends to the outside of 'em, too."

"But they couldn't have taken Chessie with them that way."

Preacher shook his head. "No, I reckon not. She's a healthy girl, not some scrawny Injun who's all bone and whang leather. Besides, Dog's still on the scent up yonder."

A few minutes later they came in sight of the canyon's end. The steep walls came together a hundred yards ahead of them. As far as Preacher could see, there was no way out.

And no sign of Chessie and her captors, either.

"I don't understand!" Oliver said. Preacher motioned for him to keep his voice down. In a hoarse whisper, Oliver went on, "They're not here, and there's nowhere they could have gone."

"They did not vanish into the air," Hawk said. He tipped his head back, studied the cliff walls, and pointed. "Look there, Preacher."

Preacher looked where Hawk was pointing and saw something odd sticking out slightly from behind a rock at the top of the cliff to the right. It was a slender, curved piece of wood, and as Preacher moved around to get a better look, he saw that other curved wooden strips were woven around it.

"Looks like a basket of some sort," he said. "I'll bet they've got it attached to a rope, and they can let it down here so they can haul themselves up out of this canyon. I reckon that must be how they got Chessie up there."

"That's . . . clever," Oliver said with grudging admiration. "I thought these Indians were utter primitives. Surely such an apparatus is beyond their capabilities."

"They're mean," Preacher said. "They ain't necessarily stupid. Anyway, folks have a tendency of findin' ways to get around, no matter what the terrain is like." He rubbed his fingertips over his bristly chin as he looked up at the mostly hidden basket. "I wish my little pard Audie was here to see this. He'd find it fascinatin'."

Hawk said, "The cliff is rough enough I can climb up there and let down the basket." He glanced at Oliver. "I know you could make the climb, too, Preacher, but I do not think Oliver could."

"I'm not going to let anything stop me from finding Chessie," Oliver snapped back without hesitation. "I can climb —"

"Take it easy," Preacher told him. "That basket ain't made for big fellas who weigh as much as we do. But the rope it's attached to is bound to be pretty sturdy, and it'll be easier for us to get up there if we let Hawk go first and throw it down to us. We can use the basket for liftin' Dog." He nodded to the young warrior. "Up you go."

Hawk nodded agreement and slung his rifle on his back. He studied the rock wall for a moment to locate the best handholds and footholds, then began to climb.

The cliff was eighty feet tall and took Hawk fifteen minutes to climb. Those minutes seemed to stretch out as they passed. Oliver paced back and forth nervously, even though in the close confines of the canyon he couldn't go very far in any direction before he had to turn back the other way.

Finally, Hawk was at the rim. Preacher held his left hand over his eyes to shade them as he peered upward and watched his son getting ready to pull himself up the last couple of feet.

That was when a bright red, hate-contorted face suddenly appeared just above where Hawk clung to the rock, and a red hand lifted a stone tomahawk and poised it to strike downward in a deadly blow.

Chapter 19

Instantly, Preacher snapped his rifle to his shoulder and pulled back the hammer, but before he could press the trigger, he realized that the angle was all wrong. He couldn't take a shot at the outcast because Hawk was in the way.

Hawk was aware of the threat, though, and as the tomahawk flashed toward his head he let go of the rock with his right hand and clung to it with his left and a couple of precarious toeholds. He caught the outcast's wrist before the blow could land and stopped the tomahawk cold. With a grunt of effort that Preacher could hear down below, Hawk twisted on the cliff face and yanked his attacker off the rimrock, then let go.

With a screech, the first outcast pin-wheeled down the eighty feet and crashed on the hard-packed dirt of the canyon floor. He landed with a soggy thud that sounded like a dropped gourd busting, and Preacher knew he wouldn't be getting back up again.

Hawk wasn't out of danger. He had pulled himself halfway over the brink, but his legs still dangled. Another of the shrieking red lunatics appeared, looming over him with a lance.

By now, though, Preacher had backed off a few steps and was in position to risk a shot. The long-barreled flintlock boomed. Shooting up at an extreme angle like that was tricky, but Preacher was one of the deadliest marksmen west of the Mississippi.

The rifle ball caught the second outcast under the chin, bored up through his brain, and blew off the top of his skull. His head jerked back but he remained on his feet for a second, already dead, before he pitched forward and plummeted into the canyon to land a few feet away from his fellow outcast.

Hawk's legs disappeared as he rolled over the edge of the rimrock. More shouts came from above. One of Hawk's pistols boomed, and a third outcast flew over the brink to fall into the canyon. This one screamed and flailed in midair, to no avail. There was nothing to stop his deadly descent. He landed face-first with bone-shattering force.

Preacher reloaded his rifle while that was going on, then gripped the weapon tightly as the sounds of battle continued above him. He couldn't see what was going on, and so there wasn't a blasted thing he could do about it.

When the yelling stopped a few moments later and the echoes died away, silence descended on the canyon. Oliver was looking up at the rimrock, too. He said in a worried voice, "Preacher . . . ?"

The mountain man didn't reply. There was nothing he could say, nothing he could do except wait.

A couple of seconds later Preacher heaved a sigh of relief when Hawk appeared at the top of the cliff, leaning out to look down at them and wave. Preacher knew the signal meant his son was all right.

A moment later the basket woven out of wooden strips came into full view as Hawk began lowering it at the end of a braided rope.

When the basket was in reach, Preacher caught hold of it and guided it to the ground. Dog sniffed and pawed at it. Preacher said, "He smells Chessie's scent on it. That proves they hauled her up in it."

Dog weighed too much for Hawk to haul him up in a dead lift by himself, so Preacher nodded toward the rope and told Oliver to climb up first. Oliver swallowed hard, looking decidedly nervous about the prospect, but he said, "I was the one who wanted to come along on this rescue mission, so I guess I can't allow my fears to hold me back. I'm really not fond of heights, though."

"It ain't too late for you to go back and join the others," Preacher told him. "You'd have to hurry, but I figure you could catch up."

Without hesitation, Oliver shook his head. "Scared or not, I'm not turning back." He grasped the rope, running his hands over its rough strands, then tightening them. "How should I do this?"

"Use the footholds like Hawk did, but you can hang on to the rope instead of havin' to find handholds. Take it slow and easy. When you're doin' something like this, it's best not to get in a hurry."

Oliver swallowed, nodded, tightened his hands on the rope, and lifted his right foot. When he had it planted solidly on a little knob protruding from the rock wall, he hauled himself up and found a good place to put his other foot.

Even with the rope to help him, it took longer for Oliver to climb the side of the canyon than it had for Hawk. The young half-Absaroka warrior had disappeared again. Preacher figured he was keeping watch for more of the outcasts. The renegades had left four men to guard their back trail and there was a chance there might be more of them waiting nearby to ambush the rescue party.

Finally, Oliver reached the top and lurched out of sight. Preacher waited, hoping the young man was just catching his breath. After several seconds that seemed longer, Oliver looked over the edge and waved, as Hawk had done earlier. Hawk appeared, too, and called, "Put Dog in the basket."

Preacher helped the big cur into the conveyance. Dog got in but whined and turned his head to look up at the mountain man. Preacher said, "I know you don't like it, old son, but it's the only way you can come with us, and we need you along. Just stay calm, and Hawk and Oliver will have you there before you know it."

Dog reared up and put his front paws on the edge of the basket. Preacher forced him to sit down again, then looked up at Hawk and Oliver and nodded. They took hold of the rope and heaved.

Dog barked unhappily as the basket lifted off the ground. "Dog, quiet!" Preacher commanded. Dog didn't bark again, but he continued growling and whining as the basket rose in front of the cliff. It twisted and tilted a little at the end of the rope, causing Preacher's jaw to tighten. He wasn't sure if he could catch Dog if the cur fell out of the basket, but he would have to try.

Dog sat still, though, and the swaying subsided. The basket reached the top of the cliff. Hawk and Oliver grabbed the handles attached to it and swung it onto solid ground. Preacher couldn't see Dog anymore, but he could imagine his old friend hopping out of the basket and shaking himself, glad to have his paws back on the earth.

Hawk let the basket down again. Preacher grasped the rope and started the climb. With his wiry strength and long years of experience at all sorts of arduous tasks, he made it to the top faster than either of the two younger men had.

Hawk was waiting for him. He leaned down and took hold of Preacher's arm to brace the mountain man as he stepped up onto the rim. Preacher looked around and saw one of the outcasts lying facedown a few yards away while Dog sniffed delicately at him. Preacher could tell from the odd angle of the Indian's head that Hawk had broken his neck.

"Seen any more of the varmints?"

Hawk shook his head. "They left four men

to watch this route and ambush anyone who came after them. They probably believe that was sufficient. We killed them all. They will not be expecting it when we catch up to them."

"Maybe not," Preacher said, "but we'll still have a devil of a time takin' 'em by surprise. As despised as they are, everywhere they turn, they wouldn't have survived this long unless they were crafty little bastards."

"They fight hard for their puny size, too," Hawk allowed grudgingly.

"Are we going to stand around and talk," Oliver asked, "or are we going to follow them?"

"We're goin'," Preacher said. "Dog, find."

As Dog loped off, nose to the ground, Preacher took a look at their surroundings. The badlands to the west, the direction Dog was heading, rose gradually in a series of twisting, razor-backed ridges. The landscape was almost barren, with no grass and only an occasional gnarled, stunted bush or tree. It didn't seem like anything, human or animal, could live here, and yet Preacher knew that a multitude of life existed in the badlands. Snakes, lizards, spiders, rats, and buzzards called this region home.

So did the outcasts. He could understand why they had drifted here. No one else wanted this hellish place. They had come here to be left alone.

Preacher would have been more than willing to do that. If Chessie hadn't been kidnapped, all the members of the expedition would be gone by now, heading on to whatever mysterious destination Edgar Merton had in mind.

Instead, the warped hatred brewing in those diseased brains had led the outcasts to strike at the people who had dared to enter their domain . . . and now this encounter wouldn't end without more killing.

Preacher, Hawk, and Oliver trotted after Dog as the big cur headed up the slope of the nearest ridge.

By the time the sun lowered toward the jagged peaks to the west, Preacher and his companions hadn't seen any more of the outcasts. In fact, if not for Dog's sensitive nose, they wouldn't have been able to tell that they were still on the right trail. The Indians were expert at not leaving any tracks. Dog had Chessie's scent, though, so Preacher was confident they were heading in the right direction.

"We're not going to find them before it gets dark, are we?" Oliver asked when they stopped to rest and drink a little from their canteens.

"Probably not," Preacher said. "They had a start on us, and they know where they're goin'. We have to take it a little slower to make sure Dog don't lose the scent. If he did, that'd mean backtrackin' and it would put us even farther behind."

"What are we going to do?" A panicky edge had crept into Oliver's voice. "We can't travel at night, can we?"

Preacher shook his head. "Not in country like this. Too big a risk that we'd fall in a ravine and break a leg."

"Then we're not going to be able to rescue Chessie from them before they have a chance to . . . to . . ."

"They've already had a chance to do that, if that's what they had in mind when they took her," Preacher said bluntly. "We got to hope they're plannin' somethin' else for her."

He didn't say it, but some of the fates those creatures might come up with for Chessie would be worse than anything Oliver was afraid of. Pointing that out wouldn't accomplish anything, though.

"We'll push on for a while," he continued, "and then we'll start lookin' for a good place to make camp."

An hour later, as shadows began to gather,

Preacher called a halt again, this time at a little notch in a ridge. A large slab of rock overhung the opening to create a cavelike space. Preacher noticed Oliver glancing up at it nervously.

"Worried that it might fall on us?" he asked.

"It does seem to be perched rather precariously up there."

Preacher shook his head and said, "It's been like that for years. Ain't budged since the last time I was through these parts and probably never will unless there's an earthquake or somethin' like that."

"But what if there *is* an earthquake?"

"Then I guess we'd have somethin' to worry about," Preacher said with a grin. "It ain't like we're exactly safe to start with, though."

"No, I suppose not," Oliver admitted. "Those . . . things . . . are still out there somewhere, aren't they?"

"Perhaps closer than we know," Hawk said.

Clearly, that comment didn't make Oliver feel a bit better.

Preacher decreed that there would be no fire, so their supper consisted of jerky and some biscuits they had brought along with them from the wagons, washed down with more water from the canteens. Dog wandered off and came back with a long-tailed rat's carcass held between his jaws. He lay down to gnaw on it and growl softly.

That made Oliver shudder. "Are you sure he really is a dog and not an actual wolf?" he asked.

"I ain't sure of anything of the sort," Preacher said. "All I know is he's a good trail partner and ain't never let me down yet. We'll take turns standin' guard tonight, but Dog there is the real sentry. He'll let us know if there's anything skulkin' around that shouldn't be."

Figuring that trouble would be less likely to crop up during the first part of the night, Preacher told Oliver to stand watch first.

"Wake Hawk in a few hours, and then I'll take the last turn. You reckon you can stay awake, Oliver?"

"I don't have any choice in the matter, do I? Our lives may depend on my alertness."

Preacher nodded and said, "Now you're startin' to understand."

He and Hawk rolled up in their blankets and went to sleep almost instantly, the way frontiersmen learned to do. Also like most frontiersmen — the ones who survived, anyway — Preacher slept lightly, so that he could be fully awake in the blink of an eye.

Dog stretched out at his side. Preacher didn't know how long he had been asleep when a low rumble from the cur's throat woke him. His eyes opened, but other than that, he didn't move. His gaze roamed around the camp, searching for any sign of trouble.

From where he lay, he could see both Hawk and Oliver. The young easterner sat on a rock on the far side of the notch. His rifle lay across his knees. Preacher's keen eyes, well adjusted to the night, saw Oliver's head turning as he looked back and forth. He was awake, and he was trying to do a good job of standing guard.

But he didn't have eyes in the back of his head, and that was where Preacher caught a hint of movement. A stray beam of starlight reached into the thick shadow behind Oliver and struck a glint of reflection from something. A knife, maybe, or the flint head of a tomahawk.

Death was afoot in the darkness, and it was creeping up behind Oliver Merton.

CHAPTER 20

Preacher whispered, "Dog, Oliver!"

The big cur leaped with the speed of a striking snake. Oliver didn't have time to let out a yell and probably didn't even see Dog coming before the animal slammed into him and knocked him sideways off the rock.

At the same time, the outcast who had been sneaking up on Oliver swung a tomahawk through the space where the young man's head had been a heartbeat earlier. The blow would have split Oliver's head open if it had landed.

As it was, the miss threw the Indian off-balance. He stumbled forward a couple of steps. Preacher lifted one of his pistols and fired. A tongue of flame a foot long spurted from the muzzle. Both balls from the double-shotted gun smashed into the outcast's chest and flung him backward.

Screeches filled the air as several more of the renegades attacked from the shadows.

Dog whirled to meet their charge and knifed among them, razor-sharp teeth slashing right and left. Preacher came up on his knees with his other pistol in his hand. A dark shape loomed over him, and he fired into the middle of it. The outcast doubled over with a groan and collapsed.

Hawk surged to his feet and leaped to Oliver's side. Another outcast lunged at them, striking downward with a tomahawk. Hawk blocked it with his rifle's barrel, then smashed the butt into the man's face and knocked him over backward. Oliver struggled to stand, then gave up the effort and fired his rifle from where he lay on the ground. In the muzzle flash, Preacher saw a hate-twisted face shattered by the rifle ball that crashed into it.

Hawk grabbed Oliver's arm and half lifted him as he backed toward Preacher. Dog fell back to the mountain man's side as well. All four of them put their backs to the rock and waited to see if the attack was going to continue.

Instead, Preacher heard the rapid slap of bare feet on rock and hard-packed dirt as the outcasts who were left from this raiding party retreated into the night. As those sounds faded, Oliver gasped, "Are . . . are they gone?"

"For now, maybe," Preacher said. "But they ain't gone far, and there ain't no way of knowin' how many more of them are out there."

"I'm not complaining, mind you, but since they obviously knew we were there, why didn't they just shoot arrows at us?"

Hawk said, "They enjoy killing too much. They like to do it at close range. I have seen enough of them now to understand that."

"Yeah, that's right," Preacher agreed. "You wouldn't think primitive varmints like that would take pride in anything, but I reckon they do. They like doin' their killin' hand to hand."

"What are we going to do?" Oliver asked. "I . . . I can feel them all around, watching us. It's awful. Like waking up and being surrounded by venomous snakes."

"You ain't far wrong with that comparison. But the only thing we can do is wait for them to jump us again, or wait until mornin', when maybe we can take the fight to them. They know these badlands too good for us to go after 'em in the dark. That'd be the same as askin' to have our throats cut."

"What you're saying is that it's going to be a long night."

"I reckon that's just about the size of it,"

Preacher said.

No one slept again that night. The men reloaded their weapons and sat with their backs against the rock and guns at the ready. Dog lay in front of them, head up and ears cocked for the slightest sound.

Once they heard a series of howls in the distance. Oliver leaned forward and asked, "Is that wolves?"

"No, it's them damn outcasts," Preacher replied.

"What are they *doing*?"

"Carryin' on about somethin'. Could be the ones who jumped us earlier got back to the main bunch and told 'em what happened. They're bound to be disappointed that we ain't either prisoners or dead."

"My God." Oliver let out a despairing groan. "And Chessie is helpless in the hands of those devils! She must be terrified out of her mind."

Preacher hoped that was indeed the case, because if Chessie was scared, it meant she was still alive. But even if she was, the creatures could take out their displeasure on her when they found out that Preacher and his companions had killed more of them.

Those bodies were heaped just outside the

notch. Hawk and Oliver had placed them there earlier while Preacher and Dog stood guard. Preacher could see the corpses, but only as vague dark shapes against the rock.

Eventually, as a faint tinge of gray that heralded the approach of dawn crept into the eastern sky, Preacher realized he could no longer see the bodies of the slain outcasts. He stiffened in surprise, then a little shiver ran through him. Sometime during the night, more of the Indians had slipped close enough to the camp to lay hands on the corpses and drag them away, all without making a sound or in any other way betraying their presence. To a man with senses as keen as Preacher's, that seemed almost impossible, but he saw the evidence of it now with his own eyes and had no choice but to trust them.

The dead outcasts were gone, and they sure as hell hadn't gotten up and walked away by themselves.

Preacher nudged Hawk and whispered, "Take a look. What do you see out there?"

"Nothing," Hawk replied, then he, too, tensed enough for Preacher to feel the reaction against his shoulder. "Nothing," Hawk repeated. "But where . . . ?"

"The others came and got 'em," Preacher said.

"What are you talking about?" Oliver asked.

"The bodies are gone."

"You mean scavengers got them, or . . . Oh no. You don't mean . . ."

"Yeah," Preacher said. "And we didn't see or hear 'em. Neither did Dog."

Oliver cursed bitterly. "What chance do we have against creatures like that?" he asked.

"As long as a fella can fight, he's got a chance. Or would you rather turn back, leave the badlands, and catch up with the rest of the expedition?"

"You mean abandon Chessie? I can't do that!"

"Oliver, you got to realize there's a chance she ain't still alive, even now," Preacher said. "I know you don't want to hear it, but it's true."

Oliver took off his hat and covered his face with a trembling hand. After a moment, he lowered his hand and said, "But there's a chance she *is* still alive, that we might be able to rescue her and bring her to safety."

"That's why we're here," Preacher agreed. "If there wasn't a chance, we wouldn't have gone after the little bastards in the first place."

Hawk added, "Until there is proof otherwise, I choose to believe that Chessie lives."

"So do I," Oliver said. "When it gets light enough, I believe we should take up the trail again."

"Then that's what we'll do," Preacher said.

By the middle of the day, the three men had penetrated deep into the badlands. When they paused to gnaw on more jerky, Oliver asked, "How will we ever find our way out of here once we've rescued Chessie?"

Preacher didn't address the assumption the young easterner made. Instead he said, "Gettin' out won't be too hard. Well, knowin' the right way to go won't be, anyway. Those damn outcasts are liable to have somethin' to say about how easy it actually is to get out."

"Assuming that we leave any of them alive," Hawk put in.

"Since we don't know how many of 'em there are, that'll be hard to say until the time comes."

"You haven't answered my question, Preacher," Oliver said.

"About how we'll know which way to go? That's easy. We'll just head northeast. That'll take us out of the badlands sooner or later and ought to put us not too far away from those hills where I told your pa and

Ryker to make camp and wait for us."

"And you'll just know which direction northeast is?" Oliver said with a puzzled frown.

"Does not everyone?" Hawk said, looking equally puzzled. "A man has but to look around to know where he is and which way he should go."

Preacher chuckled. "You let Hawk and me worry about that, Oliver. We ain't the sort to get turned around very easy."

"But if something were to happen to the two of you?" Oliver persisted. "After all, this is a dangerous errand on which we're bound. You can't guarantee anyone's survival."

Preacher couldn't argue with that statement. He pointed at the sun and told Oliver, "You steer by that. This time of year it comes up a ways north of due east, so if you aim toward the sunrise every mornin', you'll get where you're goin'."

Preacher didn't add that if he and Hawk were dead, it was highly unlikely Oliver and Chessie would survive on their own. Although he supposed that stranger things had happened. None that he could recall right offhand, however.

They pushed on. The badlands lay in a band twenty miles wide and forty miles long that stretched west into the foothills of a range of snow-capped peaks. Preacher, Hawk, and Oliver could see those mountains ahead of them, and in the clean, thin air, they looked almost close enough to reach out and touch. Preacher knew that a lot of rugged terrain lay between him and his companions and those mountains. He hoped they wouldn't have to cover all of it before they caught up to the outcasts and their prisoner.

At midafternoon, Dog suddenly let out a whine and stopped as he was about to enter a long, narrow defile. Preacher halted, too, and held up a hand in a signal for Hawk and Oliver to do likewise. His eyes narrowed as he peered along the gash in the red sandstone. The outcasts ground the rocks into powder and plastered it all over their bodies so they could blend into their surroundings and not be seen until it was too late. Preacher searched intently for ambushers lurking inside the defile.

He didn't see any of the outcasts, but he spotted something else, a flash of blue that didn't belong here in these dull surroundings. He pointed it out to Hawk and Oliver and whispered, "Either of you recognize that?"

"Good Lord!" Oliver said. "That . . . that's

the same color as the dress Chessie was wearing the last time I saw her!"

He started to spring ahead, but Hawk was too quick for him. The young warrior caught hold of Oliver's arms from behind and dragged him back.

"Wait!" Hawk said through clenched teeth. "Rushing into that canyon may be just what they want you to do."

"But . . . but that could be Chessie!" Oliver struggled to get loose, but Hawk's grip was too strong.

"I'll go take a look," Preacher said. "You two stay here. Come on, Dog."

The mountain man and the big cur started forward between the steep stone walls. Their gazes roamed constantly from side to side and up and down. The spot of blue was fifty yards into the canyon, partially concealed by a large rock. As they neared it, Preacher tried to decide if there was a body inside the cloth, but from where he was, he just couldn't tell.

Finally, he and Dog were close enough for Preacher to reach out and snag the fabric with the muzzle of his rifle. He pulled it into the open and felt relief go through him as he realized it was a dress, all right, but it was empty. He half turned and held the rifle out so Hawk and Oliver could see the garment.

"Oh my God," Oliver said in a voice choked by emotion. "It's hers! It's Chessie's dress!"

"Yeah, but she ain't in it," Preacher said. "And she ain't here, either." He took the dress from the end of the rifle and looked it over. It was dirty and torn in places, and it had a long rip down the front of it. That made his mouth tighten into a grim line. The Indians had torn the dress off Chessie, but that didn't mean they had done anything else to her. They could have wanted the dress to leave here as a means of taunting their pursuers.

Or as bait for a trap, he realized suddenly as he heard a faint grating sound from somewhere above him. He reacted instantly, yelling, "Dog, out!" as he flung himself toward the canyon mouth.

Almost as quickly, he stopped short as rocks plummeted down from above. One great bound had carried Dog past the area where they were falling, but Preacher saw he wasn't going to make it in time and threw himself back the other way. A terrible rumble filled the narrow canyon and rebounded from its walls. Rocks the size of fists pelted Preacher and made him stumble, but luckily none of them struck him in the head and knocked him unconscious. If that had happened, he would have been buried forever.

With the rockslide getting worse all around him, he gathered his strength and launched himself into a headlong dive, not knowing if it would carry him beyond the worst of it or doom him. But it was his only chance, so he took it.

When he landed, he kept rolling. A slab of rock as big as he was slammed into the ground mere feet away. He covered his head with his arms as best he could and felt rocks hammering at him. Finally he came to a stop and lay there choking and coughing as roiling clouds of dust clogged his mouth, nose, throat, and lungs. Gravel slid around him, half burying him. Preacher was too stunned to move, other than to shake from the racking coughs.

After an unknowable time, the air began to clear and the mountain man's coughing subsided slightly. He gathered his wits and his strength and managed to lift his head and look around. He had to blink several times to clear enough of the dust from his eyes so he could see. When he shook his head, more dust from his hair swirled around his face and made him cough again.

He needed to stop that, he thought.

A few yards away, a wall of boulders and smaller rocks completely filled the defile at the spot where he had found Chessie Dayton's dress, confirming that the garment had been the bait in a trap. The outcasts had sprung that trap, but it had failed. He was battered but alive.

Alive . . . but cut off from Hawk, Dog, and Oliver.

CHAPTER 21

Preacher clawed his way out of the gravel that had slithered around him and covered nearly half his body. When he was free, he staggered to his feet. He had flung his rifle out in front of him when he tried to dive out of the way of the rockslide. It took him only a moment to locate the weapon, lying apparently undamaged on the ground a few yards away. He picked it up and quickly checked it to make sure he could use it if he needed to. As soon as he got a chance he would give the rifle a good cleaning, but that would have to wait.

Right now he had to figure out a way to get free from this impromptu prison.

"Hawk!" he called. "Oliver! Can you hear me?"

No answer came back from either young man. Preacher frowned. From where he had left them, they ought to be able to hear him. The rockslide barred his path, but it shouldn't stop sound from getting out of the canyon.

Which meant Hawk and Oliver *couldn't* answer his shout, and he couldn't think of any reasons for that other than bad ones.

Preacher didn't waste any more time or energy yelling. He spotted the brim of his hat sticking out from under a rock and tugged it free, then slapped it against his leg to get some of the dust and dirt off it. He wasn't sure he accomplished that task, but he clapped the hat back on his head anyway and looked up to study the rock wall confronting him.

It rose a good twenty feet, but even though it was steep, Preacher thought he could climb it. The tricky part would be doing so without causing the rocks to start sliding again. He could break an arm or leg if he was part of the way up and got caught in such a collapse.

He turned his head to look the other direction along the narrow gash in the earth. If he had been alone, he would have explored the rest of the defile to see if there was another way out. Right now, though, he was worried about Hawk and Oliver and Dog and wanted to find out what had happened to them. He slung the rifle on his back, approached the wall of rocks, and searched for a route that looked like he could climb it safely.

There wasn't going to be anything safe about this, the mountain man reasoned. He decided on a likely-looking spot and started to climb.

Preacher tested each rock before he trusted his weight to it. They had packed down pretty solidly when they fell. Slowly, he made his way up. Now and then one of the stones shifted slightly, causing gravel and dirt to trickle down, and each time that happened Preacher froze until he was sure it was safe to go on. Sweat ran down his lean cheeks and made gullies in the thick layer of grayish-brown dust that covered his face.

At last he was close enough to the top that he was able to pull himself up and peer over it. He halfway expected to see bodies sprawled in the canyon mouth, but the opening was empty. That was a relief, in a way, but it also added to Preacher's worry. Where had his companions gone?

Moving slowly and carefully, he pulled himself up farther and swung a leg over the crest of the rockslide. His impatience grew stronger as he began the descent. When he was halfway to the ground, a rock the size of a man's head rolled under his foot.

Thrown off-balance, Preacher didn't try to catch himself. Instead he leaped out, landed with one foot on a boulder, and pushed off. That sent him clear of the small slide that tumbled down behind him. He landed on the canyon floor, rolled, and came up on both feet.

He was out of the trap but not out of danger. However, a quick look around didn't reveal any lurking threats at the moment, so he hurried forward. As he approached the mouth of the canyon, he heard a low growl and exclaimed, "Dog!"

The big cur responded with a yip. He sounded all right, which made Preacher eager to see for himself. He stepped out of the defile and looked to his right. Dog stood there with the fur on his neck ruffled up in anger. Beside him, facedown, lay the unmoving form of Hawk That Soars.

Preacher's heart slugged hard in his chest when he saw his son lying there motionless like that. Dog backed away from the young warrior as Preacher hurried over and dropped to his knees beside Hawk.

Preacher had the presence of mind to say, "Dog, guard," which was exactly what the big cur had been doing already. With him there, no one would have been able to approach Hawk's body except Preacher.

The mountain man placed a hand on Hawk's back and sighed in relief as he felt movement. Hawk was still breathing. Preacher took hold of his shoulders and rolled him over. Hawk was unconscious, but except for the bloody welt on his head where something had hit him, he didn't appear to be hurt.

Preacher looked around, not seeing any sign of Oliver Merton. Not far off, though, a welter of what looked like bare footprints marred the dust. Preacher straightened and went over to study the marks. Maybe half a dozen of the outcasts had been here. A pair of grooves in the dirt showed where something had been dragged along for a few feet before all the sign disappeared on a stretch of rocky ground.

To Preacher's experienced eyes, the scene might as well have been a page from a book. After springing the avalanche trap on him, the outcasts had attacked Hawk and Oliver. Hawk had been knocked out, but Dog, having barely escaped from the rockslide, had protected him from the Indians.

Oliver hadn't been so lucky. Preacher didn't see any blood on the ground, so he figured the young easterner had been rendered unconscious and taken prisoner. His captors had dragged him away, and by now there was no telling where they were. Probably wherever they had left Chessie under guard while they tried to wipe out their pursuers.

A soft groan made Preacher turn around. Hawk was starting to stir. Preacher went over and knelt beside him. As he did so, Hawk's eyes popped open. He tried to surge up from the ground.

Preacher's firm hand on his shoulder stopped him. "Take it easy," the mountain man said. "You got another good wallop on the noggin. Keep that up and your skull's liable to start gettin' a mite mushy."

"Oliver!" Hawk gasped.

"Gone."

Hawk raised himself again, but this time only on one elbow so he could look around. "Dead?" he asked.

"Gone," Preacher said again. "Looks like the outcasts took him." A bleak cast came over his face as he added, "I reckon we've got two prisoners to rescue now."

Hawk sat up with his back braced against a rock while he regained his wits and strength. He told Preacher, "We heard the rockslide start, but there was no way we could reach you. Dog came running out, but then a huge cloud of dust billowed up and we could not see what had happened."

"Yeah, that dust damn near choked me," Preacher said. He patted his shirt, which caused a pale puff to rise from the buckskin. "I've still got a heap of it on me."

"As soon as that happened, the outcasts attacked us," Hawk went on. "I don't know how many. A dozen, perhaps. Too many for us to fight, although we tried. I remember one of them flung a tomahawk at me . . ." Hawk shrugged. "That is all I know until I woke up with you looking at me."

Preacher nodded. "That tomahawk glanced off your head and knocked you colder'n the snow up on those peaks yonder. But Dog stood over you and kept the varmints from killin' you."

"They could have killed both Dog and me if they had tried hard enough," Hawk said. "For some reason they *chose* to leave us alive and take Oliver with them."

"They're playin' with us. This is probably the most sport they've had in a long time. They took Chessie and used her to lure us into this wasteland. Now they've got Oliver, too, and they figure we'll keep comin' after 'em. They're tryin' to pick us off one by one and make the game last as long as they can." Preacher mulled that over for a moment, then added, "Which makes me hope they ain't hurt Chessie too bad. They want to get all of us together sooner or later and then have their real sport with us."

"Torture," Hawk said. "And probably cannibalism, as well."

"Wouldn't doubt it," Preacher agreed. "We ain't gonna let things go that far, though."

"Can we still trail them?"

"Dog will see to that, once you've rested up enough."

Hawk moved as if he was about to stand up. "I can go after them now. I'm fine —"

Preacher put a hand on his shoulder and held him down again. "I can tell by your eyes that you ain't fine," he said. "Chances are that things are still pretty fuzzy for you. Just give it a little time."

"Chessie and Oliver may not have that time," Hawk said with a frown.

"It ain't gonna help 'em for you to pass out again, neither. Just sit there and rest."

Hawk didn't look happy about it, but he did what Preacher said. Since the two of them had never met until Hawk was nearly grown, the usual bond between father and son had never really existed where they were concerned. Preacher felt what he believed was a paternal instinct, a primitive urge to protect Hawk, but at the same time they were more like partners. Friends . . . maybe. Preacher wasn't sure how Hawk felt about him. But he was certain Hawk wasn't going to obey his orders out of any sense of duty to a parent. That sort of feeling might not ever be present between them.

A short time later, Preacher got Hawk to gnaw on a little jerky. When the food didn't make him sick, Preacher decided it would be all right for him to get up and move around again. A glance at the sky told him there wasn't much more than an hour of daylight left, but that was an hour they couldn't afford to waste.

"Dog, find Chessie," the mountain man ordered. "Find Oliver."

Dog trotted around the area for a few minutes but always came back to the spot where the tracks indicated that the outcasts had dragged Oliver away. Preacher suspected that the big cur could no longer find Chessie's scent, probably because they had taken her on through the gorge that was now blocked by the rockslide. But the Indians who had taken Oliver prisoner had been forced to follow a different route, and that was the one Dog trotted off on now.

They would all wind up at the same place, Preacher thought, so it didn't really matter how they got there.

The trail writhed like a snake through the badlands, climbing gradually but steadily, until Preacher and Hawk followed Dog to the top of a rise and found themselves looking out over what appeared to be a vast, storm-tossed sea. Waves leaped high and receded into the distance. But instead of the enigmatic blue-green and the constant ebb and flow of the ocean, this "sea" was tinged a hellish red and didn't move. It was made of bare rock and looked like something that ought to be located on some far planet, not on Earth.

As they gazed over that nightmarish landscape, Hawk muttered, "How can anyone be found in such a place?"

"That's why it's a good thing we got Dog on our side," Preacher said. He glanced down at the big cur, who had sat down and also looked out at the badlands. A little whine came from the furry throat. "Although it sounds like he don't like it much, neither."

"Nothing truly human could live out there. Those outcasts, as you call them, have become lower than beasts, Preacher." A note of urgency came into Hawk's voice. "We must find Chessie. And Oliver, too, of course."

"We will. Dog, find."

Dog didn't move right away. It was unheard of for the big cur not to obey Preacher's commands instantly. His hesitation now was a sure sign of just how uneasy this place — and the creatures they pursued — made him. But after a moment Dog stood up and padded down the slope in front of them into a gully that twisted across the badlands. Preacher and Hawk followed, eyes straining for any hint of trouble in the fading light.

Once the sun slipped behind the mountains to the west, darkness fell like a stone. Preacher and Hawk had to stop, even though Dog could have continued to follow Oliver's scent. The shadows were too thick for them to see where they were going, the risk of injury too great.

This would be yet another night for Chessie as a prisoner of the outcasts. At least she would have Oliver for company now. Preacher was convinced both of them were still alive. If they were dead, the outcasts would leave their bodies — or pieces of bodies — where Preacher and Hawk would be sure to find them, just to torment the pursuers.

They stopped to make a rough, cold camp. They had barely eaten anything today, and both Preacher and Hawk felt exhaustion tugging at them. Some hot food and coffee, followed by a good night's sleep, would have made a world of difference . . . but Preacher didn't think any of those things were in the cards for him and his son tonight.

"Get some sleep," he told Hawk when they had each eaten a strip of jerky and a cold, hard biscuit. "I'll wake you later."

"I can stand first watch," Hawk offered.

"You're the one who got knocked in the head today. I just got walloped by a bunch of fallin' rocks. I'm bruised up a mite, but that's all."

"You will be stiff and sore in the morning, old man."

"Maybe so, but I won't be mushy in the head like some fellas who are part Absaroka."

"Only the white man part of my head is mushy," Hawk said.

Preacher had to laugh at that.

He sat down on a rock with his rifle across his knees and Dog beside him. Hawk stretched out, and despite the uncomfortableness of the rocky ground, within minutes he was sound asleep, judging by the deep, regular breathing Preacher heard emanating from him. Preacher drew in a deep breath himself and looked up at the sky, where millions of stars swam in the endless black.

Except the black wasn't endless. Low down in the sky to the west was a very faint, arching band of orange light. Preacher frowned when he saw that, and without thinking about what he was doing, he got to his feet.

A few yards away, the gully's bank had caved in partially at some point in the past. Preacher was able to climb that irregular slope, even in the darkness. When he reached the top, he peered toward the light that he could see more clearly now.

The outcasts were nothing if not confident, even arrogant. They had built themselves a big campfire over there, and the light from it reflected into the sky plainly enough for Preacher to see it with no trouble. Obviously, the outcasts didn't care about that.

Or maybe this was another trap, Preacher thought. That was entirely possible.

But he didn't care. He slid back down into the gully and went quickly to Hawk's side, even though the young man had been asleep for only a short time. Preacher knelt and put a hand on Hawk's shoulder. Hawk woke instantly, his hand tightening around the butt of the pistol he held.

"Take it easy," Preacher said. "It's just me. I know where the outcasts are, and likely where they have Chessie and Oliver, too."

"How —" Hawk began.

"I saw the light from their campfire, a mile or so west of here. And that's where we're headed, right now."

CHAPTER 22

"This is a trap," Hawk said as he, Preacher, and Dog made their way carefully toward the orange crescent low in the sky marking the location of the outcasts' camp. They had to move slowly because there was always the danger of stepping on a razor-sharp rock, breaking an ankle in an unseen hole, or plunging into a crevice hidden in the shadows.

"You're probably right," Preacher replied, "but we've got to take that chance. Otherwise we may be trackin' 'em for days through this hellhole, and there's no tellin' what might happen to Chessie and Oliver durin' that time."

"You said the outcasts will keep them alive until they have all of us prisoner."

"Yeah, I figure that's what they're plannin', but you know how notional Injuns can be, and these outcasts are even crazier than usual. All it would take is for one of 'em to lose his temper for some reason and he'd be liable to split Oliver's skull with a tomahawk."

"I am half-Indian, you know," Hawk said coolly. "Do you believe me to be . . . crazy?"

"Well," Preacher said with a grin in the darkness, "you partnered up with me, so some folks would say that's enough evidence right there that you ain't right in the head."

Hawk just blew out an exasperated breath.

They moved on, their pace slow enough and the terrain rugged enough that it took them more than an hour to reach the area where the outcasts' campfire reflected its glow into the sky. They were even more cautious as they approached. At last the two men and the big cur stretched out on their bellies and peered over the crest of a ridge at a broad sinkhole that nature had scooped out of the badlands.

Jagged cliffs surrounded the natural amphitheater. Crude huts fashioned from twigs and branches and mud were visible here and there. At the moment, the big campfire dominated the scene. Preacher wasn't sure where the outcasts had found enough wood to build such a blaze. It must have taken them a lot of searching and gathering.

The flickering glare from the dancing flames spread out around the camp and illuminated most of the area. Preacher saw forty or fifty warriors scattered around. He didn't try to get an exact count. Some of the men squatted on their heels and passed around a pipe. Others danced, their movements weird and jerky. Some gnawed on food; Preacher couldn't tell what it was they were eating, and he wasn't sure he wanted to know.

He didn't see any children, but there were a few women around, as naked as the men. The women were as squat and ugly as the men, too, and it would have been hard to tell them apart at a distance except their heads weren't shaven and they had not daubed the red powder all over their bodies. That powder might have some spiritual significance for the warriors, Preacher thought, as well as its practical purpose in making them blend into the red sandstone background here in the badlands. It was possible the women weren't allowed to use it because of that.

As one of the women walked past a man hunkered on his haunches, he reached up, grabbed her, and flung her down roughly on the ground. Instantly he threw himself on top of her and began rutting with her, in plain sight of the others. The woman didn't seem upset. In fact, she barely seemed to notice what the man was doing to her. No one else paid any attention to it, either.

Preacher tasted the bitterness of disgust in his mouth. Calling these creatures *animals* was being unfair to actual animals, he thought. They were no better than the worms of the earth. Even that might be too generous a comparison.

He turned his attention to the reason he, Hawk, and Dog were here. Off to one side of the fire, Chessie and Oliver lay with their hands and feet bound. Chessie was clad only in her undergarments now, her dress having been left behind in the gorge to serve as bait in that failed avalanche trap. Oliver's hat was gone. Preacher saw dark smudges on the faces of both captives, but he couldn't tell if the marks came from dirt or dried blood. Might easily be both, he knew.

"They are alive," Hawk breathed.

"Yeah." Preacher had seen faint movements from both prisoners. "Hard to say from here, but it looks like maybe they ain't been roughed up too much."

"If they have mistreated Chessie —" Hawk began in a growling voice.

"Don't worry about that now," Preacher told him. "We got to concentrate on gettin' 'em away from here safely and then out of these badlands before those varmints can catch up to us."

"If we kill them all, we will not have to worry about that."

"Yeah, that's the simplest solution, but there may be a mite too many of 'em for us to do that. And there's probably more of them hidden around here that we can't see, just waitin' for us to show up."

"Then what are we going to do?"

"I been thinkin' on that," the mountain man said. In fact, Preacher's brain had been working quickly. He didn't see any way of accomplishing their goal without taking some big chances.

Big risk, big reward, he told himself. When you didn't really have any other options, that was the best way to look at things.

"When somebody's fixin' to spring a trap on you, the best thing to do is somethin' they ain't expectin'," Preacher said. "They figure we'll try to sneak in there, turn Chessie and Oliver loose, and sneak back out with 'em."

"Is that not what we need to do?" Hawk asked with a frown. "I have heard how you slipped into the camps of the Blackfeet and slit their throats without being discovered. They were so terrified of you they began to call you the Ghost Killer. I have heard the stories many times."

"Yeah, that's true, but the Blackfeet were asleep and not expectin' trouble. I'd need to be a real ghost to get in and out of that camp down there without bein' seen."

"So what do you think we should do?"

"What they *won't* be expectin'," Preacher said, "is for me to waltz right in there like I ain't the least bit worried about what they're gonna do."

Hawk stared at him in the faint glow that came from the fire in the camp below. After a moment, the young warrior said, "You cannot do that. They will kill you."

"They might if I just stood there and let 'em. But when they come after me and all hell breaks loose, it'll be your job to get Chessie and Oliver and then light a shuck outta there. When they realize what's goin' on, that'll distract 'em enough for me to make a break, too. We'll rendezvous up here and head out of these badlands as fast as we can."

Hawk thought about that for several seconds, then said, "We will not have time to get away unless you keep them distracted. You plan to trade your life for those of Chessie and Oliver, Preacher. You cannot make me believe otherwise."

The mountain man chuckled. "You ain't givin' me enough credit. Sure, there's a lot of those fellas, but they're all scrawny. I can handle 'em. You just wait and see. Or rather, don't wait. You'll need to get outta these parts as fast as you can."

"And you claim that Indians are notional," Hawk muttered. "This *notion* of yours is insane."

"You have a better idea?"

Hawk's silence told Preacher that he didn't.

"One thing you need to do before you go," Preacher went on. "Let's get some rock, crush it, and smear it on you."

"You mean I should make myself look like one of *them*?" Hawk's tone made it plain how revolting he found that idea.

"Well, there ain't time to do it up proper so you could actually pass for one of 'em. For that we'd have to cut all your hair off, and anyway, you're taller and sturdier than any of them. But if you look a little like them, it might give you a few extra seconds 'fore they notice you. That could come in handy."

"I do not like this idea," Hawk said ominously.

"It'll work. Just make sure you tell Oliver and Chessie who you are right away, so they'll cooperate with you and won't slow you down."

Hawk was still muttering under his breath as they retreated from the top of the ridge. Preacher found a place where several chunks of sandstone had already flaked off the wall of a gully. He gathered up some of them, then used the brass ball on the handle of his knife to grind them into a fine powder while Hawk stripped off his buckskin shirt and leggings, leaving him clad only in a loincloth. He told Preacher, "This is as far as I go."

"Shouldn't be too noticeable," the mountain man agreed. "Hold out your hands."

He scooped the powder into Hawk's outstretched hands. The young warrior began spreading the stuff over his body while Preacher ground up more pieces of sandstone. Dog sat nearby with his head cocked quizzically to the side, as if he couldn't figure out what these crazy humans were doing.

When Hawk had used the powder to cover the front half of his body and as much of the back half as he could reach, he pulled back his long black hair as tightly as he could and bound it with a strip of rawhide, then rubbed the powder into it as well. When looked at from the front, he didn't exactly appear shaven-headed, but his hair wasn't too obvious at first glance.

"I still believe you are risking too much," he told Preacher.

"And it's still the best chance we got to rescue those two, unless you happen to have a company of soldiers in your back pocket." Preacher grinned. "That's right, you ain't *got* a back pocket."

He led the way toward the outcasts' camp, altering the route based on what they had seen earlier so they came out as close as possible to the spot where Chessie and Oliver lay. They were about to slip up behind a couple of boulders when Preacher heard a faint scuffing sound. He recognized it instantly as a bare foot sliding on rock and twisted toward it. His knife seemed to leap from its sheath into his right hand as his left hand shot out in front of him.

The move was guided entirely by instinct. Preacher's eyes had spotted the deeper patch of darkness shaped vaguely like a man, and his nerves and muscles realized it was an outcast sentry before his brain even had time to grasp that fact. His left hand closed around the crazed renegade's throat, choking off any outcry before it had a chance to escape.

At the same time, Preacher brought the knife up and felt the blade go smoothly into the man's belly. He ripped one way and then the other and felt the hot, wet sprawl of entrails slithering over the back of his hand like snakes. The man jerked and spasmed and died in the mountain man's iron grip. He pulled the knife free and lowered the carcass to the ground behind the boulders.

"That's one we won't have to kill later," he whispered to Hawk, adding with a touch of grim humor, "You'll have some company while you're waitin' for me to circle around to the other side and make my move. We want as many of those varmints rushin' away from Oliver and Chessie as we can get."

"You will not throw your life away without a fight, will you?"

"Son, I ain't hardly done anything in my life without a fight, and I sure as hell ain't fixin' to start now." Preacher put a hand on Hawk's shoulder for a second. "You'll know when to move. You won't be able to miss it."

He started to turn away, then paused and added, "Dog, you stay with Hawk."

The big cur whined.

"I know, you want to go with me, but Hawk's liable to need your help more." Preacher scratched behind Dog's ears, then dropped to one knee and hugged the animal. Dog licked his whiskery face. Preacher stood up, vaguely embarrassed by that display of emotion — and he wasn't a man who embarrassed easily.

"How long do we wait for you to join us?" Hawk asked.

"Don't wait," Preacher said. "I know what I said about us rendezvousin', but that ain't gonna work. Just light out as fast as you can and keep goin'. I'll catch up to you where Merton and Ryker are camped in the hills, if not before."

Hawk nodded. He seemed to be struggling with what to say, so he didn't say anything. After a moment he just nodded again, and Preacher drifted back into the shadows and disappeared.

Preacher circled the camp, pulling back well away from it because he didn't want to stumble over any more sentries and risk giving away his position. When he judged that he was on the far side from where Oliver and Chessie were being held prisoner, he began to move in.

This time it was the sharp reek of long-unwashed flesh that warned him. He stopped in midstep and let his senses range around him until he was confident that the outcast guard posted in this area was to his right and in front of him, just a few steps away. Preacher shifted slightly to the side and saw the man's silhouette against the fire's glow. The guard was looking away from him and clearly had no idea that Preacher was so close.

He died without knowing, as the mountain man's left arm looped around his neck and clamped across his throat like an iron bar. Preacher's knife drank blood again, this time heart's blood as the blade slid between ribs and its tip pierced that vital organ. The man slumped against Preacher, his life there one second and then gone the next without warning.

Preacher's path into the camp was clear now. He wiped the blood from his knife on the leg of his buckskin trousers, then sheathed the blade. His rifle was slung on his back. He pulled both pistols from behind his belt and rested his thumbs on the hammers. The guns were loaded and primed. He drew the hammers back.

Then he took a deep breath, smiled in the darkness, and strode out quickly from cover into the garish firelight. Grinning, he raised his voice and announced loudly, "Howdy! My name's Preacher, and I'm here to kill *all* y'all sonsabitches!"

CHAPTER 23

For a heartbeat, surprise froze everyone in the camp in their tracks.

Then one of the outcasts screeched and charged at Preacher, brandishing a tomahawk. The mountain man let him take a couple of steps, then raised the pistol in his right hand and fired. One ball smashed the outcast's sternum while the other ripped deep into his guts. The man stumbled and went down.

The gunshot jolted the rest of the outcasts into action. They swarmed toward Preacher in a howling, bloodthirsty horde. He fired his second pistol and brought down another of the creatures, this one with blood gouting from holes in his chest. Preacher jammed the empty pistols behind his belt and reached back to grasp the rifle's barrel. He brought it around in front of him and fired from the hip. The ball tore through the body of another outcast. He had killed three of them in less than ten seconds.

Preacher shoved the rifle behind him on its sling again and drew his knife, while at the same time pulling his tomahawk from behind his belt with his other hand. He leaped to meet the closest group of the charging outcasts, striking so swiftly with the two weapons that it was difficult to follow his movements. The knife's keen edge sliced across the throats of two men in one swiping slash, causing them to gurgle and stagger as they pawed futilely at the crimson flood pouring from their necks. The tomahawk shattered one man's jaw and split the skull of another on the backswing. Preacher kicked one of the outcasts in the belly, and when the man doubled over, the tomahawk swooped up and then down, taking him in the back of the neck with such force that it bit deep enough to sever his spine.

Preacher backed off quickly, leaving howling, mad renegades after him. He bounded to his left, forcing them to change directions to come after him. Several men tried to block his path, but he zigzagged through them, striking right and left with the knife and tomahawk and leaving more crumpled bodies in his wake. It was a macabre dance of bloody violence, and no one was more graceful and fleet of foot than Preacher, nor more deadly.

Even in the midst of battle, though, he was able to cast a glance across the camp toward the spot where he had last seen Oliver and Chessie. Nearly all the outcasts had rushed to confront him when he sauntered in so boldly, but a couple of warriors had stayed behind to guard the prisoners. Preacher caught a glimpse of a red-daubed figure darting toward them. The sentries saw Hawk as well, took him for one of them at first glance, and looked again toward the chaos on the other side of the camp.

Hawk's knife raked across the throat of one guard. As the man's knees buckled and blood geysered from the gaping wound, the other guard saw what was going on and tried to recover. He was no match for Hawk's speed, however, and an instant later the young man's knife was buried in the second guard's chest.

Two women who were nearby saw the guards die and began to scream. With all the commotion in the camp, those cries went unnoticed for a moment. Then several men realized something else was wrong and turned away from the larger group trying to corral Preacher.

As they wheeled toward the prisoners, they were met by a gray, fanged flash who drove among them in a flurry of snapping and slashing teeth. One man went down, hamstrung, while the bones in another's forearm were snapped by the crushing power of Dog's jaws. As the man staggered, Dog fastened his teeth in his groin and ripped out a large chuck of it, causing the man to fall to his knees and scream hysterically.

Hawk scooped up a fallen tomahawk and threw it with deadly force and accuracy at the third man. The tomahawk buried itself in his forehead.

Preacher caught only glimpses of that action, since he had his own hands full with trying to avoid the other outcasts and killing the ones he couldn't dodge. As a younger man, he had wintered sometimes with friendly tribes, and often he had played the games the men devised, which usually involved running around and trying to keep some object away from the other competitors.

The object in play tonight was Preacher's life. He darted, ducked, and whirled, and as he did, he struck with the knife and tomahawk and sent more of the outcasts to whatever hell was waiting to claim them.

However, more of the creatures were joining the fray and it was getting more difficult to find a place to move. Preacher was almost surrounded.

Given that, it was time to go on the offensive again. He let out a yell of his own and charged straight at several of the outcasts who were closing in on him. They flinched in surprise, and before they could stop him, he was among them.

One man tried to thrust a lance at him, but Preacher knocked it aside with the tomahawk, and his knife drove in and out of the man's chest with blinding speed. He swung the knife around and slashed it across another man's face, laying it open to the bone and almost severing his jaw. The man's shriek of agony was a bubbling horror. Preacher ducked under a swung tomahawk and brought his knife up under the man's chin, angling the blade up into his brain. With his broad shoulders, Preacher bulled between two more men and thrust his knife into the back of one of them before ripping the knife free.

He found himself in the open again, and that gave him a chance to look across the camp and see that Hawk had cut the bonds holding Chessie and Oliver. Both of them were on their feet, running away, while Hawk and Dog held off a group of the outcast women who tried to pursue the escaping prisoners.

One of the creatures leaped at Preacher's back and wrapped arms and legs around the mountain man. The impact made Preacher stumble forward a couple of steps. The outcast let go with one hand and clawed at Preacher's face. Preacher felt the sting of its teeth on his neck. Feeling the same sort of primitive horror he would have felt if a rabid animal was trying to bite him, Preacher raised his knife and stabbed behind him, hoping to catch the outcast in the face with the blade. The creature let go of him and fell back, and when Preacher glanced over his shoulder he saw the outcast pawing at a ruined right eyeball that dangled from its socket, scooped out by the knife's tip.

Preacher threw one more look toward the far side of the camp and didn't see Hawk, Dog, Oliver, or Chessie. He hoped that meant all of them had gotten away successfully and were even now fleeing through the night, away from this hellish den of subhuman fiends.

Then the outcasts closed in around Preacher again, forcing him to pay attention to them as they tried to kill him.

As he had indicated to Hawk, he'd had every intention of surviving this rescue attempt. He had believed that he could hold the outcasts at bay long enough for Hawk to free the captives and get away from the camp, and once that was accomplished, Preacher would fight his way free.

He was beginning to see that maybe he had underestimated the number of enemies he would be facing. All the outcasts who had been standing guard around the camp had been drawn in by the commotion, and with them added to the warriors who were already there, the odds against the mountain man were simply overwhelming. Preacher had gotten himself out of plenty of dangerous situations in the past, but this spot might just be too tight.

That didn't mean he would stop fighting, or that he regretted his actions. If he wound up trading his life for those of Chessie and Oliver, then so be it. He'd had to try to save them. Even though he bore no responsibility for any of this, Preacher had long since learned that he couldn't turn his back on folks in trouble. The Good Lord had made him that way, and who was he to argue with the Lord?

That was the last thought that went through his brain before something smashed into his head and sent him spiraling down into a darkness from which there was no escape.

■ ■ ■ ■

That was what Preacher had figured, anyway, in that last fleeting instant of consciousness, but as it turned out, the black void that claimed him wasn't the endless oblivion of death after all. A tiny light flickered far in the distance and ever so gradually grew larger until it struck against Preacher's consciousness like a physical force. Pain surged up inside him and was most welcome, because it told him he was still alive.

His eyes were closed, but he could see the light anyway and he felt heat beating at his face. His eyelids slitted the tiniest bit but he didn't see anything except a fierce orange glare. Thunder boomed and pealed inside his skull, but it was just the sound of his pulse, he realized. He was upright somehow, his head hanging forward loosely. He forced his eyes open more and finally figured out that he was looking at the fire in the outcasts' camp. He was tied to something behind him, but he couldn't tell what it was.

He was the prisoner now of these horrible creatures.

Dreadful screeches went up from somewhere nearby. He must have moved his head just enough to demonstrate that he had regained consciousness, and some of the outcasts had noticed it. They wouldn't have wanted to carry out any of their bizarre, barbaric practices on him while he was passed out. That wouldn't have been good sport at all. But now that he was awake, he was fair game again, he supposed.

Before this night was over, he might be wishing that they *had* killed him earlier.

But while breath remained in his body, hope lingered, too. Several of the naked, crimson-daubed figures began to caper around in front of him, showing that they held him in contempt . . . at least as long as he was tied up. If he had been free, likely it would have been a different story. Preacher ignored them and concentrated instead on figuring out as much as he could about his situation. He had to know what was going on if he was going to have any chance of getting out of this.

He paid no attention to the pain throbbing inside his head, either. He had been hurt plenty of times in his life and knew he wasn't going to die from this injury. It was an annoyance more than anything else.

He moved his head and felt the rough surface behind it. His arms were pulled back around something thicker than a tree trunk — not that there were any trees in this wasteland other than some stunted, gnarled ones — and his wrists were tied together. The backs of his hands rubbed against stone. The outcasts had tied him to a rock. His ankles were bound, too, by what felt like a strip of rawhide.

Given enough time, he might be able to scrape those bonds over the rough surface enough to wear through them, but that would take hours, if not days, and he doubted if the outcasts would let him live that long. He had ruined their plan to bring all four captives together and make them watch as one by one they met grisly fates, so Preacher figured these twisted creatures would go ahead and take out their anger on him for that.

Since they already knew he was awake and more and more of them were gathering around him, he lifted his head and gave them a defiant glare, then looked around the camp. The only thing he was worried about was discovering that he wasn't the only captive, so he was greatly relieved when he didn't see Hawk, Dog, Oliver, or Chessie anywhere in the outcasts' village.

At least they had gotten away. Preacher had known he could count on Hawk.

The crowd of hopping, jabbering renegades that had gathered in front of Preacher suddenly fell silent and parted ranks. One of the crimson warriors strode through the opening toward the mountain man. This newcomer was taller and somewhat straighter than the others in body, but his face held the same brutal bestiality. The outcasts came from many different tribes, so it was difficult to determine which band one of them had belonged to originally. Something about the look of this man made Preacher believe he was a Cheyenne, though.

That was confirmed when he spoke. Preacher understood the Cheyenne tongue as well as he did those of all the other tribes, and he recognized it immediately when the man began talking, although being around the outcasts had garbled the language somewhat and given it a strange accent.

"You are man called Preacher," the man said in a guttural voice. "I see you one time many moons ago. You kill many of my people."

"I kill anybody who needs killin'," Preacher replied. "Red, white, it don't matter none to me."

"You kill many of . . . *my* people," the leader of the outcasts, for that was what he appeared to be, repeated as he gestured to indicate the creatures gathered around him.

That went along with what Preacher had heard in the past, that the outcasts considered themselves their own tribe now, regardless of their origins. "Now my people . . . kill you."

"You're welcome to try, old son," the mountain man replied. His voice was calm, without even a trace of bravado. "If you really want to be sportin' about it, though, you'll untie me and give me a knife or a tomahawk. You could bet on how many more of you I'd kill before you finally put me down."

The outcast stepped forward and hit Preacher across the face. Although he wasn't as tall or heavy as Preacher, he was powerfully built and the openhanded blow rocked Preacher's head to the side. He tasted blood in his mouth.

"You never hurt any of my people again," the man said. "We cut you apart, little bit at a time. Toes first, then fingers. Burn the cut-off place so they not bleed." A hideous smile curved the outcast's lips. "You live *long* time, Preacher. You hurt long time."

"Do your worst, you crazy son of a bitch." Preacher said the last part of that in English, since there wasn't really a Cheyenne equivalent.

The head man turned away and waved his

arms as the crowd pressed in behind him. He yelled something Preacher couldn't make out. The words sounded like nonsense to him. The other outcasts understood it, though. They scattered, scurrying away. The leader looked back at Preacher and sneered one more time, then walked toward the fire and circled it to go to one of the huts.

They were going to let him stew in his own juices for a while, Preacher thought. They might even wait until morning to get started on their torture.

Many years earlier, the Blackfeet had tried something similar. The mountain man's mortal enemies had captured him and tied him to a stake. When dawn came, they intended to heap wood around his feet and set it on fire, burning him alive.

Preacher had had something to say about that, however. In fact, he'd had a *lot* to say. Remembering a street preacher he had seen in St. Louis before he ever came west the first time, he began to spew words, "preaching" nonstop to the Indians for hour after hour. They feared harming a crazy man, since they believed that such individuals were protected by the spirits, so in the end they had let him go. That was how he had gotten the name Preacher, and it had stuck with him ever since.

In this case, such a tactic wouldn't help him. The outcasts wouldn't be leery of hurting him if he pretended to be insane. They were so warped that if he tried it, they would just enjoy torturing him to death that much more.

Taunting them into letting him fight for his life might be the best way of insuring a quick death. But if there was the slimmest chance of turning the tables on them and getting away, he wanted to take it. The outcasts' leader might be too cunning for him to pull that off, though.

For now he tested the strength of the bonds that held his wrists and ankles. He had to be discreet about it, because two outcasts stood fifteen feet away, holding lances and watching him with utter hatred on their faces. They looked like they would be happy to ram those weapons into him if he gave them the slightest excuse.

Whoever had tied him up had done a good job of it. The rawhide was tight and had no give to it. Preacher knew he couldn't scrape through it in time to save himself from the agonizing, ignominious end the outcasts had planned for him. He wondered, however, if he could scrape his wrists enough to make them bleed. The moisture might make the rawhide stretch enough for him to twist out of it. That would take hours, too, but not as long as the other way.

He began rasping his wrists against the rock to which he was tied, but since he could barely move his hands, it didn't take him long to realize that he had set himself an impossible task. Preacher wasn't the sort of man to despair, but if he had been, a feeling of hopelessness might have been creeping into him right about now.

The fire died down, and the outcasts didn't feed more wood into the flames to build it up again. Probably their supply was limited. There was no real threat in these badlands that needed to be kept at bay by a big fire, so Preacher figured by morning it would be burned down to embers. Many of the outcasts were lying down on the bare ground and going to sleep, but he knew some of them would be standing guard over him for the rest of the night. They didn't want to take a chance on being cheated out of their fun.

He let his head hang forward again, not out of any sense of giving up but rather from sheer exhaustion. The pain inside his skull had subsided to a dull ache, and it no longer sounded like someone was hammering on a drum in there every time his heart beat.

A howl made him open his eyes and lift

his head. He looked up, toward one of the jagged cliffs that surrounded the camp. That seemed to be where the sound came from. A hint of movement caught his eye. Preacher's muscles stiffened as he saw an animal of some sort up there. The creature sat down, tipped its head back, and howled again. None of the outcasts paid any attention to it. They acted like it wasn't uncommon to hear wolves in this wasteland.

But that was no wolf, Preacher thought. That was Dog. He had recognized the big cur's howl as soon as he heard it. Now, as he watched, Dog stood up, whirled away, and disappeared from the top of the rock.

He would be back, though. Preacher was confident of that. And there was a good chance Dog wouldn't be alone . . .

CHAPTER 24

Preacher didn't know whether to cuss or feel relieved. He had told Hawk to take Chessie and Oliver and get out of the badlands as fast as they could. He supposed it was barely possible that Dog had come back to the outcasts' camp on his own, but in his gut, Preacher didn't believe that at all.

Hawk was somewhere nearby, waiting for an opportunity to rescue him, and there was a good chance Chessie and Oliver were with him.

During their war against the Blackfeet, Preacher had seen plenty of evidence of how stealthy and dangerous Hawk could be. And Hawk had heard all those stories about how his father had slipped into Blackfoot camps and slit throats without being discovered. The youngster probably had something similar in mind tonight, Preacher thought.

But the outcasts were even more crazed and deadly than the Blackfeet. If Hawk were to be captured, he and Preacher were probably doomed, and that meant Chessie and Oliver were doomed as well, because the two of them would never be able to make it out of the badlands on their own.

So everything was up to Hawk now. Preacher pretended to be asleep, because he wanted the outcasts to think he was no longer a threat of any kind. That way more of them would doze off, and the ones who remained awake might not be as alert.

The way Preacher's head drooped forward, his thick, dark hair hung down and partially concealed his eyes. He was able to leave them open slightly, just enough for him to see the two men with lances, who were watching him. They leaned on their weapons, and he could tell that lassitude was stealing over them. They were still awake, but they weren't as focused on him as they had been at first.

It took every bit of his self-control not to react at all when he felt something tug at the rawhide strips binding his wrists. The movement was faint but persistent. Someone was using a knife to cut through those bonds. Had to be Hawk, he thought.

The boy was going to turn him loose so they could fight side by side. That wasn't a bad idea. Preacher's hands were a little numb from being tied so tightly. He began to flex his fingers in an attempt to get more feeling back into them. The rawhide around his wrists would still be just as tight, because Hawk was cutting the strip that ran between them, but at least his arms would be free. He would force his hands to work if it meant getting hold of a weapon again.

The rawhide parted. Preacher's arms sagged slightly, but not enough for his guards to notice. He kept them pulled back so the creatures wouldn't realize what had just happened. A moment later he felt the same sort of tugging on the rawhide around his ankles and knew Hawk was cutting through those bonds as well.

Then he got a shock. Something moved behind the two guards. A dark shape rose, seemingly out of the ground itself, and hands suddenly shot out and gripped their necks. A dull thud sounded as their skulls clunked together. The guards dropped their lances, which clattered against the ground and made enough noise to cause Preacher to wince. The guards slumped down, unconscious, and they would never come to because the shadowy figure bent over them had slashed their throats with two swift moves.

Hawk. Preacher recognized his son now.

But if Hawk had just killed the two guards, who was setting him free?

The bonds holding his legs to the rock came loose, and a second later a familiar voice whispered, "Here," as the handle of the knife that had accomplished that task was pressed into the mountain man's hand. The voice belonged to Chessie Dayton, even though Preacher had a hard time believing the girl was capable of pulling off such a dangerous job.

He didn't doubt the evidence of his own ears, though — or the welcome feel of the knife's bone handle in his fist.

Hawk faded back into the shadows, which made Preacher believe the young warrior's plan was just starting. He stayed where he was, pretending to still be tied to the rock, just in case any of the other outcasts woke up enough to glance toward him. The two men Hawk had killed looked like they were sleeping, and the faint noises of their deaths didn't seem to have aroused any of the others.

Minutes crept past with maddening slowness. Preacher didn't know if Chessie was still there behind the rock to which he was tied or if she had slipped away. Nor did he know where Hawk and Oliver were or what they were doing.

Then he heard an unmistakable sound he had heard hundreds, maybe even thousands, of times in the past: the fluttering whisper of an arrow flying through the air. It was followed instantly by a soft thud. Preacher looked in that direction and by the fading light of the fire saw a shaft sticking up from the back of a sleeping outcast.

The man wasn't sleeping anymore, however. Preacher could tell from the arrow's location that it had pierced the creature's heart, killing him in his sleep.

Another arrow flew and a second outcast died without ever knowing what had hit him. What Hawk was doing would be discovered eventually, but clearly he intended to cut down the odds as much as possible before that happened. A grim smile tugged at the mountain man's mouth as he watched four more of the outcasts meet their fate. Hawk's aim was lethal.

But then one of the arrows striking home was enough to wake a nearby sleeper. That man pushed himself up a little, gazed around, and then stiffened as he spotted the arrow protruding from the chest of a man a few yards away. He leaped to his feet and opened his mouth to yell.

Before he could say anything, his head seemed to explode as a chunk of rock heaved from the clifftop struck it. The rock made quite a racket as it fell to the ground next to the collapsing body. *That was one hell of a good toss,* Preacher thought as he stepped away from the rock where he'd been tied. Several of the outcasts were awake and starting to scramble to their feet now, so the time for stealth was over.

More rocks plummeted down from the cliff closest to the fire. Oliver must have gathered quite a supply of them while Chessie was sneaking into the camp to free Preacher. Most of the falling stones missed, of course, but enough of them found their targets to crush more skulls and break more bones. The outcasts ran around madly, screeching in terror as death rained down on them seemingly from the heavens.

Death moved swiftly among them on the ground, too. Preacher darted here and there, cutting throats and plunging the knife into the hearts of his enemies. Most of them never saw him coming. They were too disoriented by the unexpected attack from above.

Then someone barreled into Preacher from the side, knocking him off his feet. He rolled and came back up just in time to duck as the leader of the outcasts swung a tomahawk at his head. The man's face was more twisted with insane hatred than ever.

Preacher swung the knife at the man's arm, hoping to cut him and make him drop the tomahawk. The outcast leaped back, though, avoiding the blade. He snarled, "Kill you now! Kill you all!"

"Come on and try, you son of a bitch," Preacher said. He wasn't completely steady because his feet were still a little numb, but he wasn't going to let the outcast leader see that.

The man lunged at him, bringing the tomahawk up and slashing downward with blinding speed. The blow would have cleaved Preacher's skull open if it had landed. Preacher avoided it with a neat twist and struck quickly himself. The knife raked across the outcast's ribs on the left side. The man didn't make a sound of pain or even seem to notice the wound as he howled, "Kill!" in the Cheyenne tongue and whirled to swing the tomahawk again.

Preacher crouched and kicked out. The heel of his boot caught the outcast on the left thigh. He'd aimed to shatter the man's kneecap but the kick missed by inches. Even so, the impact was enough to make the creature stagger back a couple of steps. He flung his arms out to keep his balance, and that left him open for a split second.

Preacher's arm whipped back and forward. The knife flew true. Propelled by the mountain man's wiry strength, the blade buried itself to the hilt in the outcast's chest. The man staggered again.

But he didn't go down. How was that possible? Preacher wondered as he watched the man right himself and stumble forward. His heart should have stopped pumping by now. He ought to be dead.

Maybe he didn't have a heart. Maybe he ran on pure madness and hate. Something was sure as hell driving him as he snarled again and lifted the tomahawk.

Preacher caught the outcast's right wrist with his left hand, stopped the tomahawk as it descended. At the same time, Preacher reached out with his right, grasped the knife's bone handle, and ripped it free. He plunged it into the outcast's chest again, then a third and fourth time. Blood welled from the man's mouth and ran down over his chin. He laughed, spraying gore into Preacher's face. Preacher held fast to the man's wrist, keeping the tomahawk away from him, as he stabbed the outcast again and again, the blade flashing back and forth.

Finally a spasm went through the leader's body. His hand opened involuntarily and the tomahawk fell from his fingers. Preacher hung on to that wrist anyway as he changed his grip on the knife, drove the blade into the right side of the outcast's neck, and ripped it to the left, opening up a gaping wound from which crimson flooded, mixing with the crushed sandstone on the man's body to form a gruesome red mud. Preacher let go of him, put that hand on the man's ruined chest, and gave him a shove. The outcasts' head man went over backward and landed with his arms and legs flung out in the limp sprawl of death.

Preacher had had his hands so full with the battle against the leader that he hadn't been able to tell what was going on around them. He had been vaguely aware of hearing some gunshots. Now when he looked around he saw bodies scattered on all sides of the dying fire. A figure ran toward him and he reached down to grab the fallen tomahawk from the ground before he heard Chessie exclaim, "Preacher! It's me!"

He wouldn't have guessed that. She was nude, or next thing to it, with only some scraps of cloth wrapped around her hips and chest. Those makeshift garments, along with all of her skin that was on display, had been coated with the crimson powder from the sandstone. That was how she had been able to crawl up behind the rock and cut him loose, he realized. Like the outcasts, she had blended into her surroundings.

"We need to go," she went on as she reached out and grabbed his left hand.

He knew she was right. Chaos gripped the outcasts' camp right now, and quite a few of them had been killed in the attack. But there were still a lot of them alive, and sooner or later they would come to their senses and stop running around like chickens with their heads wrung off.

When that happened, they would look to start killing again.

"Come on," Preacher said as he ran toward the path that led out of this sinkhole. He held on to Chessie's hand, and she did an admirable job of keeping up with him, even though it had to hurt running on the rocky ground with her bare feet. They left the tumult behind them and vanished into the shadows.

CHAPTER 25

Even though it was still several hours until dawn and thick darkness cloaked the badlands, Preacher had an idea of where he was going. Once he had been over a piece of ground, as he and Hawk had been hours earlier when they approached the outcasts' camp for the first time, he knew instinctively which way to go. The stars functioned as a map for him, as well, and he could steer unerringly by them.

Hawk shared those abilities, as Preacher knew quite well, so the mountain man wasn't surprised a few minutes later when his son's voice called quietly, "Preacher! Here!"

He and Chessie paused as three shapes loomed out of the shadows — two human and one animal. Dog let out a pleased little bark at seeing Preacher again.

"Chessie!" Oliver said. "Are you all right?"

"I'm fine," the girl said. "Just a little . . .

uncomfortable."

Preacher figured the discomfort stemmed from the fact that Chessie was almost buck naked, which had to be embarrassing or downright chilly — or both. But whatever it was, Oliver took immediate action to address the problem, whipping his coat off and stepping forward to wrap it around Chessie's shoulders.

"Thank you," she murmured.

Hawk grunted, probably unhappy that Oliver had moved so quickly to gain Chessie's favor.

Preacher didn't figure they had time to worry about such things now. He said, "Where are the gal's clothes?"

"Right here," Oliver said. He picked up a bundle he had set down when he took off his coat.

"Miss Chessie, put your shoes back on. We ain't got time for anything else right now, I reckon. Sorry."

"It's all right," Chessie said as she took the bundle Oliver handed her and unwrapped the underclothes — the only garments she had left — from her shoes. She pulled on socks and then the shoes. "I should be able to move faster now."

"That was the idea," Preacher said. He cocked his head to listen. He could still hear the furious, hysterical howling of the outcasts in the distance. He wasn't sure, but he thought the racket *might* be coming closer. "We'd best get movin' again."

The five of them headed northeast, with Preacher and Dog leading the way. Chessie and Oliver came next. He held her arm to help her over the rough terrain. Hawk brought up the rear.

"That was mighty good aim on that first rock you chunked down, son," Preacher commented. "It busted that varmint's head clean open."

"Oliver did that," Hawk said with what sounded like grudging admiration. "It was his idea."

"I was extremely lucky," Oliver said. "If we'd had a catapult, like the ancient Romans and Greeks I've read about, we could have really bombarded that camp."

"You won't find no ancient Romans in these parts," Preacher said. "They'd have to be plumb loco to wander all the way to the Rocky Mountains!"

Then he recalled what he had discovered in a hidden valley a couple of years earlier and decided he shouldn't be quite so quick to declare certain things impossible. There was no telling what you might run across in these mountains.

Preacher kept the others moving at as fast a pace as possible given the darkness and the landscape, while Dog ranged ahead to scout for trouble in their path. Whenever they paused to rest, Preacher listened for the sounds of pursuit. He didn't hear any and hoped that meant either the outcasts had lost their trail or even decided not to come after them.

Unfortunately, it could also mean the vicious little bastards were sneaking along behind them, waiting for a good time and place to strike, so Preacher didn't let the others linger too long when they stopped to catch their breath.

The eastern sky began to turn gray, and not long after that a faint tint of orange and gold and pink appeared on the horizon. The sun would be up in a while. Once that happened, it would be more difficult for the outcasts to sneak up on them without being seen. That meant if the creatures were close enough to launch an attack, they would probably do it pretty soon.

"Everybody, be on your guard," Preacher said. "There ain't no tellin' what those varmints —"

Even as he spoke, a dark shape sailed at him from the top of a rock, arms spread out like wings, and for a second it was like some unholy bird of prey was swooping down on him.

Preacher saw the thing from the corner of his eye in time to twist around and bring up the knife he carried. The outcast who had jumped him had no chance to do anything except impale himself on the blade, which went into his body with a solid *thunk!*

Preacher yanked the knife free and shoved the dying creature aside. "Watch out!" he called to his companions. He knew the man who had attacked him wasn't alone.

The outcasts didn't need to be quiet anymore. They screeched madly as they came pouring out of cracks and crevices in the riven earth and leaped over boulders. Preacher had been forced to flee from the camp without his rifle and pistols, but he had the knife Chessie had used to cut him loose and he had also scooped up the tomahawk the outcast leader had dropped before dying. With those weapons, the mountain man whirled to meet the attack, shoving Chessie behind him as he did so.

The guns carried by Hawk and Oliver roared as they opened fire. They didn't have time to reload since the assault was so fierce, but they flipped the pistols around and used them as clubs to shatter the skulls of any outcasts who came within reach.

At the same time, the two young men positioned themselves so that they formed a rough triangle with Preacher. Chessie was in the middle of that triangle. She had picked up a rock and stood ready to bludgeon any of the outcasts who came near her. As daring as her actions had been earlier, Preacher had no doubt that she would go down fighting if it came to that.

Maybe it wouldn't. He and his companions had already inflicted a great deal of damage on the outcasts in the past twenty-four hours, killing quite a few of them and wounding many more. They hadn't been an overly large group to start with. If they had any sense, they might realize that they were paying too high a price to satisfy their bloodlust.

But if they'd had any sense, they probably wouldn't have been shunned and driven out of their original tribes in the first place. Expecting any sort of logic or reasoning from them was like expecting it from a rabid skunk. Once aroused to fury, they no longer possessed even a primitive sense of self-preservation.

So all Preacher and the others could do was to continue fighting as long as they drew breath. Slashing with the knife and the tomahawk, the mountain man forced back the tide of crazed killers on his side of the triangle. Hawk battled with the same sort of savage ferocity and efficiency.

Oliver lacked their skill and experience, and although he tried to maintain his position, he was forced to give ground. As he did so, his foot slipped and he staggered backward. Two of the outcasts rushed in at him. Oliver tried to catch himself but lost his balance and sprawled on the ground.

One of the outcasts screeched triumphantly and lifted a lance in both hands, poised to drive it through Oliver's body. Before he could strike, Chessie leaped at him and swung the rock she held. It crashed against the man's head with a crunching sound. The lance slipped from suddenly nerveless fingers and landed crossways on top of Oliver.

He snatched it up and thrust it into the belly of the other outcast. The man howled in agony and fumbled for a second at the shaft lodged in his guts before his knees buckled and he collapsed. Oliver rolled out of his way and grabbed the lance again, planting his foot against the outcast's body to give him leverage. He pulled the weapon free and surged up, thrusting with the sharp, bloodstained shaft again and driving another outcast back.

Maybe it was seeing one of their number struck down by a female, but for whatever reason, the remaining outcasts decided they had had enough. One of them leaped onto a rock and bounded away, and the others followed suit, bouncing across the badlands in a bizarre exodus visible in the grayish light of approaching dawn. Preacher watched them go and muttered, "Good riddance. If I never lay eyes on those varmints again, it'll be too soon."

Oliver dropped the lance he'd been wielding and grabbed Chessie's shoulders as she suddenly sagged. The rock she had used to kill one of the outcasts thudded to the ground beside her feet. As he held her up, Oliver asked anxiously, "Chessie, are you all right?"

"Yes, just . . . very tired," she said. Even though the red dust covered her face, Preacher could tell how pale and drawn she was from exhaustion and the strain of this night.

Oliver slid his arm around her shoulder and pulled her against him. Chessie sighed as she leaned into his chest. Preacher saw Hawk frowning and managed not to chuckle. He didn't figure Hawk had ever had much of a chance with Chessie to start with, no matter how smitten he was, and now there was no chance at all.

Preacher recalled how Chessie had played up to Hoyt Ryker back in St. Louis and continued to keep both Ryker and Oliver on the string during the expedition. He didn't think very highly of such behavior, but after tonight, he couldn't fault Chessie's courage. The girl had grit, that was for sure.

Hawk grimaced and bent to the task of cutting throats, finishing off the outcasts who were wounded but still alive. Then he said, "We should go."

"You're right about that," Preacher said. "We still got some ground to cover before we're outta these badlands. I don't think the outcasts will come after us again, especially once we're back out on the prairie, but I'll feel better about it when we are."

"Just lean on me," Oliver told Chessie. "We'll make it. And thank you for saving my life."

"I didn't —" she began.

Preacher said, "Oh, I reckon you probably did. That fella would've had that lance inside Oliver in another second."

"I didn't even think about it. I just . . ." Chessie shuddered.

"You just did what you had to," Oliver told her, "and I'll always be grateful to you."

"Come," Hawk snapped. "We need to get

out of this place."

They did so, walking steadily through the rough terrain as the sun climbed above the horizon. Golden light flooded the plains as they left the badlands — and all the evil that nightmarish place contained — behind.

CHAPTER 26

"Whose idea was it to make you look like one of them red devils?" Preacher asked Chessie as they walked toward the rising sun. The mountain man could already see the low, dark, irregular line in the distance that marked the location of the hills where he had told Edgar Merton, Hoyt Ryker, and the others to wait.

Before Chessie could answer the question, Oliver said, "It was all her idea. Hawk and I tried to talk her out of it, but nothing we could say changed her mind."

"It just made sense to me," Chessie said. "I couldn't sneak up on the guards and . . . and dispose of them the way Hawk did, and we needed Oliver up on the cliff to throw the rocks down. He's a lot stronger than I am. But I was able to cut those bonds holding you, Preacher."

"You sure did," he said with a nod. "Did a fine job of it, too."

He held up his hands and flexed the fingers. He had already used the knife to cut the rawhide straps off his wrists, being careful about it because he didn't want to nick an artery, but the ugly marks they had left were still visible on his skin. His boots had protected his ankles.

Hawk dropped back from time to time and checked their back trail, but there was no sign of the outcasts coming after them. Out here on the open prairie, it would have been difficult to approach without being seen. The outcasts were creatures of rocks and crevices and shadows, and Preacher was glad to leave them there.

He told Chessie, "We can stop anytime you want, so you can get your, uh, what you got left to wear back on."

"What I'd really like is to wash off all this *dust,*" she said. "Will there be a stream in those hills where I can bathe?"

"We'll do our best to find one," the mountain man promised.

"I think I'd rather wait until I'm clean, then. Even though I know it's absolutely scandalous for me to be in this . . . disheveled condition . . . around you gentlemen." She sighed. "Not that there's much left after all the times I've had to tear off part of my garments for some other purpose."

Oliver chuckled and said, "Chessie, I do believe that you're blushing."

"She is covered in red dust," Hawk said with a solemn frown. "How can you tell?"

Preacher thought that he was going to have to have a talk with the boy about taking everything so literally. But before he could say anything, he spotted a reflection from the rising sun on something in the distant hills.

"Look yonder," he said, pointing it out to the others. "That'll be where the rest of the bunch is waitin' with the wagons."

"Thank goodness," Oliver said. "We shouldn't have any trouble finding them."

That simple thing, the sun glinting on metal, seemed to boost not only their spirits but their strength. Their strides had renewed energy as they walked toward the hills.

The trek seemed to take longer than it should have, but Preacher knew that was because they were all worn out. Also, in this clear air, things usually appeared closer than they really were.

The day grew warmer as the sun rose higher in the sky. Finally, the wooded, rocky slopes were close. Preacher happened to be looking up at the area where he had spotted the sun glinting on something earlier when he saw a puff of gray smoke shoot out from the trees.

"Down!" he ordered.

He flung himself forward. At the same time, Hawk leaped at Oliver and Chessie, spreading his arms to grab both of them and pull them to the ground with him. As Preacher landed on his belly, he heard the distant report of a shot and the hum of a rifle ball passing close by. The sound wasn't followed by the thud of lead striking flesh and bone, so he knew the shot had missed.

That didn't mean it would be the last shot, though. Where there was one ambusher, there was usually at least one more.

"Hawk!" Preacher said. "Give 'em somethin' to think about!"

From his prone position, the young man was already drawing a bead with his rifle. "I saw the powder smoke," he told Preacher just before he squeezed the trigger. The long-barreled flintlock boomed.

"Oliver, Chessie, you two stay down and crawl backward," Preacher called to them. "Maybe you can get out of range."

"All right, Preacher, we understand," Oliver replied. He sounded a little shaken, but he had already demonstrated his ability to stay coolheaded under fire, so Preacher hoped he would continue like that.

With Oliver and Chessie backing off, the

mountain man powered to his feet and sprinted to the left, figuring he would draw the ambushers' fire. From the corner of his eye, he saw that Hawk was on his feet and heading right.

Another shot blasted from the hillside. Dirt kicked up a few feet to Preacher's right. He dodged in that direction, then instantly back left, and the feint worked. A second shot ripped past his right ear.

Then there was a lull as Preacher continued running toward the base of the hill. Two men up there, he thought, based on the timing of the shots.

Instinct made him veer again. This time the ball plowed up ground to his left.

Another lunge carried him into the brush at the bottom of the slope. He dived low and kept his head down as he crawled through the growth. A rifle ball whipped through the brush and cut off some branches, but it didn't come close to him.

So far all the ambushers' shots seemed to have been aimed at Preacher, which made him hope that he was the main target and the hidden riflemen wouldn't make a try for Oliver and Chessie. The brush was thick enough that he couldn't see Hawk anymore, but he had a hunch the men would gun the young warrior down if they got a chance.

Preacher could think of only one person in this neck of the woods with any reason to want him dead: Hoyt Ryker. Ryker could have posted men here to ambush them if they showed up, while taking Edgar Merton and the rest of the expedition deeper into the hills. Preacher wouldn't put something underhanded like that past Ryker. Not for a second.

The guns had fallen silent except for an occasional shot that rattled harmlessly through the brush. The ambushers were firing blindly now. They were probably getting nervous, too, since they couldn't see Preacher and didn't know whether they had hit him. For all they knew, he could be creeping up the hill toward them right now . . .

Which was just what he started to do.

Nobody was better than Preacher at moving through undergrowth without making a sound or giving his presence away in some other fashion. He couldn't rush, but he didn't waste any time, either, since he was all too aware that Oliver and Chessie were out there in the open. He hoped they had been able to pull back far enough that the rifles could no longer reach them.

A faint noise from his left made him look in that direction. A gray muzzle poked through a gap in the branches. Dog whined.

Preacher was glad the big cur was all right. He knew Dog was eager to get in on the action. With a grin, he said in a low voice, "Dog, hunt!"

Dog moved through the brush as silently as Preacher himself, a gray ghost gliding through the shadows. Preacher resumed his stealthy advance toward the top of the hill.

The shooting stopped completely, which made Preacher think maybe the ambushers had given up and decided to retreat while they still could. He hoped that wasn't the case. He wanted some answers, and grabbing at least one of the riflemen would be the best way to get them.

Preacher had lost sight of Dog, but he wasn't surprised when a startled yell suddenly erupted above him on the hill, followed by a snarl and a burst of cursing. The ambushers hadn't gone anywhere after all, and clearly Dog had hold of one of them.

Preacher leaped to his feet and bulled through the brush, no longer caring whether he made any noise. He almost paid for that when a pistol went off practically in his face. The roar clapped against his ears like giant fists, and he felt the sting of burning bits of powder against his face.

The next instant, he rammed his shoulder

into the man who had fired the pistol and bowled him over. The gun went flying, but the man grabbed hold of Preacher's leg and gave it a desperate heave. The mountain man tried to keep his balance, but he went down, too. The man yanked a knife from his belt and thrust it at Preacher's face.

Preacher knocked the blade aside with the tomahawk and would have smacked the man on the head with the backswing if the ambusher hadn't writhed around and buried a knee in Preacher's belly. The blow drove the air out of his lungs and doubled him over for a second.

That was long enough for his opponent to grab the wrist of the hand holding the tomahawk, roll on top, and clamp his other hand around Preacher's neck.

The ambusher was big and strong. Preacher looked up at him and saw the sunlight that came through the trees casting a dappled pattern over a rugged face. Preacher recognized him as one of Hoyt Ryker's men, just as he'd suspected. He couldn't recall the man's name, but it didn't matter. The varmint was doing his dead-level best to choke the life out of him.

With the man's weight pinning him down, Preacher couldn't reach the knife stuck behind his belt. But he was able to ball his left hand into a fist and launch a short, sharp punch that drove solidly into his opponent's jaw. That knocked the man to the side. Preacher bucked up from the ground and threw him off. The man rolled, came up on his knees, and then tried to scramble upright and flee rather than continuing the battle. Preacher tackled him around the knees from behind.

This time when the man fell, his head thudded against the trunk of a fallen tree. He went limp, and for a second Preacher though the ambusher had managed to bust open his skull and kill himself. Then he saw the man's back rising and falling. The fella didn't seem on the verge of regaining consciousness anytime soon, though.

Preacher stood up and listened. Dog's snarling and growling had gone silent. "Dog, where are you?" Preacher called. A quiet little bark answered him.

Preacher pushed through the brush and found Dog sitting beside the body of another man. This one's throat was a bloody ruin. He wouldn't be answering questions or doing anything else ever again, except providing a meal for scavengers.

"Preacher?"

That was Hawk's voice. Preacher turned and went back to the man who'd been knocked out. Hawk stood over him, holding a loaded pistol ready.

"Are there any more of them?" Hawk asked.

"I don't think so. Didn't sound to me like more than two rifles goin' off."

"The other one?"

"Dead."

"But this one lives. I assume you want to find out why he and his friend tried to kill us."

"I reckon I know why," Preacher said, his voice flat and grim. "Because Hoyt Ryker told 'em to."

CHAPTER 27

Preacher sent Hawk to check on Oliver and Chessie. While the young man was doing that, Preacher rolled the unconscious ambusher onto his back and then sat down on the log to wait for the man to regain consciousness.

It didn't take long for Preacher to grow impatient. He started prodding the prisoner's shoulder with the toe of his boot. After a few of those none-too-gentle nudges, the man groaned a little and moved his head from side to side. Preacher would have dumped a bucket of water in the man's face if he'd had one, but failing that, he continued the prodding until the ambusher rolled onto his side and started cursing bitterly. The man abruptly fell silent when he lifted his head, opened his eyes, and found the mountain man grinning down at him.

It wasn't a friendly grin.

"Best not get rambunctious, mister,"

Preacher warned. He lifted the tomahawk he held. "Try anything funny and I'll stove your head in. You know I'll do it, too."

The cursing resumed. Preacher let it go on for a moment, then said, "You and me are gonna have a talk."

"I don't have a damn thing to say to you," the man responded. A hate-filled grimace pulled his lips back.

"I reckon you do."

"Go ahead and kill me!" The man let out a humorless laugh. "I can't talk then, can I?"

"I don't plan on killin' you unless you don't give me no choice." Preacher paused. "But I might let my friend here gnaw on you for a while. Dog!"

The big cur stepped forward and snarled. Slobber dripped from his muzzle as he thrust it over the man's face. The razor-sharp fangs were only inches away.

The ambusher's bravado vanished. He tried to cringe away from Dog, but his head was right up against the log and he couldn't move.

"Get that beast away from me!" he cried in a shaky voice.

"So you're thinkin' about tellin' me what I want to know after all?" Preacher said.

"Just . . . just keep him away!"

Dog snarled. He looked like he was ready to rip the man's face to shreds . . . although he would never do that without an order from Preacher.

"I don't know if he's gonna listen to me," Preacher drawled. "Once a wild animal gets a taste for blood, it's mighty hard to keep him from goin' after it again."

"I'll tell you whatever you want to know!" the prisoner wailed.

"Dog!" Preacher said sharply.

Instantly, Dog stopped snarling and stepped back. He was still close enough to attack in the blink of an eye, though, and the tense way he stood, with the hair ruffled up on the back of his neck, revealed just how much he wanted to do exactly that.

"I don't recall your name, mister," Preacher went on.

"It's Hopkins. Thad Hopkins." The man swallowed hard and couldn't take his eyes off Dog's threatening stance.

"Who was your friend?"

"Brill . . . Jim Brill."

"Ryker left you here, didn't he?"

Hopkins swallowed again. "Yeah. It was all his idea."

"To ambush me, if I showed up."

"That's right. We were supposed to kill you . . . and the Indian. Your boy."

"I know who you mean," Preacher said, his voice cold and hard now. The ambush directed at him didn't bother him so much; people had been trying to kill him for more years than he could count. But Hopkins and Brill had intended to murder Hawk, as well, and that rubbed Preacher the wrong way. "What about the other two?"

"You mean young Merton and . . . and the girl? We weren't supposed to hurt them, just grab them and bring them back to Ryker."

"And where is he now? Deeper in the hills?"

Hopkins hesitated and licked his lips. Preacher had a hunch the man was about to try to lie.

"Dog."

The one word was enough to make the big cur lean closer to the prisoner and bare his teeth again.

"No, they . . . they were going on," Hopkins said, in such a hurry to get the words out that they stumbled from his lips. "To where Merton planned to go all along."

"Where's that?"

"Some place called . . . the Black Hills."

Preacher frowned. The Black Hills were still several days' journey to the north. Folks had started calling them by that name because of how dark they were with their thickly wooded slopes. They weren't actually black but more of a dark green. Preacher knew them better, though, as Pahá Sápa, a region held sacred by the Sioux. They believed the hills were the center of the universe and the spirits that guided their lives dwelled there, and no outsiders were ever permitted to set foot in them.

Edgar Merton's expedition had already clashed with the Sioux. Trespassing in the Black Hills would put a gigantic target on them and have every warrior for five hundred miles eager to lift their scalps.

"What the hell is in the Black Hills that Merton's after?" Preacher asked.

Hopkins shook his head. "I dunno, Preacher. I swear. Now, how about gettin' this beast away from me?"

"One more thing," the mountain man said. "Merton's been playin' his cards mighty close to the vest this whole trip. How come he up and decided to share where he's goin' with Ryker just now, while me and Hawk and Oliver were gone?"

Hopkins licked his lips and swallowed again. Preacher could tell that he didn't want to answer the question, and the implications of that hesitation made fresh anger well up inside the mountain man.

"Dog," Preacher said in a hoarse whisper.

"No!" Hopkins cried as Dog leaned still closer. "I'll tell you, Preacher, but I swear it wasn't my idea and I didn't have anything to do with it. It was all Ryker's doing."

"Keep talkin'," Preacher said. His voice was just as much of a growl as Dog's.

"Ryker . . . well, he kind of roughed up the old man to make him talk. I'm not sure exactly what he did because they were inside that covered wagon, but Merton yelled like it was pretty bad. After a while he stopped yellin' and Ryker came out and said we were pushin' on to the Black Hills."

Preacher had heard someone approaching through the brush and trees as he talked to Hopkins, so he wasn't surprised when Hawk, Oliver, and Chessie arrived in time to hear what the prisoner was saying.

Oliver's eyes widened at the mention of Ryker torturing his father. Anger darkened his face as he stepped forward and exclaimed, "You son of a bitch! I'll kill you!"

Hopkins cringed. "It wasn't me, damn it! I never touched your pa, kid. It was Ryker and nobody else."

"But you worked for him," Oliver said as he made a visible effort to control himself.

"So did all the other fellas."

"And you tried to kill Preacher just now!"

Hopkins couldn't deny that. He didn't even try.

Oliver tightened his grip on the rifle he carried. He looked like he was ready to lift the weapon and kill Hopkins. Preacher made an unobtrusive gesture to his son. Hawk stepped in front of Oliver.

"I don't blame you for bein' riled up," Preacher said, "but this fella still needs to answer some questions."

"He's a murderous animal, no better than those outcasts," Oliver said. "He ought to be exterminated."

Oliver didn't try to force the issue, though. Preacher clasped his hands together, leaned over Hopkins, and asked, "Did Merton tell Ryker what he's after in the Black Hills?"

"If he did, Ryker didn't tell any of the rest of us," Hopkins replied. "I give you my word on that, Preacher. The rest of us are just as much in the dark about it as you are."

Preacher looked up at Oliver. "Did your pa ever say anything to you about the Black Hills?"

"Not that I recall." Oliver had calmed down some, and his voice was fairly steady as he went on, "Father talked about a lot of the places he'd been out here when he was younger, but nothing about anywhere called the Black Hills."

Preacher held up a hand and said, "Hold on a minute. Your pa spent time out here on the frontier?"

"Yes, when he was a young man, before he married my mother. He went intending to make his fortune as a fur trapper."

Preacher grunted in surprise. "No offense, Oliver, but he sure didn't strike me as the sort of fella to do that."

"Well, he discovered he wasn't cut out for it," Oliver admitted. "He returned to the East and wound up being quite successful in business. He was better suited for that, no doubt about it. But earlier, he was young, you know? Adventure and excitement held a certain appeal for him. I'm not sure that ever went away completely. I remember there would be times, when I was young, that he would get this faraway look in his eyes and say he would like to go west again, that he wanted to go back and find what he'd left behind . . ." Oliver shook his head. "But I have no idea what he was talking about, or even if it was anything specific. It could have been just . . . the feeling he had out here."

"Maybe," Preacher said as his eyes narrowed. He didn't believe that Edgar Merton would have gone to the trouble, expense, and danger of outfitting this expedition and accompanying it if he hadn't been after something in particular, rather than just trying to recapture the excitement of his youth.

The mountain man turned his attention back to Hopkins and asked, "When did Ryker and the others leave?"

"Early this morning," the man replied. "Jim and me were supposed to wait here for a couple of days and take care of you and the Indian if you showed up."

Oliver said, "It didn't bother you that Ryker was telling you to commit cold-blooded murder?"

"Kid, I've ridden with Ryker long enough to know I didn't want to cross him. That seemed like a quick way to wind up dead. You don't know how snake-mean that fella can be."

"I know, all right," Preacher said. "Comparin' him to a snake probably ain't fair . . . to the snake."

CHAPTER 28

They had to go after Ryker, of course; there was no question about that. The man's bad intentions were out in the open now. As soon as he got what he wanted, he would finish off Edgar Merton. Preacher was sure of that.

For now, though, according to Hopkins, Merton was still alive. Hopkins had gotten a glimpse of him in the wagon as the rest of the expedition set off toward the Black Hills, leaving the two ambushers behind.

That meant he was still of some use to Hoyt Ryker, probably to lead the others to a specific spot. But once Merton had outlived his usefulness . . .

With Brill dead and Hopkins a prisoner, Ryker had six men left. Not terrible odds when Preacher and his companions caught up to them. In fact, if they could rescue Edgar Merton, the numbers would be almost even.

"Did Ryker leave horses for you and your partner?" Preacher asked Hopkins, who had proven willing enough to cooperate that the mountain man had allowed him to sit up.

"Yeah. They're tied back on the other side of this hill."

"Two horses," Hawk said. "Not enough for all of us without riding double."

Hopkins frowned and said, "Wait a minute. There are five of us."

Hawk put a hand on his knife and gave the man a cold stare. He didn't say anything, but he didn't have to in order to make a shudder go through Hopkins.

"W-wait a minute," the man began to babble. "I helped you. I told you everything you wanted to know. You can't just . . . just . . ."

"Take it easy," Preacher said. "You tried to kill us, mister. Hawk could cut your throat and never lose a minute's sleep over it. To tell you the truth, I reckon I could, too. But you might be of some use to us later on, as long as you cooperate. Give us any trouble and we'll leave you for the buzzards. Don't doubt that for a second."

"No trouble," Hopkins said. "I don't owe Ryker or any of those other boys a damned thing!"

Anybody who would betray his comrades

that easily would turn on anybody else he threw in with, Preacher mused, so he knew better than to trust the man. For the moment, though, Hopkins was too scared to do anything except what he was told.

"Tie his hands behind his back," Preacher said to Hawk.

"You intend to leave him alive? Even worse, to bring him along with us?"

"Like I said, he might be able to give us a hand when we catch up to the rest of the bunch."

"He will slow us down." Hawk frowned as he studied Preacher for a moment. "But you are not in a hurry to catch them, are you?"

Oliver looked surprised to hear that. "What?" he said. "We have to help my father as soon as possible!"

"Ryker ain't gonna hurt your pa any more than he already has," Preacher said. "He needs him, or he'd already be dead. Hate to be so blunt about it, Oliver, but them's the plain facts of the matter."

"Ryker could have killed Father after they left here."

"Why would he wait? Why not do it as soon as he found out that your pa was headin' for the Black Hills?" Preacher shook his head. "No, there's got to be more to it than that, and that's why he'll keep your pa alive."

Oliver turned to Hawk and demanded, "Why did you say Preacher doesn't want to catch them?"

"I said he does not want to catch them *too soon,*" the young half-Absaroka warrior replied as he finished lashing Hopkins's wrists together with rawhide thongs behind the man's back. "He wants your father to lead Ryker to whatever was his objective all along, and lead us there at the same time."

Oliver looked at Preacher. "Is this true?"

The mountain man shrugged. "We're all headed for the same place," he said. "And I don't mean whatever's on the other side of the divide, although that's true, too. We might as well hang back, let your pa and Ryker get where they're goin, and make our move then, when we find out what it's all about."

"I don't like it," Oliver said, shaking his head. "I don't like it at all."

Before they could discuss it any further, Chessie came out of the brush where she had gone to put her clothes on. Even under the circumstances, Hopkins's eyes had almost bulged out of their sockets when he'd seen her crimson-dusted near-nudity covered up only by Oliver's coat. Even now she wore only her undergarments, again with the coat over them, because her dress had been lost back in that avalanche.

She must not have overheard any of the conversation she had interrupted, because she asked Preacher, Hawk, and Oliver, "Have you decided what we're going to do?"

"Evidently we're going to take our time rescuing my father," Oliver said with a bitter edge to the words.

"What?"

"Preacher thinks it would be better to let them reach these so-called Black Hills first."

Chessie looked at Preacher. "But why?"

"You can tell her all about it, Oliver," Preacher said. "Hawk and I are gonna go find those horses. Keep an eye on Hopkins while we're gone."

"All right, fine," Oliver said, not trying to keep the sullenness out of his voice.

As Preacher and Hawk walked up the hill, out of earshot of the others, the young man said, "I understand why you believe your course is right, Preacher, but it would be better to cut that man's throat and catch up to Ryker as soon as possible. You gamble with all of our lives to satisfy your own curiosity."

"Maybe," Preacher allowed, "but just bein' born puts you in the game with the highest stakes of all."

It didn't take long for them to find the two horses and bring them back. Preacher said, "Oliver, you and Chessie ride double on one of 'em. Hawk and me will take turns on the other horse." He looked at Hopkins. "You're gonna be hoofin' it."

"That's cruel," Hopkins said.

"You ain't tryin' to breathe through a second mouth cut in your throat, so I wouldn't be complainin' too much if I was you."

Hopkins shut up after that, but he still had a sullen expression on his face.

Oliver mounted up first, then took Chessie's hand and helped her climb onto the horse in front of him. He took the reins in his right hand while he slid his left arm around her to steady her.

Hawk frowned at this arrangement but didn't say anything. Preacher hoped the youngster was starting to realize there was no future for him and Chessie. There never had been.

Preacher motioned Hawk into the other horse's saddle, then put a hand on Hopkins's shoulder and gave him a push toward the bottom of the slope.

"Let's go," the mountain man said. "It's

still a good ways to the Black Hills."

They covered several miles that afternoon. As they headed north, Oliver asked, "What's in these so-called Black Hills, anyway?"

Preacher explained the beliefs the Sioux held about the region, then said, "I've heard tell of a few fellas tryin' to do some trappin' in there. There are plenty of creeks runnin' through those hills, and that means plenty of beaver. I never ventured very far into 'em, myself. Heard too many stories about men who lost their hair for gettin' greedy. And it just didn't seem right, knowin' the way the Sioux feel about the place."

"Surely you don't believe it's true, though," Oliver said.

"You mean about the Pahá Sápa bein' the home of the spirits?" Preacher chuckled. "I've never run across any proof that it *ain't* true."

"But those are heathen beliefs," Chessie said.

"From time to time, I been accused of bein' a heathen. I figure there's worse things. Mostly, though, it seems the only way to really find out the truth about what's on the other side of the divide is by dyin', and I ain't quite ready to do that yet. So I'm content to be mystified for now." Preacher grinned. "Audie taught me that highfalutin word. It's a good one."

By evening, they had left the small range of hills behind and were back out on the prairie. As twilight settled down, they made a cold camp. Hopkins was exhausted from walking and had a headache from banging his head on that log. He stretched out on the ground and fell asleep almost instantly. Preacher had walked the same distance, but his muscles were like rawhide and he barely felt the effort.

They would split the guard duty into three shifts among Preacher, Hawk, and Oliver. Chessie insisted that she could take a turn, but Oliver wouldn't hear of it.

"After everything you've been through, you need to rest," he told her.

"I haven't been through that much more than any of the rest of you," she said.

"You were held captive by those terrible creatures longer than we were. You must have been terrified."

"I was," Chessie admitted. "But then Hawk freed us, and that was a wonderful feeling."

Hawk didn't say anything, but Preacher could tell he was pleased by Chessie's words.

The night passed quietly, as Preacher expected. He couldn't rule out the possibility of the outcasts leaving the badlands and coming after them, but it seemed mighty unlikely because so many of them had been killed by the mountain man and his companions.

Nor was there much chance of the Sioux they had clashed with earlier pursuing them. Of course, they might run across *another* band of Sioux. The tribe roamed all over these northern plains and up into Canada. But if that happened, it would be pure bad luck, with no way to foresee it.

Hoyt Ryker and the rest of his bunch were well ahead. Preacher wasn't worried about them. Ryker wasn't going to slow down or turn back until he found out what was so important to Edgar Merton. Just as Preacher had anticipated all the way back in St. Louis, Ryker had seized the first good chance to betray his erstwhile employer. He wouldn't abandon the search for answers now.

And neither would Preacher.

Chapter 29

Preacher wasn't the sort to take pity on a fella who'd done his damnedest to kill him, but the next day he allowed Thad Hopkins to ride the second horse for a while anyway. Hopkins had been stumbling along in obvious exhausted misery for most of the day when Preacher dismounted and told the man to take his place.

Hawk and Oliver scowled when he did that. Preacher knew both young men would have left Hopkins for the buzzards if it were up to them, but that didn't bother him. He had never lived his life by any code except his own.

During the afternoon, a range of small mountains became visible on the northern horizon. Chessie saw them and asked, "Are those the Black Hills?"

"That's them, all right," Preacher replied. "Beautiful country, once you get amongst 'em. You can see why the Sioux would think there was somethin' sacred about them."

"Will we be there by nightfall?"

Preacher shook his head. "No, not hardly. We'll be doin' good to get that far by the end of the day tomorrow. Might even be the next day."

"But they look so close!"

Oliver said, "Distances are deceptive out here. So are the way things look. Those mountains are probably a lot bigger and more extensive than they appear from here, aren't they, Preacher?"

"Well, they ain't as big as the Tetons, over west of here," the mountain man replied. "They're tall enough to be mountains, in spite of the name folks have hung on 'em, but when it comes to mountains out here on the frontier, they're on the small side. Plenty big and rugged enough, though, if you've got to climb 'em. You'll see when we get there."

Oliver gestured toward the wagon tracks they had been following for the past two days. "Will we be able to follow the trail once they get into the mountains?"

"Should be able to. There are only certain ways you can take wagons in there." Preacher looked up at Hopkins on the second horse. "How were you and Brill supposed to find Ryker and the others if you didn't catch up before they got to the mountains? Did Ryker mention any landmarks Oliver's pa might've told him about?"

Hopkins frowned in thought, then said, "He figured we'd catch up. But he did say, in case we didn't, that we ought to look for a place where two creeks flow in from the west through some deep gulches and come together to make one. Does that make sense to you, Preacher?"

"Reckon maybe it might. I recollect a place like that from the last time I was through these parts. Pretty rough country thereabouts."

"Can you find it again?" Oliver asked.

"I've been there before," Preacher said, as if that answered the question. Which, as a matter of fact, it did.

They made a cold camp again that night and stood guard in the same shifts as the night before. The next morning, they resumed the northward trek with the prisoner walking again.

Being able to ride for a while the day before seemed to have lifted Hopkins's spirits. As he trudged along between Preacher and the horse Hawk was riding at the moment, he said, "You know, I could walk a lot easier if you'd untie me."

"Your legs ain't tied," Preacher said. "You

ain't havin' to hop along."

"Yeah, but it's really awkward and uncomfortable with my arms pulled back and my hands tied behind me. You could tie them in front of me."

"Which would also make it easier for you to grab a gun or a knife." Preacher shook his head. "If you'd shot me like you did your damnedest to, I reckon that would've been pretty uncomfortable for me. Like I've told you before, Hopkins, just be grateful you're still alive. I'm the only one who wanted to keep you that way."

"This is true," Hawk said solemnly from horseback.

Hopkins sighed, kept his mouth shut, and plodded on.

As Preacher expected, by the end of the day the Black Hills appeared to be just as far away as ever. Chessie was discouraged by their apparent lack of progress, even after a long day of traveling, but Preacher assured her that the next day, they would be able to tell a difference.

That turned out to be the case, as by midday the mountains were noticeably closer, but even so, the group's approach was maddeningly slow. It was late in the afternoon of the third day after escaping the outcasts before they actually drew near the wooded slopes.

When they were still a mile out, Preacher called a halt and announced, "This is where Hawk and me will be leavin' the three of you."

Oliver, Chessie, and Hopkins all stared at him in confusion.

"We're gettin' close enough that somebody with a spyglass might be able to spot us if we kept goin'," the mountain man continued. "Oliver, you and Chessie will ride in front, like you're prisoners. Hopkins, you bring up the rear. Your hands will be tied to the saddle, so don't get no ideas."

Oliver said, "If he's behind us, he could turn and gallop off before I could stop him."

"And he'd be stuck tied to that horse out here in the middle of nowhere with no weapons and no supplies." Preacher smiled coldly at Hopkins. "You can try it if you want, I reckon, but you'll stand a lot better chance of comin' through this alive if you do what you're told."

"I don't see how you figure that," Hopkins said with a bitter edge in his voice. "Even if you're able to get the better of Ryker and the others, which doesn't seem very likely to me, you'll just kill me when it's over."

Preacher shook his head. "Cooperate and

I'll turn you loose. You've got my word on that." He rested his hand on the knife at his waist. "If that ain't to your likin' . . ."

Hastily, Hopkins held up a hand and said, "No, that's all right. I suppose I don't have much choice but to go along with what you want."

"No other *good* choice," Preacher said.

Hopkins shrugged. "Tell me what to do."

Hawk dismounted and untied the prisoner's bonds. Hopkins climbed onto the horse, grimacing at the painful play of stiff muscles. Hawk used the same strips of rawhide to lash the man's wrists to the saddle in front of him. Hopkins winced as Hawk pulled the rawhide even tighter than before.

"My hands are gonna get so numb they'll fall off."

"You complain more than an old woman," Hawk said.

Oliver asked, "What are you and Hawk going to do, Preacher?"

The mountain man gestured. "We'll circle around on foot and come at the hills from a different angle, keepin' low so we'll be hard to spot. Wait here an hour to give us time to get there, then go straight on." Preacher pointed. "Head for that little notch. We'll be somewhere close by, keepin' an eye on you. If Ryker left anybody behind to meet you, we'll deal with 'em. If not, we'll join up again and make camp, then push deeper into the hills tomorrow usin' the same method, you three on horseback and me and Hawk lurkin' around the vicinity."

"What about that other man?" Oliver said. "Brill. If there's anyone waiting, they're bound to notice that he's not with us."

"Anybody from Ryker's bunch will figure Brill got killed when him and Hopkins ambushed us. They'll believe that Hawk and me are dead, too, otherwise Hopkins wouldn't be waltzin' up with the two of you as his prisoners. Make sense?"

"Yes, I suppose it does. If one of Ryker's men spotted you and Hawk with us, he'd hurry back to Ryker and warn him."

Preacher nodded. "Yep. You gonna behave, Hopkins?"

"What choice do I have?" the man asked sullenly. "You'll probably be somewhere close by, ready to put a rifle ball through my head if I try to double-cross you."

"Now you're catchin' on," Preacher said with a grin. "Come on, Hawk. You, too, Dog."

The two men and the big cur turned and trotted off at right angles to the course the group had been following. Hawk asked, "Are we far enough out that they will not see us if they wait at the edge of the hills?"

"Yeah, at this range they wouldn't be able to make out any details, even with a spyglass."

"And you are convinced they might be watching this approach?"

"That notch is the best way into the Pahá Sápa," Preacher said. "If Edgar Merton's been here before, and if Ryker's forcin' him to show the way, that's most likely the way he'd go. You can't plan for everything, though. Just take your best shot and move on."

Hawk said nothing in response to that. Most fathers gave their sons advice on various subjects, Preacher thought wryly. When he found himself giving advice to Hawk, it was usually on ways not to get killed.

But then, he had never been one to do things the way most folks did.

At first glance, the prairie appeared to be flat and open, with no hiding places, but actually there were swales and creases to it that allowed Preacher and Hawk to approach the Black Hills with less chance of being seen, especially if they kept low. They trotted for a mile or so after leaving Oliver, Chessie, and Hopkins, then turned and began working their way toward the mountains. The course they followed approached the notch at an angle. A ridge thrust out just west of there and gave them some cover.

The climb up the west side of the ridge wasn't easy. Dog had more trouble than the two men. Preacher had to help the big cur from time to time, but he wasn't going to leave his trail partner behind. It already bothered him enough that he had been away from Horse for several days now. He hoped that Ryker hadn't tried to mistreat the big, rangy stallion.

Of course, anybody who tried to bother Horse was probably letting himself in for some bad trouble. Horse could take care of himself.

They reached the top and bellied down behind some rocks to watch the trail that went through the gap in the thickly wooded hills. Preacher looked to the south, his eyes narrowing as he studied the landscape intently. After a few minutes, he grunted and told Hawk, "Here they come."

"I see them," the young man said. "Oliver and Chessie look like prisoners, the way their heads are down and their shoulders droop."

"Yeah, they're puttin' on a good show," Preacher agreed. "And Hopkins is doin' his part."

"Do you really intend to let him live?"

"I gave him my word, didn't I?"

"He tried to kill you."

Preacher shrugged. "Lots of folks have tried to kill me. I'll admit, most of 'em I put under. But some either got away or I let 'em go. I never lost any sleep over it." The mountain man shook his head. "Anyway, a varmint ornery enough to throw in with Hoyt Ryker is likely to try somethin' sooner or later. A snake ain't a snake just 'cause he says he ain't. If Hopkins double-crosses us, I'll kill him and won't lose no sleep over *that,* neither."

A few minutes later, the three riders moved through the notch without being challenged or met by any of Ryker's men. Atop the ridge, Preacher motioned for Hawk and Dog to follow him and moved to intercept Oliver, Chessie, and Hopkins.

CHAPTER 30

The riders had disappeared into a thick stand of trees. It took a while for Preacher, Hawk, and Dog to work their way down from the ridge and reach those trees. As they walked through the growth, Preacher's keen ears heard the sound of horses stomping and blowing up ahead.

As Preacher and Hawk emerged into a clearing, Thad Hopkins said sharply, "All right, you two, that's far enough."

Preacher stopped short. His hand went to the tomahawk stuck behind his belt, and beside him, Hawk started to lift his rifle. Both of them froze when they saw Hopkins standing there with a pistol pressed against Chessie's temple. His other arm was wrapped tightly around the girl's midsection, nudging upward against the undersides of her breasts.

Oliver lay sprawled on the ground nearby, senseless, with blood oozing from a welt on the side of his head where something had walloped him, probably the gun that was now in Hopkins's hand, threatening Chessie.

"Put all your weapons on the ground," Hopkins snapped. "Don't try anything, or I'll blow this little whore's brains out."

"Remember what I said about a snake bein' a snake?" Preacher said to Hawk. "Varmints just can't help theirselves."

Hopkins said, "That's enough talk. Do what I told you."

He ground the pistol harder against Chessie's head to emphasize his point, making her cry out in pain. A low growl sounded in Hawk's throat. He leaned forward, caught up in the emotions raging through him. Preacher said quietly, "Best take it easy, son. Hopkins ain't got nothin' to lose. He'll do what he says."

"Damn right I will."

"If he hurts Chessie," Hawk said, "he will die, too. Long and painfully."

Hopkins smirked and said, "I reckon that's probably true. But the girl will be dead, too, and there won't be a damned thing you can do about that, redskin. Now drop those weapons!"

Preacher sighed. Slowly, so as not to spook Hopkins, he pulled the tomahawk from behind his belt and the knife from its sheath and tossed them on the ground about halfway between him and Hopkins. Hawk followed suit, lowering the rifle's butt to the ground and then letting it fall over. He tossed his pistol, tomahawk, and knife near Preacher's weapons.

"Don't go thinkin' about siccing that wolf on me, either," Hopkins cautioned. "No matter how fast he is, he can't get me before I pull this trigger."

"You got the upper hand," Preacher said. "How'd you go about that, anyway?"

A gloating grin stretched across Hopkins's beefy face. "That boy's a damned fool. I acted like I was sick and needed to get down from the horse. He cut me loose, and I was able to grab his gun and clout him with it. That's all it took."

Preacher glanced at Oliver and shook his head. He'd expected better from the young man. Unfortunately, even though being on this expedition had toughened up Oliver to a certain extent and educated him as well, he was still an easterner at heart and subject to momentary lapses of reason.

"I guess you didn't kill him because Ryker told you to bring him and the girl back. You figure he's worth somethin'."

"I guess we'll have to wait and see."

Hopkins laughed and tightened his grip on Chessie. "But one way or another, this little gal's going to be worth something to me — you can bet on that."

"You don't reckon Ryker's gonna let you have her, do you? There ain't a chance in hell of that. He's had his eye on her ever since St. Louis."

"Maybe, maybe not. He's liable to be grateful to me. After all," Hopkins said, "I'm the one who's gonna kill you and the redskin. Now back away from those guns."

Hopkins must have realized that he had one shot in Oliver's pistol and two enemies facing him. Even if he was able to fatally wound one of them, the other would kill him. The gun in Hopkins's hand wasn't really worth anything to him except as leverage while it was held to Chessie's head.

But if he could get Hawk's pistol as well, he might have a chance to shoot both of them. It would be a miracle if two rushed shots found their marks and brought down Preacher and Hawk, but stranger things had happened.

"You'd better think this through, Hopkins," Preacher said. "You can still put down that gun and work with us —"

"You would let him live after this?" Hawk exclaimed in amazement.

The boy had a lot to learn about manipulating a situation to his advantage, Preacher thought. He said, "As long as he's got Chessie, we got to do what he says."

"That's right," Hopkins crowed. "Now back off!"

Preacher had seen something in Chessie's expression. Her face was pale and drawn, and she was obviously scared, as most folks would be with a gun pressed to their head. But anger burned in her eyes as well. Preacher had seen for himself what sort of gumption the girl had. She was on the verge of making a move, and he would be ready when she did.

"Come on, Hawk," he said. "Let's back away like the man says."

Keeping his hands half lifted, Preacher took a couple of steps back. Still growling in anger and frustration, Hawk did likewise. Hopkins forced Chessie forward, toward the guns lying on the ground.

She had taken only a couple of steps when her foot caught a dead branch lying on the ground and she stumbled heavily. Preacher knew it was an act, that she had done it on purpose. Hopkins might have realized that, too, if he'd stopped to think about it, but instead he burst out, "Damn it, watch what you're —"

The gun muzzle had wavered away from Chessie's head. She twisted and rammed her left shoulder into Hopkins's chest, which made his grip on her loosen. With a cry of effort, she tore free and dived away from him.

Hopkins hesitated, torn between swinging the gun after her or jerking it back toward Preacher and Hawk, and that split second of indecision was enough for the mountain man to spring forward, scoop up the tomahawk, and throw it. The tomahawk revolved perfectly in the air one time, then it thunked into the middle of Hopkins's forehead, splitting the skull and lodging in his brain. As he was dying, his eyes widened grotesquely and crossed as they tried to look at the tomahawk. His arm jerked and the pistol went off. His knees buckled. He pitched forward onto his face, driving the tomahawk even deeper in the sundered gray matter inside his skull.

A few more involuntary twitches and he was dead.

"Dadgum it," Preacher said. "I was hopin' to kill the son of a bitch before he got a shot off. No tellin' how close Ryker is and whether or not he heard that."

Hawk knelt at Chessie's side and took hold of her shoulders to roll her over and make sure she was all right. She sobbed and threw her arms around him, clinging to him as reaction set in now that she was out of danger, at least relatively speaking. None of them would be truly out of danger until they had dealt with the threat of Hoyt Ryker and his men.

Hawk was pleased by the way Chessie turned to him, Preacher noted as he bent over and wrenched the tomahawk free from the dead man's skull. Hopkins stared up sightlessly at him. Preacher said, "Don't look at me like that, old son. I told you what'd happen if you tried to double-cross us."

The opportunity for Hawk to comfort Chessie didn't last long. Oliver suddenly groaned as he began to come to, and Chessie cried, "Oh!" and pulled away from Hawk. She sprang to her feet, ran to Oliver's side, and dropped to her knees. She took hold of him and lifted him so she could rest his bloody head in her lap.

Preacher managed not to laugh at the disgusted frown on his son's face.

"Oh, Oliver!" Chessie said as she leaned over him. "Are you all right?"

He opened his eyes and blinked up dazedly at her. "Wha . . . wha' happened?" he asked.

"That terrible man Hopkins hit you and took me hostage," she explained. "But Preacher came along and killed him."

"I . . . I didn't mean for him to get loose . . ."

Preacher hunkered next to the two of them and said, "You can't trust a skunk like Hopkins, not ever. Make use of 'em if you can, but don't never trust 'em. A sore head's a small price to pay for learnin' that lesson. Reckon you'll remember?"

"I will," Oliver promised. Some color was coming back into his face now. "I'll remember. And I'm sorry, Preacher."

"Do better next time," Preacher said. "Meanwhile, how long are you plannin' to lollygag around with your head in that gal's lap?"

Oliver and Chessie both started to turn pink. She helped him sit up. He was clearly a little dizzy, but he insisted, "I'll be all right." He turned his head to look at Chessie as something occurred to him. "Did Hopkins hurt you? If he did, I . . . I'll . . ."

Hawk said, "You will do nothing. The man is already dead."

"I'm fine, Oliver," Chessie assured him. "He didn't have a chance to hurt me."

"No thanks to me," Oliver said as a sullen frown appeared on his face.

Preacher and Hawk walked over to the horses as Oliver and Chessie continued talking, their voices too low now to be understood. Hawk walked around the horses and checked the cinches on the saddles. While he was doing that, he said quietly to Preacher, "His carelessness could have gotten them both killed."

"Yeah, that's true," the mountain man agreed. "But she'll forgive him. Quicker than he'll forgive himself, I imagine. But that's their lookout, not ours. We still got to find Ryker, Merton, and the others."

That distracted Hawk from thoughts of the conversation going on between Oliver and Chessie. He said, "Those creeks Hopkins spoke of, in deep gulches coming in from the west and joining together . . . do you truly know this place?"

"I do," Preacher said. "It's a ways north of here. Take a couple of days to get there, more than likely. If that's where Hopkins and Brill were supposed to rendezvous with Ryker, we'll find the bunch waitin' there. One thing about it, it's a pretty wild place. Plenty of cover, so we ought to be able to get close without Ryker knowin' we're around."

"Do you believe that is where Edgar Merton was bound for all along?"

"Could be."

"What is there about it to make it so important for him to return?"

"I reckon we'll find out when we get there," Preacher said.

Chapter 31

They left Thad Hopkins's body where it had fallen and pushed on a couple of miles deeper into the Black Hills before finding a place to camp for the night. It had been several years since Preacher had been here. He was reminded once again what a beautiful part of the country this was, with thick forests, stark, rocky upthrusts, and cold, clear, fast-flowing streams. It was easy to see why the Sioux considered these hills sacred.

Since they weren't out on the open prairie anymore, for the first time in several days Preacher built a small fire so they could have hot food and coffee for supper that night, using the supplies that Hopkins and Brill had brought along in their saddlebags. They had pitched camp under some overhanging rocks, so the flames couldn't be seen from very far away and the rocks would disperse the smoke.

Oliver had been moping about the way he'd allowed Hopkins to get loose, but the meal seemed to lift his spirits some. He and Chessie sat close together as they ate, which probably made him feel better, too.

"I should give you your jacket back," she said. "It'll probably get cold at night here in the mountains."

"All the more reason for you to keep it," he told her. "I'll be fine."

Preacher said, "Hopkins and Brill had blankets with 'em. Either of you can wrap up in them if you need to." He added wryly, "Might be a good idea to check 'em for crawlin' varmints first, though."

"What about you and Hawk?" Chessie asked. "Won't you get cold?"

"We'll be fine. We're used to livin' out in the open like this."

Hawk said, "I am Absaroka. I do not feel the cold."

Which was a bald-faced lie, Preacher thought. Without a doubt, Indians were more accustomed to physical hardships than folks from back East like Oliver and Chessie, but that didn't keep them from getting cold. That was why they always had plenty of soft, thick buffalo robes in their lodges and tepees. Hawk wasn't going to admit that in front of Chessie, though.

Preacher thought he might need to have a talk with the boy. Hawk couldn't help it that he was attracted to Chessie, but he ought to be smart enough to see that she had her attention focused on Oliver Merton. Being determined was one thing; being downright muleheaded was another.

Preacher allowed the fire to burn down to embers after the meal was over. Chessie rolled up in a blanket and fell asleep right away, apparently exhausted by another long day and yet another dangerous ordeal that easily could have resulted in her death. Preacher didn't know what she had expected when she'd decided to come along on this expedition, but more than likely she had realized by now that she'd bitten off a pretty big chunk of trouble.

As he sat by the glowing coals of the fire, his thoughts turned from Chessie to Edgar Merton. It had come as a surprise to him that Merton had spent time on the frontier. Obviously, something important had happened while Merton was out here, or else the man wouldn't have been so determined to return years later.

Usually, when a man was haunted by something to that extent, one of two things was responsible, Preacher reflected: love . . . or money.

He wondered which one had brought Edgar Merton back to the Black Hills.

When it came time to arrange the guard shifts that night, Oliver said, "After what happened earlier, are you sure you trust me to keep watch, Preacher?"

"Yeah, I do," the mountain man replied. "You made a mistake. Everybody does, sooner or later. Just don't make the same one again."

Hawk said, "Some mistakes can get you killed. Or worse, others."

Oliver nodded sheepishly. "I know. I'd never have forgiven myself if that bastard had hurt Chessie. If there was some way to send her back to St. Louis, just like that, where she'd be safe again, I'd do it in an instant."

Preacher wasn't sure Chessie had been all that safe on her own back in St. Louis, although he was confident Red Mike would have tried to look after her. If she and Oliver both survived this expedition, she might be better off than she would have been under any other likely circumstances.

If it looked like the best deal to her, would she betray them and go back to Hoyt Ryker? Preacher didn't believe she would. Like Oliver, Chessie seemed to have grown up some during this hazardous journey. But he supposed only time would tell.

The night passed quietly, during Oliver's watch as well as the others, and in the morning the group pushed farther north into the mountains. The supplies Hopkins and Brill had brought along were running low, but that afternoon Hawk brought down a young deer with an arrow and they had fresh meat for supper, as well as enough to take along with them for the next day.

After they had eaten, Oliver said, "We've seen several creeks since we got into these hills. How do you know we're headed for the right place?"

"Won't know for sure until we get there," Preacher replied. "And I won't claim I've been over every foot of ground in these parts. Pert near, though. And I only remember one spot where two creeks come in from the west like that in deep gulches and flow together in a deep hollow surrounded by hills. The Sioux call the place Owayásuta. Hard to translate exactly, but it sort of means to approve of something . . . the way they want the spirits to approve of them."

"But if we get there and don't find my father and Ryker and the others?"

"Then we'll keep looking," Preacher said.

As things turned out, it never came to

that. The next day, as the group was making its way in a generally northward direction, allowing for the terrain, Hawk paused, lifted a hand and pointed, and said, "There."

Preacher had spotted it at the same time as his son. A tendril of gray smoke climbed into the sky ahead of them, visible above the tops of the pine, spruce, and bur oaks that covered the slopes of the valleys folding into each other.

"What is that?" Oliver asked.

"Somebody's got a good-sized fire goin' a mile or so ahead of us," Preacher said.

"Indians? As you said, they consider this their domain."

Hawk snorted and said, "Not even the Sioux would be so careless. Smoke like that in the middle of the day is the work of white men."

"Then we've found them," Oliver said with excitement creeping into his voice. "Who else would be here in these mountains?"

"Well, I've heard tell of a few fellas who came here to trap," Preacher said, "but unless they were real greenhorns, they'd have enough sense not to tell the world where they are. I reckon I agree with Hawk. Ryker and his bunch have stopped for some reason, and they're big enough fools to have built a fire like that."

"Maybe we can rescue my father and deal with them, then." Oliver paused and frowned. "I hadn't really thought about it, but . . . we're going to have to kill them, aren't we? We can't just take my father away from them and go on. They'll come after us."

"Afraid you're right," Preacher said, nodding. "If Ryker's got his hands on somethin' he thinks is valuable, he ain't the sort to let go of it without a fight."

"But we're outnumbered."

"Not as badly as we were against the outcasts," Hawk pointed out. "There were many of them and a few of us, and yet here we are."

Oliver looked at Chessie and said, "You were the one who told my father to talk to Ryker. I got the feeling that you two were . . . friends."

So the youngster wasn't quite as thickheaded as he seemed sometimes, Preacher thought.

"I didn't know what sort of man he was then," Chessie said with an embarrassed look on her face. "And we were never that close, anyway. After everything that's happened, Oliver, I don't care what happens to Hoyt Ryker, and that's the truth. I swear it.

If he got the chance, I'm sure he would kill the three of you." She swallowed hard. "And whatever he had in mind for me, I know it wouldn't be good."

Preacher said, "You can bet a brand-new hat on that. All right, we've done some plain talkin' here, and I reckon we all know where we stand. What we need to do now is find out why Ryker and his bunch have stopped, and then we'll figure out what to do about it."

Oliver looked worried. "Do you think something's happened to my father? If he can't give Ryker directions on where to go next, that could mean he's . . . he's . . ."

"We'll find out," Preacher said again, "and there ain't no use in worryin' until then."

They moved out, heading toward the smoke. When they were half a mile away, Preacher called a halt again and said, "Ryker will have guards posted, more than likely, so the rest of you will stay here while I go scout around a mite."

"I should come with you," Hawk said immediately.

The mountain man shook his head. "I don't cotton to the idea of leavin' Oliver and Chessie here on their own. Dog will come with me, in case I run into trouble."

Hawk didn't like the decision, but he

didn't argue with it. Instead he said, "You should take a pistol with you."

"Now, that I'll do," Preacher agreed.

Oliver handed him the pistol the young man had been carrying. Preacher tucked it behind his belt, then said quietly, "Come on, Dog." With the big cur beside him, he loped off into the forest and within moments could no longer see the others behind him, which meant they couldn't see him, either.

No one alive could move through the wilderness with more stealth than Preacher, which was one reason his enemies among the tribes feared him so much. Dog had learned to be almost his equal. The two of them circled the smoke to come at it from a slightly different direction, and it wasn't long before they were looking out through small gaps in thick brush at Hoyt Ryker's camp.

Ryker and his companions had brought the wagons to a halt on a relatively level bench that thrust out from the side of a mountain. The area in front of the wagons was open ground, which meant it would be difficult to approach from that direction.

Behind the camp, however, a rocky bluff rose almost perpendicularly to a height of a hundred feet. Preacher studied it intently for a moment, then shifted his attention to the men moving around the wagons and the campfire.

He saw Pidge, who seemed to have recovered from the wounds he'd suffered earlier in the journey. Three men tended to the mules or repaired harnesses, while one squatted next to the fire and watched a coffeepot sitting at the edge of the flames.

That left Ryker and one more man unaccounted for. Preacher had a hunch the missing member of the expedition was standing guard somewhere nearby. But there was no sign of Edgar Merton, and Preacher figured Ryker was probably wherever the wealthy easterner was.

That made him look toward the covered wagon. He couldn't see into it from where he was, but after watching the vehicle for several minutes, he saw Hoyt Ryker climb over the tailgate and drop to the ground. Ryker didn't look happy, and when Pidge approached him, Ryker snapped at him. Preacher could tell that even though he couldn't make out the words. Pidge stood there looking a little like a whipped dog as Ryker stalked away.

That made Preacher even more interested in the wagon with its canvas cover. Since Edgar Merton wasn't anywhere else around the camp, that was really the only place he could be. That is, if Merton was still alive . . .

Preacher knew he was going to have to get a look into the wagon to find out.

CHAPTER 32

Oliver and Chessie looked up in surprise from the log where they sat when Preacher stepped out from the trees. Hawk looked like he was expecting his father, though, so Preacher knew the youngster had heard him coming.

Oliver stood up and asked, “Did you find them?”

“Yeah, their camp’s right out in the open,” Preacher said. “With that smoke comin’ up, it wasn’t hard to find.”

“And my father? Did you see him? Is he all right?”

The anxious questions tumbled out of Oliver’s mouth. Preacher answered honestly, “I didn’t see him. I think he must’ve been in the wagon. Ryker climbed out of it while I was watchin’, and he seemed upset about somethin’.”

A stricken look appeared on Oliver’s face. “Father’s dead,” he said in a hollow voice.

"Ryker tortured him, and now he's died from whatever that bastard did."

"You don't know that," Chessie told him as she took hold of his arm with both hands and squeezed it in an effort to comfort and reassure him.

"The gal's right," Preacher said. "Somethin' must be goin' on, or else Ryker wouldn't have stopped and pitched camp in the middle of the day like this, but we don't have any way of knowin' what it is until I get a look inside the wagon."

"If he's there, and if he's alive, you can rescue him," Oliver said. Now there was a note of excitement in his words.

"It ain't gonna be that easy." Preacher went on to describe the layout of the camp and the surrounding area. "I can't just waltz in from the front, but that cliff in back of the wagons is rough enough I ought to be able to climb down it once it gets dark."

"You mean not until nightfall?"

"If I tried to make that climb in broad daylight, anybody who happened to glance up would spot me," Preacher said. "Then I'd be a sittin' duck."

Hawk said, "You should let me climb down the cliff and look in the wagon, Preacher. I am younger."

Preacher glared at him. "Are you sayin' I

ain't as spry as I used to be?"

"No, but you *are* older."

"Not so old I can't do what I set out to do." Preacher looked at Oliver. "Here's the thing, though. Even if your pa is in the wagon and is all right, relatively speakin', he won't be able to climb back up that cliff with me. That just ain't the sort of thing he can do."

"You're saying you'll have to *leave* him there?"

"For now," Preacher said.

"But that doesn't help us at all!"

"It helps us if we know he ain't dead," Preacher said bluntly. "Then we can figure out a way to get him away from Ryker."

Oliver sighed and said, "I suppose you're right. But I don't like the idea of leaving him in Ryker's hands any longer than we have to."

"And we won't. Right now, though, there's nothing we can do except wait for it to get dark."

"I can think of one more thing," Chessie said.

"What's that?"

"We can pray that Mr. Merton is still alive and well."

Oliver was still tense as dusk settled down

over the landscape several hours later. He assured Preacher that he understood the situation and would go along with whatever the mountain man decided. But that didn't stop him from being nervous and eager to learn his father's current condition.

Preacher gnawed on one of the pieces of venison they had cooked the day before and brought along with them. They would have a cold camp again tonight. They were too close to Ryker's camp to risk a fire, no matter how welcome it would have been. The light of the flames or the smell of the smoke could have given them away. Even though Ryker's men were far from experienced frontiersmen, they would be alert for anything like that.

Night had fallen but the moon had not yet risen when Preacher got ready to take his leave. "Dog, stay with Hawk," he told the big cur. Tonight he would be on his own, as he always was whenever he ventured like this into the enemy's den.

"You can still send me to make this scout," Hawk said.

"No, I'll do it. You stay here with Oliver and Chessie. I'll be back."

"If you have not returned by morning, I will come and find out why," Hawk promised.

"If I ain't back by mornin', chances are I ain't comin' back. But we ain't gonna dwell on that, 'cause I don't intend for it to happen."

Chessie stepped up to the mountain man, put her arms around him, and gave him a hug. "Be careful, Preacher," she said.

He gave her an awkward pat on the back and said, "Don't worry, I will be."

"Do not believe him," Hawk said. "He has never been careful in all the time I have known him."

"Which ain't been all that long," Preacher reminded his son. He slapped Hawk on the back, then shook hands with Oliver.

"Find my father," the young man said.

"I intend to."

Preacher nodded, even though they weren't able to see him very well in the darkness, and faded away into the shadows.

Even though a thick blackness cloaked the hills, he had no trouble finding where he was going. His sense of direction was unerring, as always. Nor was it long before he had the light of Ryker's campfire to steer by. The orange flames leaped high and cast a glow into the sky above the camp.

Preacher hoped that glow didn't reach all the way to the cliff looming behind the wagons. If they spotted him climbing down, it would be the same as if he had a giant target painted on him.

Reaching the top of the cliff behind the camp proved to be a long, difficult task. Earlier, Preacher had scouted out some possible routes, but he didn't know which ones would take him where he wanted to go until he tried following them, so he had to backtrack several times when trails played out and the slope was too sheer for him to keep going.

Finally, long after night had fallen, he stretched out on his belly and peered over the brink at the camp below. The fire had burned down, and most of the men had rolled up in blankets and gone to sleep. At least one guard was posted; Preacher spotted a tiny coal in the bowl of a pipe clamped between the teeth of a man sitting with his back against a wheel on one of the supply wagons. Preacher saw the coal brighten and dim and knew the man was puffing on the pipe. The fella probably had a rifle across his lap, too.

Preacher waited to make sure the camp was going to remain quiet. While he did, he studied the face of the cliff as best he could in the poor light. Earlier, when he had looked at it in daylight, he had seen how rough and seamed it was. Climbing down in darkness would require him to feel around for hand- and footholds, but he was confident he could find plenty.

Satisfied that the time had come to make his move, he swung over the edge and began his descent.

It was slow, treacherous going. In some places the rock crumbled in his hand when he tried to put his weight on it, which left him clinging to the cliff face with his other hand while he searched for a more secure hold. When that happened, gravel clattered down and the sound made Preacher's jaw tighten grimly, but there were enough night noises that it seemed to blend in. No cries of alarm came from the camp below.

Time was deceptive in such a situation. Preacher wasn't sure how long he had been on the cliff when he realized the ground was just a few feet below him. He let go and dropped the rest of the way, landing as lightly as a big cat. His knees flexed, and he bent to put a hand on the ground and steady himself.

He saw the covered wagon twenty yards away, silhouetted against the faint glow from the campfire's remaining embers.

With all the considerable stealth at his command, Preacher moved toward the vehicle. The tailgate was raised and fastened in place. He paused beside it and listened intently. The sound of deep, somewhat irregular breathing came from inside. The wagon's interior was absolutely stygian. Preacher could tell someone was inside, but there was no way to be certain who it was.

Then as he listened, he heard the occupant let out a low moan. It was difficult to tell from such a sound, but he thought it came from Edgar Merton. Whoever it was shifted around and moaned again, as if in pain and trying to find a more comfortable position. That also made Preacher think it was Merton in the wagon.

He crouched and peered underneath the heavy vehicle. Men often slept underneath wagons when they were camped. Enough light from the coals filtered under this one for him to see that nobody was there.

Straightening, he listened to the man's breathing for a moment longer, then grasped the tailgate, put a foot on the wagon's frame, and pulled himself up and over. There was only one way to make sure the man was Edgar Merton.

He waited to see if there was any reaction from the sleeper. The man shifted again and muttered something. Preacher eased closer and drew his knife. He had been in situations like this many times before, drifting through the darkness like a phantom, knife in hand, but in those cases he had been bent on killing an enemy, not rescuing a friend. He let the sound of the man's breathing guide him as he weaved noiselessly through the supplies and other goods stored inside the wagon until he was kneeling beside the bunk where the man slept.

Still working by sound rather than sight, Preacher leaned closer and held out his left hand. When he felt warm breath brush against his palm, he dropped the hand and clamped it over the man's nose and mouth.

The sleeper came awake with a start but didn't try to fight or bolt up from the bunk. Preacher rested the tip of his knife against the man's throat and whispered, "Better listen close, mister, and do what I say. I'm gonna ask you a question, and then I'm gonna take this knife away so you can move your head. Are you Edgar Merton?"

Preacher pulled the blade back a little. The man on the bunk nodded rather weakly.

Of course, it was possible he was lying about his identity. Preacher rested the knife against the man's throat again and went on, "I'm gonna take my hand away from your mouth now so you can talk to me and convince me you're tellin' the truth. If you try any tricks, I can cut your throat from ear to ear before you even let out a squawk."

He kept the knife in place and lifted his hand. In a half sob, half whisper, the man said, "Preacher?"

"That's right."

"Oh, thank God, thank God." It was Edgar Merton's voice; Preacher was sure of that. "I was sure you and Hawk were dead. I was afraid . . . my son was, too, even though Ryker promised . . . that he would keep Oliver safe. Is . . . is Oliver all right?"

Preacher noted that Merton didn't say anything about Chessie. The man didn't sound like he was in good shape, though, so Preacher supposed he could be forgiven for not thinking about the girl. Merton's hoarse, hesitant words revealed the strain he had been under.

"Oliver's fine," Preacher said. "All four of us are. How bad are you hurt?"

"I . . . I don't know. I've been . . . blacking out. When Ryker said . . . we were going on without waiting for you and the others to get back . . . I argued with him, and he got angry. He hit me and told me . . . I was going to tell him my secret . . . and when I refused, he hit me again and again . . ."

An exhausted sigh came from Merton. Just talking a little had worn him out. But even though Preacher felt sorry for the man, there was more he had to know.

"You told him you wanted to go to a place in the Black Hills."

"Owayásuta . . . I had no choice. He would have killed me. But I was . . . stubborn and . . . wouldn't tell him anything else. He doesn't know . . . why we're going there."

Preacher would have liked to know that himself, but he didn't figure this was the time or place to try to convince Merton to tell him. The use of the Sioux name was proof that Merton really had been here in the past, though.

Preacher asked, "How come Ryker stopped and made camp here in the middle of the day?"

"I don't know . . . I blacked out again . . . for a long time."

Ryker knew where they were going but not exactly how to get there, Preacher thought. With Merton unconscious and unable to give him specific directions, Ryker had decided it was better to wait, rather than risk getting hopelessly lost in country unfamiliar to him.

"How bad are you hurt? Do you have any wounds?"

"My head . . . bled a lot . . . when Ryker

hit me. I haven't really felt right . . . ever since."

"But you can walk?"

"I don't know. I feel . . . awfully weak. I can . . . I can try, though. Are we going to . . . get out of here?"

"Not just yet," Preacher told him. "I hate to say it, but there ain't no way to get you out of here right now, Mr. Merton."

The man groaned softly.

"But that don't mean we won't come back for you," Preacher went on. "We'll figure out a way to get you loose from Ryker. You just got to hang on until then."

"All right," Merton said, although it sounded like it took quite an effort to get the words out. "Not . . . too much longer, though. I'm not sure . . . how much longer I can last . . ."

Preacher wasn't sure about that, either. He was determined to get father and son back together, though, and to see that Hoyt Ryker got what was coming to him for his treachery and brutality.

A second later, though, that determination hit a rough spot in the trail as a footstep sounded at the back of the wagon and a harsh voice demanded, "What's goin' on in there? Merton, who the hell are you talkin' to?"

CHAPTER 33

Preacher didn't recognize the voice. It didn't belong to Hoyt Ryker. More than likely, the guard who had been sitting over next to one of the supply wagons had heard him and Merton talking.

He tensed, his hand tightening on the knife's handle as he readied himself to whirl around and spring through the opening at the rear of the wagon. If he could kill the guard without *too* much commotion . . .

"Wha . . . what?" Merton said, sounding completely confused. "Is that you, Father? . . . No, I haven't seen Mother . . . Here's my little dog."

The man at the back of the wagon snorted contemptuously and muttered, "Bastard's out of his head and talkin' to himself. Ryker shouldn't have knocked him around so much."

Footsteps receded into the darkness.

Preacher let out a breath he hadn't realized he was holding. Edgar Merton fumbled at his arm in the darkness, caught hold of it, and squeezed it without much strength but hard enough to make Preacher aware the man knew what he was doing.

That had been a clever gambit on Merton's part. Preacher wouldn't have thought Merton was coherent enough to pull off the deception, but he had.

Leaning closer again, Preacher whispered, "That was quick thinkin', Merton. Now I've got to ask somethin' of you that you probably ain't gonna like."

"What do you . . . want me to do?" Merton asked.

"Cooperate with Ryker. Keep tellin' him how to get where he wants to go."

"If I . . . tell him everything . . . he won't need me anymore. He'll kill me!"

"Don't tell him what the secret is. Hold back enough to keep yourself safe. But as long as the bunch is camped here, we can't get you away from him. We need a better spot before we make our move."

For a long moment, Merton didn't say anything. Then he replied softly, "I understand. We have to . . . bide our time. It's . . . not easy."

"No, it ain't."

"I can't let him . . . have it. I worked . . .

too hard . . . waited . . . too long . . .”

Merton’s voice was just a breathy murmur now. Preacher figured he was on the verge of passing out again — or maybe just falling asleep. Natural sleep might be the best thing in the world for him right now. Preacher patted the older man’s shoulder in the darkness and told him, “Hang on, Edgar. We’ll get you out of this, and you and Oliver will be together again.”

“All for Oliver . . . Did it all for him . . .”

Merton was quiet then, but Preacher could still hear his faint breathing. Better to let him rest for now.

He wondered if Merton would remember any of this conversation in the morning. That beating Ryker had given him could have broken something in the man’s head. It was possible Merton might not ever be right again.

They would have to wait and see about that, Preacher told himself. Right now, his main concern was getting back out of the camp without being caught.

He went out the front of the wagon this time, keeping the vehicle between him and the guard. Once he was on the ground again, he dropped to hands and knees, then his belly, and began crawling toward the cliff. Reaching it without incident, he stood up and tried to make out the handholds and footholds he had used coming down. The mountain man could see in the dark almost as well as a cat, so after a moment he started up confidently.

The climb up took just as long as the one coming down. Finally, Preacher grasped the rim, pulled himself up and over the edge. He rolled away and was well clear before he stood up, because he didn't want his moving shape to blot out any of the stars if one of the men below happened to be awake and for some reason looked up.

It had been a successful foray into the enemy camp, and Preacher was relieved to have found Edgar Merton still alive. But at the same time, it was frustrating that he'd had to leave Merton behind as a prisoner. Merton had suffered greatly at Hoyt Ryker's hands, and while Preacher knew Ryker intended to keep Merton alive, Ryker's temper had gotten out of control before and might again at any time. It might not take much more abuse to finish off Merton.

They were another day, maybe a day and a half, from the narrow valley the Sioux called Owayásuta, with the twin gulches with their fast-flowing creeks running off to the west. Those gulches were choked with brush and dead trees, Preacher recalled from the last time he had passed through these parts. He had no idea why that spot was important to Edgar Merton, but it seemed to have a powerful hold on the man.

Preacher tried to recall if there was a good place between here and the expedition's destination where he and his companions could try to rescue Merton. He remembered a long ridge with a narrow cut through it that was the only way to get through without going a dozen miles east or west. If he and the others could get ahead of the wagons, they could set up a trap there. He, Hawk, and Oliver could leap from the cutbanks down onto the wagons and kill or knock out the drivers. That would swing the odds in their favor before Ryker and his men knew what was happening.

Those thoughts went through Preacher's head as he made his way back to the spot where he had left the others. By the time he got there, he had decided that the rough plan forming in his mind represented their best chance of saving Edgar Merton and dealing with the threat of Hoyt Ryker and his men.

Dog lifted his head and whined as Preacher stepped out of the trees. Hawk came lithely to his feet and told Oliver and Chessie, "Preacher is back."

Oliver scrambled up and asked anxiously, "Is he alive? Is my father all right?"

"He's alive," Preacher said. "I ain't sure you could say he's all right, though. He took quite a beatin' from Ryker."

Oliver cursed in bitter fury and said, "I'll kill that bastard. I swear I will."

"You may get a chance," Preacher told him. "I had to leave your pa with them. I didn't want to, but the shape he was in, there was no way I could get him out of that camp and up the cliff. I have an idea how we can get him back and deal with Ryker and his bunch, though."

"You mean kill them," Hawk said.

"I imagine it'll come to that, yeah."

"They've got it coming," Oliver said. "Tell me what he said. You did talk to him, didn't you?"

Preacher said, "Yeah, I did." He gave Oliver the highlights of the conversation. Chessie came to Oliver's side, and when Preacher talked about Ryker's abuse of Edgar Merton and how the older man was barely coherent, she slipped an arm around Oliver's waist and hugged him to comfort him.

"He may be in bad shape, but he still thought fast enough when he had to," Preacher went on, telling them about Merton's ploy when the guard came over to the wagon. "He's bound and determined to make it through this. Whatever he's after here in the Black Hills, he intends for you to have it, Oliver. He says he's done all of this for you."

"Risked his life and probably lost it, you mean." Oliver sounded bitter again. "We should have stayed back East. We were doing fine there. Nothing is worth what we've gone through on this expedition."

"If you had stayed in the East, Oliver," Chessie said quietly, "you and I never would have met."

"Well, that's true, I suppose." He put his arm around her shoulders. "And I wouldn't want that. I can't imagine not being with you, now that I've gotten to know you. I just wish things had turned out differently."

"That's my fault," Chessie said, sounding miserable now. "I'm the one who got your father involved with Ryker. I . . . I really didn't know what kind of man he was."

Preacher thought she sounded sincere. He could have told them all along that Hoyt Ryker was a snake, and had in fact tried to do so. But there was no point in dwelling on that now. They needed to deal with the situation the way it was, not the way they wished it might have been.

"Best get some more rest," he told the others. "We're gonna be movin' out as soon as there's enough light to see . . . and I don't need much light for that. We have to get in front of Ryker's bunch. I've got an idea about how we can jump them."

He gave them a quick summary of the plan that had formed in his head, and then they all turned in. Preacher knew where their enemies were, and it hadn't appeared that Ryker or any of his men would be budging from their camp tonight. It was possible some Sioux warriors could come along, but that was unlikely as well since they rarely entered the hills except for religious ceremonies. If they had seen Ryker's big campfire earlier, though, they might come to investigate and see who was interloping on sacred ground.

If any Indians came around, Dog would alert them, Preacher knew, so he rolled up in a blanket as well and fell asleep immediately, with the frontiersman's knack for that. He wouldn't need someone to rouse him. He had the knack for waking up whenever he wanted to, as well.

Because of that, when he opened his eyes and sat up sometime later, just the faintest tinge of gray lightened the eastern sky as the stars began to fade. Preacher got to his feet, touched Hawk lightly on the shoulder, and when the young man sprang up, also fully awake in an instant, Preacher said, "See to the horses. We'll be hittin' the trail in just a little while."

Hawk tended to the chore without saying anything. Preacher let Oliver and Chessie sleep a few minutes longer, then woke them as well. Both yawned in weariness. Emotionally, they were eager to pull ahead of Ryker and his men and get ready to rescue Oliver's father, but their bodies were still in a state of near exhaustion after everything they had gone through.

If they could hang on for a while longer, Preacher thought, maybe sooner or later there would be a chance for all of them to get some real rest. Until then they would just have to find the strength to go on.

Preacher was standing off to the side and gnawing on a small piece of jerky when Chessie came up to him. Quietly, so that Oliver and Hawk wouldn't overhear, she said, "You think I'm a terrible person, don't you?"

"After you risked your life to help me get away from those blasted outcasts, that ain't very likely."

"But I got us into this mess to start with by urging Mr. Merton to hire Ryker."

Preacher shrugged in the predawn gloom. "You said you didn't know what sort of fella he was. I ain't got any reason to believe you're lyin'."

"I had my suspicions," Chessie said, "but Hoyt could be so charming when he wanted to. I . . . I honestly didn't believe Oliver could ever be interested in . . . someone like me . . . at least seriously. I wanted to find out, but I thought that . . ."

"You thought you'd hedge your bet by playin' up to him and Ryker both," Preacher finished for her when her voice trailed off. "Plenty of women have done that in the past. I reckon men probably do it, too, sometimes. After all the grit you've showed, I ain't holdin' no grudges against you, Chessie, if that's what you're worried about."

"And what about Hawk? I can tell by the way he looks at me sometimes that he . . . he . . ."

The mountain man chuckled. "He's been smitten with you ever since he first laid eyes on you back in St. Louis. I reckon he knows you don't feel the same way about him, but that don't mean he has to like it. A man'd have to be damn lucky to have every gal he falls in love with during his lifetime feel the same way about him. That just ain't gonna happen. Sooner Hawk learns that lesson, the better."

"What about you, Preacher? Have all the women you've ever loved been in love with you, too?"

Preacher frowned. He wasn't sure he had actually been in love except for Jennie, all those years ago, and that had been a boy's love for the first girl he had known intimately. What he'd had with Hawk's mother, Bird in a Tree, might have turned into love if they had been together longer, but Preacher's fiddle-footedness had prompted him to move on even before he knew about the baby growing inside the young Absaroka woman. So he didn't have an answer for Chessie's question, and if he did, he probably wouldn't feel like sharing it.

"We need to get on the trail," he said, knowing that he sounded gruff. "Ryker ain't gonna wait around, and we got to get ahead of him if we're gonna have a chance to save Oliver's pa and ever find out what this whole blasted mess is about."

CHAPTER 34

Oliver and Chessie rode the two horses while Preacher, Hawk, and Dog ranged ahead on foot, finding the best route through the rugged terrain. Preacher swung to the east of the spot where Ryker's camp was located, giving it plenty of room. He figured that he and his companions had gotten started earlier than Ryker's bunch likely had, and they could move faster, too. Taking wagons through the mountains was a slow process.

By midmorning, Preacher believed it was safe to assume they were now ahead of the expedition. He angled back slightly to the northeast. That took them toward Owayásuta and also toward the long ridge where he planned to spring a trap on Hoyt Ryker and rescue Edgar Merton.

When he called a halt so they could rest, Oliver objected. "We should keep going," the young man said. "We can't afford to waste any time. The sooner we jump Ryker and his men, the sooner we can free my father."

"The rest is more for the horses than for you," Preacher said. "We're liable to need them. I hope we don't have anybody comin' after us, but if we do, your pa will have to ride. He ain't in shape to do anything else."

"I thought we were going to kill all of them."

"That's the plan . . . but plans have a way of not always workin' out."

When they started again, Hawk asked Oliver, "Are all white men as bloodthirsty as you?"

"Why don't you ask Preacher about that? He's white. And you're half-white, remember?"

Hawk shook his head. "Preacher may have been born white, but now he is just Preacher, not white or red or anything else. And I know nothing of that side of my own heritage. I was raised Absaroka. As far as I am concerned, they are my people, not anyone else."

"Well, I can't answer your question," Oliver said in a surly voice. "I just know I've got a score to settle with Hoyt Ryker, and any of his men who get in my way are going to regret it."

Preacher let that bit of bravado pass without responding to it. So far, with the one exception when he had fallen for Hopkins's trick, Oliver had come through and performed well when he needed to. With any luck, he would continue to do so.

By midafternoon, Preacher was able to point out the ridge. Beyond it, more of the thickly wooded mountains rose. Looking at them, Preacher spotted the pass above the little valley that was their ultimate destination.

"Once we've got your pa away from Ryker, it'll take us most of a day to get there," he explained to Oliver.

Hawk spoke up. "If we do not kill Ryker and all his men, the ones who are left alive will come after us."

"I don't doubt it," Preacher said with a nod. "But we'll stomp them snakes when we come to 'em."

Later, when they drew near the ridge, Preacher saw the cut that he remembered and led his companions toward it. It looked like someone had taken a giant knife and slashed through the ridge, leaving a narrow passage about a hundred yards long and barely wide enough for a wagon and a team of mules to pass through it.

Preacher walked through the cut first, followed by Oliver and Chessie leading the horses, with Hawk and Dog bringing up the rear. Once they were on the other side of the ridge, Preacher looked around and found a good spot for the horses in a clearing hidden by trees and brush.

"You'll have to stay here and keep an eye on them," he told Chessie. "The three of us will be up on those banks, waitin' to ambush Ryker. Hawk, you take the west bank. Oliver and me will be on the one to the east."

Oliver pressed one of the extra pistols they had gotten from the dead Hopkins and Brill into Chessie's hands. "It's loaded," he told her. "I'm not going to leave you here without some way to protect yourself."

"But don't use it unless you have to," Preacher added. "Sound carries a long way out here."

The banks on the sides of the cut were twenty feet tall, which meant the three men would be ten or twelve feet above the drivers when the wagons rattled through.

"You'll have to be careful timin' your jumps," Preacher went on to Hawk and Oliver. "If you miss it's liable to ruin everything."

"I will not miss," Hawk said confidently.

"Ryker has six men left, not countin' him. He'll probably be in the lead with one of the other men, and that leaves two to bring up the rear. We can't waste any time gettin' rid of the men on the wagons, because it won't take long for the rest of 'em to start shootin' at us. At that point it'll just be a matter of who's the better shot."

"I want to take the wagon that has my father in it," Oliver said.

Preacher shook his head. "No, that one will be in the lead. I'll take care of it and make sure it comes to a stop. Once it does, the other wagons can't keep goin', no matter whether you've dealt with the drivers or not. You'll take the middle wagon, Oliver, and Hawk, it'll be up to you to stop the third one."

That was the safest position for Oliver, Preacher thought, but it would expose his own son, Hawk, to the fire of the men riding behind the wagons. As for himself, once Ryker and the other man realized the wagons were under attack, they would whirl their horses around and charge back, more than likely with guns blazing.

He and Hawk would just have to be ready for that, the mountain man thought.

Preacher looked at the sky, saw the sun dropping toward the peaks in the west. There was a good chance the expedition wouldn't reach the ridge before darkness fell. Would Ryker stop and make camp again, or would he push on? Preacher thought it was unlikely Ryker would risk traveling at night. Even so, they had to be ready.

"We need to climb up onto those banks," he told Oliver and Hawk once Chessie and the horses were safely hidden in the trees. "It may be a long night, but we can't risk Ryker slippin' past us. The ridge is too steep to take wagons over it, but we shouldn't have any trouble gettin' up there."

"If I see or hear them coming," Hawk said, "should I signal with the call of a night bird?"

"That'll work. And I'll do the same. Come on, Oliver."

They parted ways, Preacher and Oliver heading for the ridge on the east side of the cut, Hawk on the west. Preacher could still see the young warrior as Hawk began to climb.

Oliver grunted and puffed some from the effort required to get to the top of the ridge, but he kept up fairly well. When they reached the top, he threw himself on the ground and lay there breathing heavily.

Preacher left the young man there and went to the other side of the ridge, which was topped with pines. The tree trunks provided plenty of cover as he stood there studying the landscape to the south.

As rough as the terrain was, he knew he might not be able to see the wagons and outriders until they were within half a mile of the ridge. That would give Preacher, Hawk, and Oliver time to get ready, but even more warning would be better.

After a while, Oliver came up behind him and asked, "Any sign of them?"

"Not yet," Preacher said. "You catch your breath?"

"I did," Oliver replied, sounding a little sheepish. "Sorry I got so winded. I guess I'm just not used to this rugged outdoor life yet."

"Six months ago, would you ever have dreamed you could do any of the things you've done in the past couple of weeks?"

"Good Lord, no! When I stop to think about it, I can still barely believe it."

"Folks are generally capable of a lot more than they think they are," Preacher said. "They just got to have a good enough reason. Before, you were out to save Chessie, then me, and now your pa. You ain't done any of it for yourself. I reckon that's a pretty good sign."

"I appreciate you saying that. I'll . . . try to live up to it."

Preacher lifted a hand and pointed. "Look yonder."

Oliver squinted, then shook his head and said, "I don't see anything."

"See those two trees stickin' up higher than the others around 'em?"

"Yes, I think so."

"Look right between 'em."

A note of excitement entered Oliver's voice as he said, "There's something moving on that slope rising behind them . . . Is that the wagons?"

"Yep. They're still more than a mile from here. As late in the day as it is, Ryker will probably stop and make camp before he gets here." Preacher did a birdcall, and when Hawk stepped out from the trees on the other side of the cut, Preacher pointed again. Hawk nodded to show that he understood and had already spotted the wagons himself. They all moved back into cover to watch for the approach of their enemies.

The sun had set but the western sky was still full of rosy light when the covered wagon came into view at the other side of the broad flat just south of the ridge. The two supply wagons followed it. All three vehicles stopped, and the men on horseback around them reined in. It looked like Ryker was going to make camp and wait until morning to venture through the cut, which was already cloaked in deep shadow. Things were playing out the way Preacher expected.

The three observers on the ridge watched as Ryker's men unhitched the mules and built a fire. Oliver said quietly, "This is difficult, knowing my father is over there in that wagon, only half a mile away, injured and needing my help."

"I know," Preacher said, "but your best chance for helpin' him is to wait until mornin' and jump that bunch like we planned."

Oliver nodded. "I understand that. But it's hard waiting."

"Bein' able to wait when you need to will go a long way toward keepin' you alive out here on the frontier."

Oliver fell silent. Preacher didn't think the youngster would be foolish enough to try anything on his own, but he figured he'd better keep a close eye on him anyway.

They still had some dried meat from the deer Hawk had brought down two days earlier. It was getting pretty tough and gamy by now but was better than nothing to gnaw on during the long night. Once Oliver was sound asleep, Preacher allowed himself to doze a little, knowing his sleep was light enough that he would wake up instantly if

Oliver moved or if Ryker did the unexpected and started through the cut during the night.

Neither of those things happened. When Oliver woke the next morning, stretched, yawned, and climbed to his feet, the sun was already up and so was Preacher. The mountain man stood in the shadows under the trees, watching Ryker's camp on the other side of the flats. He heard Oliver moving behind him and said without looking around, "I was just fixin' to wake you. Looks like that bunch is gettin' ready to break camp. They'll be comin' through here before too much longer. We'd best get ready."

Oliver looked in the direction of the clearing where they had left the girl, the horses, and Dog. "I wish I knew that Chessie made it through the night all right," he said.

"If there was any trouble, I reckon we would have known about it," Preacher said. "She would have fired that pistol. Gal's got a lot of grit. You'd probably do well to remember that if you're thinkin' about marryin' her one of these days."

"I never said that," Oliver replied, looking a little uncomfortable.

"Well, maybe you ought to give it some thought. Now, come on."

As they moved to the edge of the bank overlooking the cut, Preacher saw that Hawk was doing likewise on the other side. He pointed across the gap to the spot where Hawk should position himself, then did the same for Oliver. Both young men stretched out flat on the ground. As the wagons approached, the men with them wouldn't be able to see anyone on top of the ridge.

Preacher took his place. They still had some waiting to do, since it would take a while for Ryker and his men to break camp and arrive at the cut. Preacher looked over at Oliver, some twenty feet away from him, and could tell that the young man was nervous, probably a mixture of worry for his father and the knowledge that soon they would be fighting for their lives again.

Preacher was calm and he had a hunch Hawk was, too. Life on the frontier taught many lessons, and one of the most important was to not fear death too much. There were so many ways the frontier could kill someone, from hostile enemies to savage animals to brutal weather, that worrying about all of them would soon drive a man mad. The key was to live as brave and honorable a life as possible, to prepare for danger without seeking it out recklessly, and to be ready to fight to the last breath. Any man who could do those things had no real reason to fear death, because he had done all he could and the rest was up to a higher power. That was the way Preacher looked at it, anyway.

A short time later, he heard hoofbeats thudding and wagon wheels creaking. The vehicles were approaching the cut. He drew his tomahawk and gripped it in his left hand. His right hand was wrapped around the butt of a charged, primed, and double-shotted pistol. He planned to use the tomahawk on the driver, then bring down at least one of the outriders with the pistol.

The noises from the wagons grew louder and began to echo. That told Preacher the lead wagon had entered the cut. It rumbled on. The sun was high enough in the sky now that the air was starting to grow warm. Preacher felt a trickle of sweat on the back of his neck where the rays were shining.

Hawk and Oliver wouldn't make their moves until he made his. He knew they were watching him. He edged forward but not enough to look over the edge of the bank just yet. He continued to judge the wagons' progress by sound.

Hoofbeats went past, a quicker, lighter rataplan from the two men on horseback leading the way. The slower, heavier thuds of the mules' hooves hitting the ground came closer. Preacher risked a look. The team hitched to the lead wagon was passing just below him. Sitting on the driver's seat, swaying back and forth a little, was the gigantic Pidge.

Preacher's jaw tightened. Despite their initial clash back in St. Louis, Pidge had taken a liking to him after Preacher had patched up the wounds the giant had suffered in the battle with the Sioux. The mountain man hated to have to kill him now. But Pidge's first loyalty was probably to Hoyt Ryker, and Preacher couldn't allow himself to lose sight of the goal, which was to save Edgar Merton. At this point, there was nothing he could do except continue with the plan.

Those thoughts flashed through Preacher's brain in the couple of seconds it took for the mule team to move on and the front of the wagon to draw even with him. Preacher couldn't wait. Gripping the pistol and tomahawk, he came up on his knees, then surged to his feet and powered into a leap that carried him away from the bank and into the air as he dropped toward Pidge.

CHAPTER 35

The big man saw him coming and gaped up openmouthed at Preacher. Preacher's boots struck Pidge on the left shoulder. It was almost like trying to budge a redwood tree, but the impact was enough to knock Pidge to the right on the driver's seat. He slid off the seat and one knee went down to the floorboard.

"Preacher, wait!" Pidge bellowed in a voice like thunder as the tomahawk flashed up and started down.

No matter how long he lived, Preacher would never know for sure why he paused. Most times, when he launched a killing stroke nothing could hold it back.

But today, the tomahawk stopped before it fell all the way and split Pidge's skull. Then Pidge surged back up, slashed the reins against the mules' behinds, and roared at them. The team responded, bolting ahead against their harness. The wagon lurched heavily as it picked up speed, throwing Preacher back against the arched canvas cover.

A mad flurry of impressions followed. Pidge kept whipping and shouting at the mules. Preacher saw the two men on horseback ahead of them jerking their mounts to the side to avoid being knocked down and trampled. He caught a glimpse of Hoyt Ryker's face with its long, curling mustache. Ryker looked shocked to see Preacher alive, but his features were also flushed with rage as he flung up a pistol and fired.

Preacher felt the ball rip through the air close to his ear. The way he was being thrown back and forth by the careening wagon, any kind of accuracy was impossible, for him as well as for Ryker, but he jerked his pistol toward the man and pulled the trigger anyway. The weapon boomed and bucked in his fist.

Then they were past Ryker and the other rider, and Preacher had no idea if his shot had found its target. A particularly hard jolt made him lose his balance. He tumbled backward into the wagon bed.

"Preacher!"

That thin cry came from Edgar Merton. He was still alive, and that came as a relief to Preacher. The mountain man rolled over, caught a glimpse of Merton propped up on one elbow in the bunk, and scrambled on hands and knees to the back of the wagon so he could peer out at the other vehicles.

The first supply wagon, which was in the middle of the little caravan, had come to a stop, halting the wagon behind it as well. Oliver stood on the driver's box, struggling with the man who had been at the reins. As Preacher watched, unable to do anything, the man struck Oliver down and grabbed a pistol from behind his belt.

When a shot blasted, though, it came from the third wagon, where Hawk appeared to have taken care of his man. The pistol in the young warrior's hand gushed flame and smoke, and the man about to kill Oliver was thrown backward by a heavy ball smashing into his chest. That sent him crashing down onto the backs of the team hitched to that wagon.

Mules didn't spook easily, but the smell of powder smoke and blood, as well as the terrible racket from gunfire echoing in the cut, was enough to make these beasts stampede. They charged ahead, trampling the man who had fallen among their legs and making certain he was dead.

Oliver couldn't do anything except pull himself up on the seat and hang on for dear life as the runaway team followed the lead wagon out of the cut.

Behind him, Hawk had grabbed the reins of the third wagon and begun whipping the team. He ducked low as pistol balls fired by the trailing riders whistled overhead. From where Preacher was, he couldn't hear that, but he knew what was happening. So far, things hadn't gone exactly as they had planned, but he, Hawk, and Oliver were still alive and they had the wagons and Edgar Merton.

Ryker and at least three more men were also still alive, though, and that meant they were a long way from out of trouble. Plus there was Chessie to consider. They couldn't leave her behind to be captured by Ryker and his men, who were already giving chase.

Preacher went back to the front of the wagon, and as he knelt behind Pidge, he saw Chessie burst out from the trees where they had left her, riding one of the horses and leading the other. Dog raced along behind them.

Chessie must have been watching and seen what was happening. Preacher had to give her credit for realizing right away what she needed to do in order to salvage the situation. At the angle she was headed, she would intercept the wagons in another hundred yards.

Preacher drew his knife and leaned forward to say over the thunder of hoofbeats, "Pidge, does this mean you're throwin' in with us?"

Instead of answering the question directly, Pidge said, "Preacher, I was never so glad to see anybody in my life! I figured for sure you were dead!" He didn't take his eyes off the mules and the ground in front of the racing wagon as he spoke.

"Well, I ain't dead," Preacher replied, "and I'd sure be obliged right now if you'd give me a reason to trust you!"

"Haven't I already done that? Didn't I just help you rescue Mr. Merton?" The giant frowned and shook his head. "Hoyt never should've hurt Mr. Merton like he did. That wasn't right. There just weren't no call for it." Finally, Pidge glanced over his shoulder at Preacher. "And you tended to me when I was hurt. Maybe even saved my life."

"I'm glad you didn't make me hurt you, Pidge." Preacher didn't mention that things would have been simpler if he and his allies had been able to wipe out all of Ryker's bunch, as they had planned. Pidge's impulsive action had disrupted that and left living enemies behind them, so they weren't by any means out of danger.

Even so, Preacher was glad he hadn't stoved in the big fella's head.

Chessie drew alongside them with the galloping horses. Preacher climbed over the seat and stood on the box, clinging to the framework supporting the canvas cover as he looked at her. Her eyes were big with fear, but she wasn't panicking. She had the horse she was riding under control.

"You all right, girl?" Preacher called to her.

She nodded, then pointed behind them. "They're coming after us!"

"I know! Ride on ahead just a little!"

She looked confused by that order, but she did what Preacher told her and urged her mount to a faster pace that brought her alongside the mules.

That made the horse she was leading gallop along beside the driver's seat. Preacher leaned down and told Pidge, "Just keep headin' north! Mr. Merton knows where we're goin'!"

"Preacher, what are you gonna do?" Pidge asked.

"Try to buy us some time!"

With that, Preacher braced himself on the edge of the driver's box, then leaped from it into the saddle of the riderless horse. A jump like that had to be timed perfectly, and even when it was, it was dangerous. Preacher landed square in the saddle, though, and found the stirrups while he was grabbing the reins. Chessie let go of them.

He hauled back on the reins, slowing the animal and turning it as the other two wagons rolled toward him. They were well out of the cut now, in a stretch of rolling ground dotted with clumps of aspen. As Preacher looked back toward the ridge, the terrain made Ryker and the other pursuers pop into view for a second, then disappear again, only to repeat that pattern a moment later.

Preacher waited until the wagon Oliver was driving rattled past him, then heeled the horse into motion again and rode alongside the vehicle with Hawk at the reins. He brought the lunging horse closer and closer until he was able to kick his feet out of the stirrups and dive again, this time *from* horseback *onto* a wagon. He landed on the supplies in the back.

Preacher pulled himself forward and vaulted over the seat back onto the driver's box next to Hawk. "How are you, son?" he called over the noise.

"How are you?" Hawk repeated. "In the middle of all this chaos, this is what you ask?"

"Well, I want to know," Preacher replied with a grin. "You hurt?"

"No! I am fine! But why did you not kill the driver on the lead wagon?"

"Because it was Pidge, and he's decided that he's on our side. Besides, he turned on Ryker and took off too fast for me to do much about it. We'll just have to change our plan to suit the way things are now."

"This is mad! We should make a stand against Ryker and the other three."

"You're probably right," Preacher admitted, "but there'll be a lot of pistol and rifle balls flyin' around if we do that, and I ain't sure Oliver and Chessie can stay outta the way of all of them!"

Hawk didn't say anything to that, which was good because he needed to concentrate on his driving, not arguing. Preacher looked down and saw a rifle lying on the floorboard at their feet. It must have belonged to the man who had been driving the wagon — who was no doubt lying dead back there in the cut where Hawk had jumped him.

Preacher had powder and shot. He reached down, grabbed the rifle, and took a look at it. Already loaded and ready to fire, he saw. He turned and climbed back over the seat into the wagon bed, then knelt next to a crate of supplies. He aimed the rifle behind them and looped his thumb over the hammer to draw it back.

As soon as the four riders topped a swell and came into view again, Preacher pulled the trigger.

The rifle boomed. Through the cloud of smoke that came from the muzzle, Preacher couldn't see the men on horseback, and by the time the smoke cleared, they were gone, having dipped back down into another swale. He began reloading.

The range had been long, and a bouncing wagon was no place from which to be shooting. Any hit would be almost pure luck, and Preacher knew it. He wasn't counting on hitting any of the pursuers, though. He just wanted to make them aware that they were risking their necks by coming any closer to the fleeing wagons.

Preacher finished reloading and cocked the rifle again. He considered resting the barrel on some of the supplies, but his grip was steadier than that would have been.

The riders popped back up. Preacher pressed the trigger as soon as he saw their hats, aiming a little high and giving the ball time to travel before the targets were fully revealed.

This time the four men stayed in sight longer . . . long enough for Preacher to see one of them fling his arms out to the side and go over backward off his horse.

"Got one of the sons o' bitches!" the mountain man exclaimed.

He grinned as he saw the others slow down and veer away. The wagon went over the crest of a rise and he couldn't see them anymore, but that last glimpse had been enough to tell him that they weren't as interested in giving chase anymore.

He hoped the man he had shot out of the saddle was Hoyt Ryker. It would have been more satisfying to kill Ryker up close, but he would take that varmint being dead any way he could get it.

Hawk kept the wagon moving at a fast clip. Up ahead on the second wagon, Oliver had finally managed to retrieve the reins, but he wasn't doing much good at controlling the mules. Luckily, they continued to run the same way the other teams were going, as did the loose horse. Chessie still rode beside the lead wagon, Preacher saw when he glanced over his shoulder.

Most of his attention was focused behind them, though. He reloaded while waiting for the riders to show up again. When they didn't, he called to Hawk, "Looks like they gave up — for now!"

"You believe they will come after us?"

Hawk asked.

"Depends on whether or not Ryker's still alive. If he is, he's crazy-mad enough to keep comin'. If he ain't, the others might decide to cut their losses the way the Sioux and the outcasts did. Right now, though, we need to keep movin' and put as much ground between us and them as we can."

CHAPTER 36

The mules weren't tireless and couldn't keep running forever. Preacher let them continue at the same pace for another mile, then whooped and hollered until he got Oliver's attention and prompted the young man to look around. Preacher motioned for him to slow down.

Oliver shouted at Pidge to do likewise, and gradually all three vehicles slowed and finally came to a halt. Chessie had reined in as well. The loose horse stopped, too, its sides heaving and wet with sweat from the hard run. The same was true of all the other animals.

"Keep an eye out," Preacher told Hawk. Loaded rifle in hand, he jumped down and strode toward the lead wagon. Pidge was climbing down from the box when he got there. Preacher didn't exactly aim the rifle at the big man, but he kept it pointed in Pidge's general direction.

Pidge didn't miss that. He said, "You won't need that rifle, Preacher. I've cast my lot with you folks."

"Thing is, I still need convincin' that you'd do that."

Before Pidge could say anything else, Oliver hurried up to the wagon. "Is my father in there?" he asked.

"Oliver?" Merton called weakly from inside the vehicle. "Oliver, is that you?"

Oliver grabbed the tailgate, pulled himself up and over it. He said, "Thank God!" in a choked voice as he caught sight of his father in the bunk.

While that reunion was going on, Pidge nodded toward the wagon and said, "That's why, along with what I told you earlier. Mr. Merton treated me decent, and he's an old man. Hoyt shouldn't oughta beat on him like that." The giant scowled at the ground. "Reminded me too much of how folks used to beat on me when I was a younker, 'fore I got too big for 'em to do that. Hoyt used to treat me decent, too. He never called me dumb, like most folks. But when I saw what he done to Mr. Merton, I knew he only treated me nice 'cause he was scared of me. He might've done things like that to me, too, if he figured he could get away with it."

"I expect you're right about that."

Preacher tucked the rifle under his arm so that the barrel pointed at the ground now.

Chessie dismounted and came over to Preacher. "Are Oliver and Hawk all right?" she asked.

The mountain man nodded. "They're fine, as far as I know. Oliver's in there sayin' howdy to his pa."

"I know. I don't want to disturb them. Oliver's been so worried about his father . . ."

"Preacher!"

The cry came from inside the wagon. Preacher stepped on the front wheel on this side of the vehicle and climbed to the box. He leaned into the opening and said, "What is it, Oliver?"

"My father! He . . . he was talking to me, and then . . . he passed out! I can't tell if he's breathing!"

Preacher set the rifle on the seat and swung into the wagon bed. He dropped to a knee beside the bunk and rested a hand on Edgar Merton's chest. The older man's face was haggard and almost as pale as the white rag tied around his head as a makeshift bandage.

"He's breathin'," Preacher told Oliver after a few seconds. "You say he was talkin' to you when he passed out?"

"That's right. He seemed coherent enough —"

"Chances are, all the excitement was just too much for him. Just let him rest. He's hurt pretty bad, though, Oliver. I reckon you know that."

"Are you saying he's going to die?" Oliver asked as he glared at Preacher.

"Nope. That ain't for me to say. I'm no sawbones. But if he's gonna have a chance, we need to get somewhere we can fort up and he can get some real rest."

Preacher's calm words seemed to steady Oliver. The young man nodded and said, "You're right. As long as any of those bastards are still alive, there's a chance they'll come after us."

"If Ryker's still drawin' breath, I can guaran-damn-tee it."

"So where should we go?"

"The place we've been headin' for all along," Preacher said.

Preacher and Hawk stood guard while the mules and horses rested. Oliver and Chessie sat on the lowered tailgate of one of the supply wagons and talked quietly. Pidge volunteered to sit inside the covered wagon and keep an eye on Edgar Merton, in case the older man woke up and wanted anything.

"We are too out in the open here," Hawk said, scowling, as he and Preacher intently scanned the surrounding landscape in all directions. "There is little cover."

"I know that, but we won't be stayin' here long," Preacher said. "Just long enough for the animals to recover a mite from that run. Then we'll push on and try to make it to Owayásuta by the end of the day. If we can, Ryker'll have a hard time rootin' us out of there." The mountain man paused. "And then maybe we can find out what's so all-fired important that Merton had to get back there after all this time."

Hawk shrugged, never taking his keen eyes off the landscape as he searched for any sign of danger. "If you killed one of the men following us, the odds are even now. Actually, they are in our favor if you count Pidge and Chessie."

"I believe Pidge is tellin' the truth about throwin' in with us. And I reckon you got to count Chessie, the way she's done her part. Her and Oliver have both growed up a lot on this trip."

"Yes," Hawk said quietly. "Despite the differences in their backgrounds, the two of them . . . fit well together."

Preacher heard the grudging acceptance in his son's voice. Hawk knew that Oliver and Chessie were going to be together — if they both survived — and there was nothing he could do about it. He didn't seem to be too upset about that realization, either.

Edgar Merton still hadn't regained consciousness when Preacher announced a while later that it was time for them to get moving again. Pidge, Oliver, and Hawk took the reins on the wagons while Preacher swung up into the saddle on the second horse. He wished he knew what had happened to his gray stallion, but for now he had to worry about saving the lives of his companions.

He told Chessie, who was already mounted, "You're gonna be scoutin' for us while Dog and me bring up the rear and watch our back trail. Think you can handle that?"

Chessie looked nervous but nodded without hesitation. "I can do it," she said, "but I don't really know where I'm going."

Preacher pointed to the pass that was visible in the distance. "Keep your eye on that," he said. "Head toward it as straight as you can. You may have to veer off now and then on account of the terrain, but get back on course as soon as you can. Pidge, you follow Miss Chessie, hear?"

"I will, Preacher," the big man said. "You

can count on me."

Preacher nodded and said, "I know that." The mountain man's confidence made Pidge beam.

The group resumed the trek deeper into the Black Hills. Preacher was a little worried about the way Edgar Merton still hadn't regained consciousness after passing out. As the day went on, Merton remained unresponsive and barely breathing, which made Preacher wonder if he was going to slip away over the divide without ever waking up again. That would be hard on Oliver, but although the circumstances always varied, that final journey was something everyone had to face sooner or later, first with their loved ones and then for themselves . . .

The longer they traveled without any sign of pursuit, the more hopeful Preacher was that his rifle shot had killed Ryker and the other men had abandoned the chase and turned back. He wasn't ready to believe that just yet, but he could sure as hell hope. The miles fell behind them, and in the middle of the afternoon they began the long climb to the pass. Their progress slowed to a crawl because the mules were already tired and the slope was steep. Preacher didn't want night to catch them still climbing. It would be better if they could at least reach the pass before having to stop.

He had reined in and turned his mount to look back down the wooded slope at where they had come from, with Dog standing and panting beside him, when a tiny flicker of movement caught his eye. Preacher squinted. Could have been a bird flitting from branch to branch, he told himself, or some other small animal moving around, but then the lowering sun glinted off something for the briefest of seconds before the reflection was gone.

That was enough.

"Damn it," Preacher said, quiet but heartfelt. Beside him, Dog growled. The mountain man glanced at the big cur. "They're too far away for you to smell 'em, but I reckon you can sense 'em anyway. We got skunks on our trail . . . the two-legged kind."

He turned and rode until he caught up with the third wagon. "They're still back there," he told Hawk. "More than a mile behind us, but they'll make that up pretty quick, as slow as we're havin' to travel now."

"Should we stop and fight them?"

Preacher peered up the slope and frowned in thought. After a moment, he shook his head.

"No, we'll keep goin'. This ain't the place

to make a stand. If we can get over the pass and into the valley, that'll be better."

Hawk nodded and slapped the reins against the team. The tired mules continued plodding up the hill.

Preacher rode on ahead to give the news of the pursuit to Oliver and Pidge, both of whom accepted it with grim-faced nods. Deep down, they hadn't really expected anything else. Then Preacher dropped back again to make sure they weren't taken by surprise.

The shadows cast by the trees were long by the time Chessie galloped back to announce excitedly, "The pass is just ahead. We're almost there." She waved at Preacher, who returned the wave and motioned the wagons on.

The sun had dipped below the peaks to the west when the wagons pulled into the pass. Huge, boulder-strewn, misshapen ridges rose on either side, but the trail between them was level and grassy. It dropped almost immediately into the valley beyond, which was already dark and gloomy at this time of day. Preacher called for the wagons to halt and loped his mount up beside them.

He looked to the west and saw the dark mouths of the two gulches where the creeks emerged to flow together into one stream meandering eastward through the valley. This was Owayásuta, the place of confirmation.

The trail down was steep, but not as bad as the one ascending to the pass. The valley was narrow and heavily wooded. If they were able to ford the creek, they could find a place that backed up to the almost-perpendicular slope on the other side, fell some trees with the axes that were in the supply wagons, and literally fort up behind a log breastwork. From there they would be able to command a field of fire both ways along the creek so their pursuers wouldn't be able to flank them but instead would have to come at them from the front. They could fill their water barrels from the creek, but food might be a problem if Ryker decided to lay siege to them.

Preacher ran all that through his mind, then said, "It'll be dark soon, but we need to keep movin'. We'll have to risk travelin' when we can't see very good. Chessie, you stay with the wagons now. I'll go on ahead. Pidge, you keep your eye right on me."

"I sure will, Preacher," the big man said.

If Preacher had been mounted on Horse, he wouldn't have worried about the big stallion being able to pick the best path down into the valley. He didn't have that sort of trust in the animal he was riding, although so far it seemed to be a good mount. As the shadows thickened, the mountain man relied on his keen eyesight and instincts to find a trail the wagons could handle.

Night had fallen by the time the group reached the valley floor and the creek that ran through it. The wagons came to a halt while Preacher explored the stream in search of a place they could ford. Several times he put the horse into the water, only to turn back when it became too deep. Finally, he located a spot where the creek was shallow enough, and the bed rocky enough, that the wagons could cross without either floating away or bogging down.

Preacher waited until the wagons were across, then dismounted and went scouting on foot for a place they would be able to defend. While he was gone, Oliver and Pidge would fill the water barrels while Hawk and Dog stood guard. Preacher believed they still had a little time before the pursuers could catch up, but it never hurt to take precautions.

It didn't take him long to come across a steep bluff that was too sheer and featureless for anyone to climb down it, so no one could attack them from behind. Two rocky promontories shouldered out from it, with a space about forty feet wide between them. Preacher went back to the others, led the wagons there, and pointed to some nearby trees.

"We'll have to fell those by starlight and build a wall with logs across that opening. Once we do that, it'll be hard for anybody to get to us, especially once the sun comes up. Pidge, fetch some axes from the wagons, and we'll start choppin'."

"I can do that, Preacher," the giant said. "I been choppin' down trees my whole life. You and Mr. Oliver and Mr. Hawk can get some rest. I don't need none."

"We'll all pitch in," Preacher said. "How many axes are there?"

"Three, I reckon."

"Then we can switch back and forth, and one man will always be restin'."

Pidge thought about that, then his massive shoulders went up and down in a shrug. "I guess that would be all right," he said.

Soon the night rang with the sound of ax blades biting deep into tree trunks. Once the trees were felled and the larger branches trimmed off, Pidge dragged them into place and arranged them to form a crude wall. He seemed as tireless as a steam engine, and he handled the heavy logs like they were child's toys.

As the moon rose, Preacher studied what they were doing and decided that while the fortification wouldn't hold off an army, or even a large group of determined men, it ought to be enough to stop three or four men, however many were left.

While Preacher and the others were working, Chessie watched over Edgar Merton. They built the log wall eight feet tall, with the gaps where the trunks were pieced together serving as natural loopholes for their rifles. It was well after midnight now, Preacher judged. In a few more hours the eastern sky would begin to turn gray with the approach of dawn.

"Oliver!" Chessie called from the wagon. "Your father's awake!"

Oliver dropped the ax he was still holding and ran toward the covered wagon. Preacher, Hawk, and Pidge followed at a slower pace. Oliver grabbed the tailgate and hauled himself inside. By the time Preacher and the others reached the wagon, the young man was kneeling beside the bunk and had caught hold of his father's right hand with both of his.

"I'm right here, Father," Oliver said. The shadows inside the wagon were so thick Merton might not be able to see him. "I'm here. How do you feel?"

"Very . . . tired." Preacher heard Merton's rasping whisper from where he stood with Hawk and Pidge at the rear of the wagon. "I think I'm about . . . done for, Oliver."

"Don't say that. You're going to be fine."

"No . . . I won't. Ryker . . . broke something . . . inside me. Getting harder to breathe . . . to think . . . so I want you to know . . . why we came here . . ."

Preacher leaned forward. He wanted to know that, too.

"Gold," Edgar Merton said.

Chapter 37

"Gold?" Oliver repeated.

"That's . . . right. Years ago . . . when I was trapping in these parts . . . I ran into some Indians . . . who chased me into this valley. I was able to . . . fight them off . . . but while I was here . . . I found a nugget that was . . . almost pure gold. It must have . . . washed down the creek . . . from one of those gulches."

"That's why you wanted to come back here? Because of the gold?"

"There could be . . . a fortune up those gulches, son."

"But you're already a success!" Oliver protested. "You've made plenty of money."

"Yes, but . . . it's *gold.*"

Preacher heard that note in Merton's voice and knew what it meant. Sometimes, the desire a man felt for something could become more important than the thing itself. He had never spent much time around men who went searching for precious metal, but he knew the hunt could take hold of them with a lust even stronger than what any man had ever felt for a woman.

"I want you . . . to have it, son," Merton went on. "It's all for you. You'll be . . . as rich as Midas! You can . . . see for yourself. I have it . . . the nugget . . . kept it all these years . . . it's in my pack. When you . . . hold it in your hand . . . you'll understand."

The older man let out a long sigh, which caused Oliver to exclaim anxiously, "Father! Father!"

Quietly, Chessie said, "Let me see . . . he's still breathing, Oliver. He's sleeping again."

"Passed out, you mean," Oliver said. "He used up all his strength spinning some foolish yarn about gold."

Preacher said, "It didn't seem foolish to him. A man can't always help what's important to him. A thing'll get under his skin and gnaw away at him for years, and there ain't a blamed thing he can do to change it." The mountain man grunted and shook his head, then went on, "Of course, if he ever gets his hands on whatever it is, a lot of the time he finds that it ain't anything like what he figured it'd be."

Chessie said, "I'll watch him, Oliver, and

let you know right away if he wakes up again."

Oliver sighed. "All right. We still have to worry about Ryker and his men, after all." He moved to the rear of the wagon and climbed out, dropping to the ground beside Preacher, Hawk, and Pidge. "Shouldn't someone be standing guard?"

"Dog would've let us know if anybody was skulkin' around," Preacher said. "But we'd best get back to that wall and get ready for trouble. It'll be here soon enough."

They had enough rifles now so that every man was armed with one as they took their positions at the barricade, and loaded extra weapons were leaned against the log wall. There was plenty of powder and shot in the wagons, and enough food to last for a week or more. Without being able to get out and hunt for game to stretch those rations, though, they might run short if Ryker and the others kept them bottled up in here for too long. They could make their water last longer, but sooner or later that would be a problem, too.

The solution, Preacher mused, would be to make Ryker and his allies reveal themselves.

Then Preacher and Hawk could go out and kill them.

"I hate waiting like this," Oliver said after a while. "Do you ever get to where it doesn't bother you?"

"You get used to it," Preacher said. "I ain't sure you ever get to where you don't feel it, though. A man never knows what life's got in store for him, but most of the time he's too busy to worry about bein' uncertain. When you're just standin' around, though, and you know folks are on their way to try to kill you . . . hard not to think about that."

More time dragged past. The sky began to lighten in the east. Pidge gave a prodigious yawn, then apologized for it.

"I'm not sleepy, Preacher," he insisted. "I swear it."

"It's fine if you are, Pidge," the mountain man assured him. "I reckon we're all a mite worn out by now."

Oliver said abruptly, "I'm not sure what my father thought I was going to do. I'm not a miner. I wouldn't know how to go about finding gold, even if there's really any around here. What do you think about that? Have you ever heard of anyone finding gold in this area?"

Preacher didn't have to answer that, because the next instant, another sound came clearly through the night and made all four men catch their breath as their muscles stiffened in surprise.

Somewhere not too far away, a man had started screaming in agony.

"What the hell!" Oliver said.

"I don't like that sound," Pidge said. "It scares me, Preacher!"

"It ain't good," Preacher agreed.

The screaming continued, but it was punctuated suddenly by a pair of gunshots. Preacher put his eye to one of the gaps between the logs and peered across the creek at the woods on the far bank. The shadows were still thick under the trees. Another shot blasted, and this time he caught a glimpse of an orange spurt of muzzle flame.

A moment later, a man burst out of the trees and ran toward the creek as if all the devils of hell were after him.

They might as well have been. Twisted gray shapes bounded out of the forest almost on the heels of the fleeing man. Preacher's teeth ground together in anger. He had believed they'd left those varmints far behind them.

"Outcasts!" Hawk said. He was looking through another gap, as were Oliver and Pidge.

"That's Hoyt they're chasin'!" Pidge yelled.

It was true. Enough predawn light had seeped into the heavens for Preacher to be able to make out Hoyt Ryker's tall form as the man ran for his life with half a dozen outcasts right behind him.

"Ryker!" Preacher bellowed. "Over here!"

Ryker splashed across the creek, water flying high around him, and veered toward the log barricade.

"Pepper those little bastards with lead!" Preacher ordered. "Slow 'em down or he won't make it!"

As much as he hated Hoyt Ryker, the idea of not offering sanctuary to the man never crossed Preacher's mind. As long as there was a chance of Ryker reaching safety, Preacher couldn't stand there and watch him being torn to shreds by the animal-like creatures that had once been human. He wondered fleetingly how many of the outcasts had followed them all the way up here in search of their primitive vengeance. More than the ones who were chasing Ryker, because more men were screaming in the gloom now, and Preacher knew that a terrible fate had befallen Ryker's companions.

A volley of shots rang out from the men behind the logs. Rifle balls raked through the group of outcasts and knocked three of them off their feet. Another stumbled but managed to stay upright. Preacher lowered his empty rifle and stuck a pistol through the gap. It boomed and cut down another of the outcasts. This time the remaining two retreated.

They had come almost within grabbing distance of Ryker, but now he was able to dash to the barricade and start climbing it. A tomahawk flew through the air and struck only a foot to his right, sticking in the log. Ryker hauled himself up and over and fell inside the makeshift fort, safe for the moment . . . but only for the moment.

Because a great howling came from the woods on the other side of the creek as the screaming of the white men fell eerily silent. The outcasts still wanted blood, and this was the only place they could get it.

None of the creatures were in sight at the moment except the ones who had been killed or badly wounded. Those four were sprawled on the ground between the creek and the barricade. Preacher said, "Get all the guns reloaded you can. Ain't no tellin' how long we've got before the rest of 'em come stormin' up here."

He stalked over to Ryker, who still lay on his back, gasping for breath after his mad dash across the creek. Ryker froze, though, as Preacher laid the keen edge of a knife across his throat.

"What happened out there?" the mountain man asked.

"Those . . . those maniacs must have been following us all along," Ryker said. "We didn't know . . . they were anywhere around. They had the others . . . before I could do anything to help them."

Preacher didn't know whether to believe that — he thought it was more likely Ryker had run for his life as soon as he realized they were in danger — but he supposed it didn't matter now.

"Step aside, Preacher," Oliver Merton said. "I'm going to kill him."

Oliver held a pistol pointing down toward Ryker. Preacher shook his head and said, "No, you ain't. I don't like the son of a bitch any more'n you do, but he can pull a trigger and that's what we need right now."

"That's right," Ryker agreed immediately. "You fellas saved my life. Any problems between us are over. I'll never cause trouble for you again. I give you my word on that."

Preacher for sure didn't believe *that.* Ryker's word was worth less than a big pile of grizzly droppings. He would betray them again as soon as he believed it was safe to do so.

That would be dealt with when the time

came. Right now, the outcasts represented a bigger threat. Preacher took the knife away from Ryker's throat and said, "I'll have one eye on you the whole time. Do anything that looks the least bit funny, and I'll kill you right away without ever askin' any questions."

"You don't have to worry —" Ryker began.

From the barricade, where he was watching the creek, Pidge yelled, "Better give him a gun, Preacher. Here they come!"

Preacher grabbed one of the extra pistols and shoved it into Ryker's hand. "Make your shots count!"

Preacher turned back to the barricade as Ryker sprang up. He thrust a rifle barrel through the gap and saw at least two dozen outcasts charging toward the barricade. They were running straight into a deadly storm of lead, but that probably never occurred to them. Their minds were too full of their killing frenzy to be rational.

The first volley of shots ripped through the attackers. Several went down as blood flew in the air. In the predawn light, it was black instead of crimson as it splattered across the bodies of the outcasts who ran behind the wounded men. That carnage blunted the charge, but only for an instant.

That delay, brief though it was, gave Preacher time to drop the empty rifle and snatch up a loaded one. The outcasts had just reached the creek as more shots rang out, this time in a ragged fashion. Preacher saw the man he had targeted double over as the rifle ball punched into his midsection. The mortally wounded outcast pitched forward into the creek.

More were down in the stream, some of them still alive and thrashing in their agony, sending sprays of water high in the air. Hawk blasted the first man across the creek, the rifle ball to the chest throwing him backward as his arms and legs flung out wildly before he splashed down on his back.

But for every outcast that fell, it seemed that two more took his place. An apparently endless horde poured out of the woods. In moments all the guns would be empty, and there wouldn't be time to reload.

Oliver's face was already grimy from powder smoke as he panted, "I have to go protect Chessie and my father!"

"The best way you can protect 'em is to stop those bastards right here!" Preacher told him. When they had finished cutting down the trees to form the barricade, they had leaned the axes against the logs. "Grab one o' those axes!"

Preacher snatched up one of the long-handled tools and swung it just as the first of the outcasts scrambled up the front of the barricade and sprang over. The ax head swept under the creature's chin and sheared right through his neck, causing his head to pop up into the air while his body flopped lifelessly to the ground with blood fountaining from the decapitating wound. Preacher let the swing's momentum carry the ax around and back up, and when it came down again it split the skull of another outcast like a man chopping open a pumpkin.

Hawk and Oliver had axes as well and flailed around them as more of the outcasts bounded over the wall. If the defenders had been fighting with knives and tomahawks, they might have been overrun and pulled down. The longer axes kept the outcasts somewhat at bay, though.

As the outcasts swarmed around Pidge, he bellowed and caught one of them by the neck with one hand. He shook the man and snapped his spine like a dog snapping the neck of a rat. Then Pidge literally *tossed* the dead man up in the air, caught hold of his ankles, and waded into the others, swinging the corpse like a gigantic club. He mowed down half a dozen men with his first swing, then did it again. He stomped into the middle of them, knocking them right and left, cracking skulls every time his massive, booted feet came crashing down.

Dog was in the middle of the melee, too, snarling and slashing with his razor-sharp teeth, hamstringing the creatures and then ripping their throats open when they fell.

Preacher had fought battles like this before, bloody contests where he was vastly outnumbered and the sleeves of his buckskin shirt were smeared with blood to the elbows. Each time he had figured he was going to die, so he might as well fight to the last breath and take as many of the enemy with him as he could. And each time, through some providence, he had survived.

So far.

Today looked like the day his luck was finally going to run out. There were just too many of the outcasts, and they were being driven on by the screeches of a gnarled older man who had jumped on top of the barricade and balanced there. Preacher caught a glimpse of him through the fighting, and for one bizarre instant, it appeared that the man had two heads, one sitting on top of the other.

As a matter of fact, the outcast had fashioned a grisly headdress out of a human skull, small enough that it could have belonged to a child. Rage welled up inside Preacher at the thought. He didn't know if the outcasts had medicine men like the other tribes did, but there was a good chance they did, and that ugly varmint had to be one. Preacher had seen in the past how a tribe's medicine man could work the warriors up into an unthinking, murderous frenzy. He had a hunch that was what was going on here, and without thinking more about it, he acted, drawing back the ax and letting it fly.

Throwing an ax was a different skill from throwing a tomahawk or knife, but Preacher had mastered just about every way there was to kill on the frontier. The ax revolved in midair and the head came around to smack cleanly into the medicine man's breastbone, splitting it wide open. The ax head lodged there as blood gushed from the wound. The medicine man's eyes opened wide. He screeched again, but this time in mortal agony. The eyes of all the outcasts turned toward him as he swayed on the barricade.

That gave Hawk, Oliver, and Pidge the chance to kill even more of them. Then the medicine man's bulging eyes rolled up in their sockets and he toppled backward off the logs.

The other outcasts wailed and began trying to flee. The older man's death meant their medicine had turned bad. All they wanted now was to get away from these accursed white men. Hawk and Oliver chopped down a couple more of them with the axes, and Pidge wrung another pair of necks.

Then the surviving outcasts were over the wall and moving so fast across the creek and away from there that Preacher knew they would never come back to this scene of ignominious defeat.

All four defenders were so splattered with blood it was difficult to tell if any of them were seriously wounded. Preacher was about to ask if anybody was hurt when another scream ripped through the air. This one came from the direction of the wagon. Preacher whirled around and looked for Hoyt Ryker. There was no sign of the man.

But Preacher knew he hadn't gone far. That was Chessie who had screamed, and the mountain man knew Ryker had to be in the wagon.

CHAPTER 38

"Chessie!" Oliver cried. He ran toward the wagon, limping as he did so because he had sustained a wound in his right thigh during the battle with the outcasts. He had taken only a few steps, though, when Hoyt Ryker appeared in the opening at the back of the wagon, his left arm tight around Chessie's throat and a knife held to her chest, the blade poised to plunge into her heart.

"Stay back!" Ryker yelled. "I don't want to kill her, but I will if I have to."

Preacher said, "You gave me your word, Ryker."

The man grinned over Chessie's shoulder. "You should've known better than to believe that, Preacher."

"Oh, I knew better, all right," the mountain man said. "I figured you'd double-cross us as soon as you got the chance. I didn't figure it'd come quite this quick, but them damn outcasts gave you a pretty good distraction, didn't they?"

"That's right, and I'm finally going to find out why we're all here. I want to know what's so important about this place. Merton must have told you by now. Spill it, and I'll let the girl live."

"What about the rest of us?" Hawk asked. "Will we live as well?"

Ryker smirked. "Well, now, that's going to be a little bit more of a problem . . ."

Pidge strode forward. "Hoyt, you shouldn't be doin' this," he said. "I thought you was a good man, the way you treated me at first."

"That's your problem, you big, dumb ox."

Pidge frowned and clenched his hamlike hands into fists. "You shouldn't ought to talk like that to me," he said as he took another step forward. "I don't like it."

"Stop right there!" Ryker ordered. "Unless you want me to gut this girl right in front of your eyes."

"Stay back, Pidge," Preacher told the giant. The sun still wasn't up, but there was enough light for him to see dimly into the wagon, behind Chessie and Ryker. He had just spotted some movement there. He didn't think any of the outcasts had made it as far as the wagons, so that left only one person who could be stirring inside the vehicle . . .

Edgar Merton stepped up behind Ryker, pressed a small pistol to the back of the man's head, and said, "Drop that knife, Ryker . . . or I . . . I'll blow your brains out."

Ryker had stiffened at the unexpected touch of the gun, but now he grinned again and said, "I thought you were either out cold or dead, Merton. I sure as hell didn't think you had the strength to get up."

"A man can . . . find the strength . . . when he needs to."

"The hell he can. I'll bet you can't even pull that trigger. You're going to pass out before you ever get the chance —"

Ryker moved suddenly, twisting toward Merton, letting go of Chessie as he jerked away from the gun and swung the knife at Merton's belly. Merton screamed as the blade sunk into flesh. The pistol sagged in his hand.

But it was still pointed toward Ryker's chest when he pulled the trigger.

The close-range blast knocked Ryker back into Chessie. Both of them toppled over the tailgate, followed by Merton. All three sprawled on the ground at the rear of the wagon as Oliver cried, "Chessie! Father!" and dashed forward.

Ryker had dropped the knife when he was shot, but it was lying on the ground next to him. He reached for it, but Preacher's boot came down first on Ryker's wrist and pinned his hand to the ground. Blood bubbled from Ryker's chest wound as he gazed up at Preacher. The color was draining rapidly from his face. He struggled to form words and finally gasped, "At least tell me . . . what it was all about . . ."

"Ask the Devil when you get to hell," Preacher said, then watched without expression as the life faded from Hoyt Ryker's eyes.

A few feet away, Chessie babbled, "I'm all right, I'm all right," as Oliver tried to help her sit up. "See to your father!"

That wasn't going to do any good, no matter what any of them did, Preacher knew. That slash from Ryker's knife had opened up Edgar Merton's belly. There was a good chance he never would have made it back to civilization alive, but now death was only moments away.

"Ol . . . Oliver," he said, groping upward with a hand.

Oliver scrambled over and caught hold of it. "I'm here, Father," he said, struggling to hold back sobs. "Hang on —"

"Oh no," Merton whispered. "I'm not . . .

going to make it. But at least . . . I can die knowing . . . you found . . . two treasures . . . the gold . . . and that . . . young woman . . ."

The long, rattling sigh that came from Merton's throat told Preacher the man was gone.

Oliver bent over his father's body and cried unashamedly. Chessie knelt beside him and put an arm around his shoulders to comfort him. Preacher, Hawk, and Pidge stood well aside so as not to intrude on the young man's grief.

"I believe I am glad that Chessie made the decision she did," Hawk said quietly to Preacher. "Oliver needs her more than I ever will. I have what I need."

"What's that?" Preacher said.

Hawk lifted a hand and made a small but eloquent gesture to indicate the Black Hills that surrounded them. "The frontier," he said. "My home."

By the middle of the day, they had laid Edgar Merton to rest here in this valley that had haunted his hopes and dreams ever since his first visit many years earlier. Pidge insisted that they bury Hoyt Ryker as well.

"He was a bad man," Pidge said with the simplicity Preacher had come to appreciate, "but there were times when he was good to me."

"And that's reason enough," Preacher agreed.

The outcasts would lie where they had fallen, and in time it would be as if they had never brought their madness into this lush wilderness.

Preacher, Hawk, and Pidge had taken down the barricade as well, so the wagons could be driven out of here. As they were getting ready to go, Oliver came over to Preacher and held out his hand.

"I found this in my father's belongings, like he said."

Preacher looked down at the object lying in Oliver's palm, a rough, mostly dull chunk of rock with brighter streaks in it. He grunted in surprise.

"It's gold, isn't it?" Oliver said.

"Well . . . in a way," the mountain man replied. "That there is a chunk of what some folks call fool's gold, 'cause people look at it and mistake it for the real thing."

Oliver stared at him for several seconds before asking, "You mean it's worthless?"

"Pretty much."

Oliver looked like he didn't know whether to laugh or cry. He settled for laughing, but there was pain in his voice as he said, "That means this whole horrible business was for nothing, doesn't it? My father spent years dreaming a dream that was false."

"He made a mistake," Preacher said. "Everybody does. But at least he died thinkin' he'd done a good thing, and that's somethin' to be thankful for." He looked over to the wagon where Chessie was petting one of the mules and talking to Pidge. As the girl laughed, Preacher said, "Anyway, your pa told you you had two treasures now, and he was half-right. That's pretty good, considerin' some folks never find even one."

A short time later, when they were ready to pull out, Preacher suddenly lifted his head and said to Hawk, "Listen."

"To what?" the young warrior asked.

"Thought I heard a horse . . ."

A gray, rangy form came high-stepping out of the trees on the other side of the creek, lifted his head, and whinnied a greeting. Dog barked and bounded across the stream to run around and around his old friend, who had been lost for days now.

"Horse!" Preacher said. "He must've been trailin' Ryker and the others the whole way." He hurried across the creek and rubbed Horse's neck while the stallion bumped his nose against the mountain man's shoulder. It was a touching reunion for the three trail partners.

When what was left of the expedition headed south, Preacher was mounted on Horse again, with Hawk riding beside him and Oliver, Chessie, and Pidge driving the wagons. All of the men had suffered minor wounds in the final battle with the outcasts, but nothing that would keep them from putting these dark, bloody hills behind them as soon as possible.

"I think I have seen enough of the white man's world," Hawk said as they rode ahead of the wagons. "We brought it back with us from St. Louis, and it fouled this land. Next time you go there, you go without me."

"Your choice," Preacher told him. "Anyway, we got to hunt up White Buffalo. I'm sure he'd be happy to have you around for a while."

"So there is no gold in the Black Hills," Hawk said, looking around. "Only the gold of fools."

"Well," Preacher replied, "I didn't exactly say *that.*"

ABOUT THE AUTHORS

William W. Johnstone is the *New York Times* and *USA Today* bestselling author of over 300 books, including the series The Mountain Man; Preacher, The First Mountain Man; MacCallister; Luke Jensen, Bounty Hunter; Flintlock; Those Jensen Boys; The Frontiersman; Savage Texas; The Kerrigans; and Will Tanner: Deputy U.S. Marshal. His thrillers include *Black Friday, Tyranny, Stand Your Ground,* and *The Doomsday Bunker.* Visit his website at www.williamjohnstone.net or email him at dogcia2006@aol.com.

Being the all-around assistant, typist, researcher, and fact checker to one of the most popular western authors of all time, **J. A. Johnstone** learned from the master, Uncle William W. Johnstone. William began tutoring J.A. at an early age. After-school hours were often spent retyping manuscripts or researching his massive American Western History library as well as the more modern wars and conflicts. J.A. worked hard — and learned.

The employees of Thorndike Press hope you have enjoyed this Large Print book. All our Thorndike, Wheeler, and Kennebec Large Print titles are designed for easy reading, and all our books are made to last. Other Thorndike Press Large Print books are available at your library, through selected bookstores, or directly from us.

For information about titles, please call:
(800) 223-1244

or visit our website at:
gale.com/thorndike

To share your comments, please write:

Publisher
Thorndike Press
10 Water St., Suite 310
Waterville, ME 04901